HUNGER

I was not listening to her words, all I could concentrate on was the burning of her flesh against mine. She loomed very close to me, so close that I could scent the aroma of her skin, her hair, her blood. I wanted to taste her again, wanted to explore and pierce that perfect body with fang and claw, to drink in her incredible life force. Slowly. Savoring her flavor, basking in her heat.

"Yes." Her answer was not communicated by voice, she was still telling me stories about the school at which she'd met Phoenix's father. Instead the unspoken word seem to fly through my veins and shout in my head. "Yes, please, let's do that again."

I leaned in close to her; her hair, soft as a cloud, brushed my cheek. My fangs began to grow and I licked my lips in anticipation of the feast. Luscious and ripe, Maggie's neck loomed in front of my eyes. I felt hypnotized by the faint beat of her pulse visible through her skin. Lovely, she is so lovely, I thought. And I must have her again.

Once more I bent my mouth to her neck, once more I drew in her blood and vitality. . . .

Books in the Vampire Legacy Series by
Karen E. Taylor

BLOOD SECRETS

BITTER BLOOD

BLOOD TIES

BLOOD OF MY BLOOD

THE VAMPIRE VIVIENNE

RESURRECTION

Published by Pinnacle Books

ONE

The ruined abbey hovered over the town; visible from almost any vantage point, it stood like a sentinel—cold, stony and vigilant. My eyes were constantly drawn to its massive arches, its empty windows and the solid rows of surrounding graves. I was never quite sure if the abbey served as a headstone for the past, a warning for the future or an example of what we had become.

Forcing my gaze away from the ruins and from the stones gently glowing in the moonlight, I sighed. The hour was late and hunger threatened. We would have to hunt soon even if it meant risking recognition or capture. I wondered, and not for the first time, how we had fallen from our once exalted state into nothing much more than cornered and frightened animals.

"I don't know, Mitch. Perhaps they're right after all. We serve no purpose in this world."

I spoke the words quietly, leaning on the railing of the small boardwalk, staring now into the dark water that flowed past us. If he heard, he gave no indication, made no response. It made no difference, we'd had this same discussion many times during the past three years.

Three years. A short time in comparison with the almost two centuries I had already lived. And yet those past three years weighed heavily on my mind and my soul. We had been running for too long, living in fear and anger among people who'd previously had no knowledge of our existence. We had spent three years looking over our shoulders, constantly waiting for the next attack, moving and hiding, but still being drawn deeper into a rapidly changing world.

I shivered and Mitch wrapped his arm around my waist, drawing me close to him, brushing his lips against my hair.

"No, Deirdre, you promised you wouldn't start again. Remember what I said when we settled here?"

I gave a small, sad smile for the memory and leaned forward again on the rail, pulling away from him slightly. "It stops here." I whispered his words to the river, understanding as I did that they meant something different to me than they did to him. Mitch, I knew, was making a stand. Whereas I was merely resting, too tired for the constant struggle, content to let the current wash over me and pull me under.

"Damned straight. We're going to win this, Deirdre. We're going to beat those bastard Others at their own game."

I nodded, took his hand and held it to my cheek. "The swans are gone," I said, changing the subject back to something safer. "I suppose they've gone someplace warmer for the winter. If so, I'll miss watching them; they seemed so peaceful, gliding out on the water."

Mitch laughed. "Hardly peaceful—they always remind me of Vivienne." Then he sobered. "Damn it. I wish I knew where she was. Not a word from her since May. I don't like it one bit."

"Nor do I, Mitch. But I feel sure she is safe. Or"—I shivered again—"we would have heard about it on the news. I am sure 'Real-life vampires would have no compunction about reporting her death. And the no-contact rule was yours, after all, so she is merely following instructions. As are they all."

"Following instructions?" He laughed again, his voice warm in the night air. "Rest assured, our Viv is merely doing what Viv wishes to do. Chances are she and Sam are holed up somewhere passing the time very pleasurably."

"What must it be like?" My voice wavered. "To live a life like hers? No guilt, no remorse, no conscience, no ghosts to haunt her?"

"Deirdre." All of Mitch's previous humor and warmth were gone. "We've been through this before too. And none of it is your fault."

My fists clenched tight around the railing and I shook my head. "No, Mitch. All of it is my fault. Eduard said as much; had I not killed Max he would not have been able to make his move."

"And if you hadn't killed Max, I'd be dead. Damn it, Deirdre"—his voice rose over the still night air—"Eduard was a lunatic. And so was Max. Regardless of all that has happened, the world is a better place without either one of them."

He turned to me, grabbing my shoulders. I could feel the tension and anger in his grip and I thought he might shake me. Instead, he pulled me close to him and rubbed his hands up and down my arms. "You can't bear the burden of all the deaths they caused, love, you just can't. I won't let you. At the very worst, you were manipulated into acting as you did."

I gave another little sad smile, knowing that I wouldn't win this argument either. Perhaps I did not want to. "You're right, Mitch. I'm just over-reacting and internalizing the conflict."

"Sounds like you've been talking to Sam," Mitch said, laughing again. Before becoming Vivienne's newest lover, Sam had worked as a psychiatrist at the institution to which Mitch had been committed for expressing his belief in the existence of mythical creatures of the night. Now Sam lived in Paris with one of us and the whole world believed in vampires. The irony of life in general and our lives in particular never ceased to amaze me.

"No. No Sam. That would be against the rules, remember? But," and I sighed, "I wish I could. I wish none of this had ever happened and the world could return to normal."

"We're working on that, Deirdre."

"Are we?" My voice rose in anger. "These creatures have managed to kill so many of us, they've cut off our finances and our ties with the rest of our kind. We have become afraid to move, afraid even to feed for fear of discovery. And worse, they have taken away the one thing that kept us safe for all these years. Human disbelief. How are we to fix that? Wiping the memory of one human is easy, but the whole world?"

Mitch knew me well enough to realize that I was not angry with him, but with the futility of our situation. "Hush, love," he said, smoothing my hair. "We'll find a way. After all, we're not dead yet—"

His body tensed and without warning, he pulled me down to the ground. I heard a sharp crack and felt a painful tug on my left arm.

The scent of blood, my blood, blossomed in the night air along with an almost tangible scent of anger and rage. They had found us here and it would all start again.

Looking up with a snarl, I saw a young man, seemingly no more than eighteen years old. Dressed totally in black, he perched on the railing, an empty crossbow gripped in one hand. He peered down at us, eyes narrowed with his smug smile.

"Bastard." Almost from out of thin air, I heard Mitch's voice and knew that he was even now changing form to meet the threat.

The man ignored him, and jumping down onto the walk, he reached into a pack slung over his shoulder to fit another sharpened stake onto the bow, aiming once again for me.

Forgetting the pain and the blood, I gave a sharp, inhuman hiss and dissolved my body into a mist, rolling across the concrete toward him.

His smile quickly turned to a gasp of amazement, then to a grimace of fear as I slowly and tortuously curled up his body and hovered around his ear.

"You cannot kill what you cannot touch." My voice was a whisper, tenuous to match my form, as quiet as the sea and as insistent. He made no sound, but he flinched and I knew that he heard. Wrapping myself around his neck, I felt the scar that made him what he was. I tightened my hold and hissed again, rewarded by the small shiver of fear and doubt that overwhelmed him.

"Other," I said, half phasing into my human form. "But," and my voice grew softer, "he is so young." Despite his current attempt on my life, our lives, I pitied him. "Why do they send them out so young? So totally unprepared?"

Another clump of mist formed into a familiar figure behind the boy, knocking the crossbow from his hands. The weapon tumbled over the wall and fell with a splash into the river. Unarmed now, the Other was less of a threat and I fully resumed my human form. Mitch did the same, grasping our assailant's arms and twisting them behind his back.

"What shall we do with him, my love? Wipe his mind and let him go?"

Mitch looked over at me and shook his head, eyes hard and merciless. "That won't work. We can't let him go, Deirdre, or he'll be back, followed by a small army. He may be the first to find us here, but he'll definitely not be the last. And if we take pity and let him go, well, you do remember what happened in London?"

I sighed. "Yes, I remember. But he's only a boy, Mitch."

"Not a boy." The gravelly words slid over gritted teeth, sounding like the hesitant, first-learned words of a beast. "I am older than either of you, and stronger than you think. And I will see you dead and rotting before I die."

With the exception of Eduard, we had never heard one of them speak before. Always they came at us, silent and sullen; always before they had fought and died without a sound. In that split second of surprise, Mitch must have loosened his hold. The man wrestled an arm away and reached into his pack, pulling out a small revolver.

I had begun to shift form, but seeing his weapon of choice, I stayed upright and solid, knowing that he could not hurt me with this. "A gun? What do you hope to do with that?" I gave a mocking laugh. "Don't they teach you any better than that where you come from, Other? You should not come hunting vampires with guns. In fact you should not come hunting vampires at all. What have any of you gotten out of this war but death?"

He smiled at me and I noticed with shock then that all of his teeth had been ground down to sharp little points. "You talk bravely for one about to die, my dear," he said. Then he aimed the gun at my heart and laughed. "Wooden bullets."

I ducked away to one side, throwing myself down to the ground again. Biting my lip, I waited for the pain and for the burn of wood into my flesh. I listened for the click of the trigger. Instead of the firing of the gun, however, I heard a struggle and feet scuffling on the pavement. Then, with an agonized groan and a sickening crack, the laughter stopped.

Mitch pulled his hands away from the boy's neck and the Other fell, eyes lifeless and teeth permanently clenched in his jack-o'-lantern grin.

"Are you okay, love?" Mitch extended a hand and pulled me up from the pavement.

"Fine," I said, dusting off my jeans and adjusting my sweater. "Thank you."

"I wish to hell he hadn't made that last try," Mitch said, kneeling next to the body and going through pockets and pack. "We might have found out more from him." He held up the wallet he found and rifled through it. "As always, no identification, no charge cards, nothing to say who he was and where he came from. Nice amount of cash, though, and that certainly never hurts." He slipped the wallet into the pack and handed it all to me. "We'll keep those this time, maybe we'll be able to find out something from the labels."

Mitch picked up the body, looking down at the anonymous face. "Funny that this one talked, don't you think? Do you suppose the other ones could speak and were simply choosing not to?"

I shrugged, ignoring the pain in my arm. "Who can tell? It all seems so pointless, so futile. They keep trying to kill us and we don't even know why."

Mitch gave a grim laugh. "Well, here's one who won't be trying again. Nor will he be reporting back. And just think of all the time he's saved us tonight—no need to go looking for prey when they come looking for you." He glanced over the railing. "Perfect timing, the tide's starting to go out. There's no one else around now and we've still got a little time to feed; he'll stay warm for a while." Then he smiled at me. "Ladies first."

I bent my head to the Other's neck, avoiding the heavy scar tissue and placing my fangs in the soft, unresisting flesh just a few inches below his ear. He was still warm, as Mitch predicted, and I drew on him hungrily, taking his blood in large greedy swallows, enjoying the warmth of its flow down my throat, eagerly anticipating the renewed strength and life it would give.

Then my eyes, almost of their own volition, opened wide and I pulled my mouth away abruptly, spitting out what little blood remained in my mouth. Choking and gagging, I doubled over and fell to the pavement, vomiting out the blood I had just drunk.

"Poison," I managed to gasp, between gulps of air. "Do not drink from him. He's poisoned."

"Son of a bitch." Mitch dropped the body and leaned over me, laying a hand on my shoulder. "Deirdre?"

I halfheartedly waved him away. "Get rid of him, just dump him, he's no good to us now." I swallowed and wiped my mouth on the sleeve of my sweater. "I will be fine in a minute," I said, "but the sun will be up soon and we must get inside."

As I struggled to my feet again, he picked up the body and hefted it into the air, tossing it over the railing and into the swiftly flowing water. We both watched it drop and sink.

"It seems such a waste," he said, "all that blood and not one drop safe for us to drink. Nothing we can do about that, I suppose."

"What will happen to the body, Mitch?"

"It should stay under long enough for the tide to carry him fairly far away. If our luck holds, he'll surface out in the middle of the North Sea, in a week or two, completely unrecognizable." Mitch wiped his hands on the sides of his jeans. "Provided, of course, that Other flesh isn't poisonous for fish. Let's go home."

TWO

We walked back to our new home, a small flat above a pub in the oldest section of town. The street was narrow, dark and paved with cobblestones; wonderfully atmospheric, it was usually deserted at this time of the night, especially now that the tourist season was drawing to a close.

The flat itself was more than adequate for our use, not a huge amount of space, but it had a bedroom and sitting area with a large fireplace, a kitchen with a long counter and a small alcove that held a table and two chairs, and an impossibly tiny bathroom. Once the front entrance was refitted with a steel door and the two windows with steel shutters, it was reasonably secure.

Home had been a foreign concept to me for most of my life as a vampire. Always, it seemed, I had been running and hiding, not really living but just existing—so very many cities, so many different houses and apartments and rooms. I remembered each and every one of them; if I closed my eyes I could recall the colors of the carpets or the patterns of the wallpaper. But they were all empty, cold and loveless. And none of them could be called home.

The longest consecutive period of my life had been spent in New York. I dwelled in a posh hotel, in an upper-floor penthouse suite, the living room of which would hold our entire flat here. Ten years spent there did not make it home. It was only when I met Mitch that I began to understand the concept.

I remembered fondly the cabin in Maine where we had dwelled together for a time, happy and safe, until events conspired to separate us once again. Even that retreat was gone now, burned to the ground as a result of my anger.

The truth of the matter was that I belonged nowhere, felt safe nowhere, except in the circle of Mitch's arms. My only home, I realized, was with him. So it did not matter how much we traveled or how many times we were forced to move as long as we were together.

We were here now, and here we planned to stay for as long as fate allowed. And in spite of the threats of Other attacks, we could still be happy in our cozy little flat.

The pub below us was called, in one of life's ironies, the Black Rose, an appellation my creator and nemesis, Max Hunter, had bestowed on me many years ago. I laughed to myself every time I passed under the sign.

My onetime business partner, Pete, had found the flat for us and negotiated the lease with no questions asked. When we arrived, we discovered with surprise and delight that he himself had bought the pub below, with the proceeds from the sale of our shared pub in London.

"I needed a change of scenery after the wife died and here seemed as good a change as any," he'd said on the night we moved in. "And it's half yours, Dottie, darlin'." He always called me the first name he'd known me as. I had been Dottie then, and Dottie I would remain. "Mind, you and Mitch want to lie low for a while, avoiding whatever trouble the two of you stirred up in the States." He gave a low chuckle, contemplating our imagined escapades. "There's no one who'll blame you. Then again," he said, winking at me, "if you're wanting to pour drinks every now and then, I won't be saying no."

For the most part, we did a little of both, staying in the flat some of the time, but putting in an appearance at the pub every so often, so as not to arouse curiosity.

We need not have worried; the people of the town took us at face value with hardly a second glance. In their eyes, we were eccentric Americans, and if we happened to look a bit like some of the people featured on the news, well, coincidences happened. And Pete had spent time here in his youth; all of the old-timers remembered him from those wild days. If Pete vouched for us, they reasoned, then we must be acceptable folk.

What Pete thought of us, whether he knew or wondered what we were and what we did, I could not bear to ask. The subject was never discussed. The place seemed safe enough, safer than many places we'd lived. Pete occupied a small room off of the kitchen and seemed happy enough, especially after he had encouraged three stray dogs to make a home in the small grassy area behind the building.

Two of the dogs were of indeterminate breed, small and wiry with bristly tangled fur. The third, and obviously the leader, looked to be a pure-blooded mastiff. He towered over the others, black, massive and threatening. Although Pete had lured this one with food and attention, the dog had decided that it belonged to me and would follow me around when permitted.

Pete had given them no names, but Mitch had christened the largest one Moe, which, he said, automatically made the other two Curly and Larry. As a trio, though, they were not Stooges. They were, instead, Hellhounds. I had come up with that title, laughing at Mitch as he had at me for not recognizing those first three names.

"Hellhounds, my love," I had said, feeling pleased that for once I knew something he did not, "the traditional guardians of vampires."

These guardians greeted us now as we unlocked the front door of the pub. Or, more properly, Moe greeted me and the other two paid their attention to Mitch. For some reason, the two smaller dogs avoided me when they could and ignored me when my presence was forced upon them. I ventured the guess that the scent of cat on me was too strong for them to feel comfortable. But they adored Mitch, fawning upon him, sensing his canine side and accepting him as their pack leader.

"So, how are you boys tonight?" Mitch said, bending down to scratch a few scraggly heads. "Want to come howl at the moon with me?" Moe yawned in response. "No? Well, that's okay, it's too close to dawn anyway. Maybe some other night."

He took the Other's bag from my hand and held it out to the dogs. As they sniffed it, the hackles on the backs of their necks rose and they all gave a low growl. "Good boys," Mitch said, giving them each a pat. "Yes, this is a bad person smell. Now"—he shouldered the pack and we started up the stairs—"it's bedtime."

I went first, followed by Mitch, who was in turn trailed by the dogs. They did not usually sleep in our flat but one or the other of them always stood guard outside the door. This night, agitated perhaps by the scent of the bag, all three of them settled down there.

When we closed and bolted the door, Mitch pulled me to him in a tight embrace. "That was just too close a call for you out there tonight, Deirdre," he said, whispering the words into my hair. "I can't bear the thoughts of losing you." Then he pulled back and stared intently into my face. "What were you thinking? Why the hell didn't you change at the end? Is your overburdened conscience giving you a death wish?"

"He surprised me, Mitch." I moved away from him and went to fasten the shutters at the windows. "First by talking. And then with those wooden bullets."

When I raised my arm, I winced, registering with disbelief the pain in my left side. I turned around and peeled back the ripped sweater from my shoulder, inspecting the corresponding tear in my arm. "In addition, this distracted me. How odd," I said, noticing for the first time the still trickling blood, "this should have healed already."

Mitch gently dabbed a finger in the blood, brought it to his lips and grimaced in disgust. "Damn bastard poisoned the stake." He tasted it again, then spat it out into his hand. "Something new for them, it seems. Poison the weapons and poison the blood," he said, going to the bathroom and washing his hands.

He came out holding the towel. "I don't like the way their attacks get more complicated, more intricate every time. I wish we knew something more than what Victor told us."

"Victor told us only what Victor wanted us to know."

"Or what little he could remember."

Victor had, at one time, been the undisputed leader of the Cadre vampires, all powerful, all knowing. But lately it seemed that his many years and the deaths of so many of his loved ones had caused him to come unhinged. He resided now in New Orleans with my daughter, Lily. "He's not himself" was the favorite phrase used these days to describe him. On the other hand, he was the one who'd managed to kill Eduard DeRouchard, the Others' leader. I had my doubts about his mental instability.

"After all this time, Mitch," I said, sliding my sweater off over my head, "I am beginning to believe that Victor's tired old man act is just that. An act."

I ducked my head and examined my arm, tentatively exploring it with the fingers of my right hand, and all thoughts of Victor and the struggles of the Cadre faded in the face of the pain. The area around the wound felt hot to the touch and tiny streaks of red were already starting to color my abnormally pale skin.

"Damn it. This should not be happening. It should already be healed. We are going to have to treat this, Mitch. Which do you think would be best, alcohol or fire?"

He shook his head. "I don't know. Maybe both. Get comfortable and I'll start."

Lying down on the bed, I put my right arm behind my head and stared at the ceiling. "I'm as comfortable as I can be, Mitch," I called to him. He was starting a fire in the hearth first. "And I'll be ready when you are."

He came over to the bed and gave me a kiss on the tip of my nose. "Let me get the medical stuff together and I'll be right back."

He gathered the necessary items and lined them up on the nightstand: a scalpel, a pair of tweezers, towels, some cotton gauze and a bottle of rubbing alcohol. Kneeling beside the bed, he began to peel back the layer of skin torn away by the crossbow shot.

I started to talk, hoping to take my mind off of the searing pain that shot through my body at his touch.

"So, do you think those wooden bullets would work?"

Mitch grunted as he picked the first few splinters of wood from the wound. "Why are you asking me? You've been a vampire for over a century now; if anyone would know, it would be you."

I bit my lip and held back tears, feeling the icy stab of the scalpel as he probed deeper. "You must remember, my love, for most of those years I did not have armed assassins hunting me down. Just a few sheriffs here and there, and one or two nosy detectives."

"Two? And here I thought I was your only detective." His tone was light, but I could feel the tension in his hands. I closed my eyes and attempted a laugh.

"Fine. I should know better than to try to fool you. You caught me in the lie. There has only ever been one detective in my life. But as for the question at hand, I have this sinking feeling they know more about us than we know about them."

"In which case," he said, nodding, following my reasoning, "the answer is yes, wooden bullets can kill us; otherwise they wouldn't be employing them. Unfortunately, that means they no longer need to deal with us up close and personal. The killing can be done at a distance even farther away than the range of the crossbow."

I sighed. "Yes, so it would seem."

"Especially if they coat the bullets with whatever it is they hit you with." He fell silent for a minute or two, studying my arm. "I think that takes care of the splinters, at least. How are you doing?"

"I'm fine Mitch."

"Liar," he said, his voice trembling only slightly

less than mine. "I hate having to hurt you, Deirdre. I'd rather cut off my own arm."

I reached up my right hand and touched his cheek. "I know, my love. But this has to be done and who else is there?"

"True," he said, "but that doesn't mean I have to like it, does it?" He wadded up one of the towels and gently lifted me to slide it under my arm. I looked away again when I smelled the strong scent of alcohol.

"Hold on," Mitch said, slowly trickling the liquid into the gaping wound. This new pain was almost welcome, a clean and cold shock to my burning flesh; still, I couldn't help letting out a small gasp. Mitch gingerly patted the area with some of the cotton gauze, then paused for a minute or two.

"It's still not healing, Deirdre. Damn, I wish Sam were here. I think," and he was silent for a second, trying to avoid the inevitable, "I think we're going to need to burn the poison out."

I understood his hesitancy. All I'd had to do was lie quietly and manage the pain. He'd had to inflict it. "Burn it out, Mitch." I touched my right hand to my lips and put it up to his. "Be relentless and I'll handle it. I've had worse, my love."

A small moan escaped his lips; then he squared his shoulders, stood up and went over to the fireplace. I didn't watch, but knew that he was heating the poker until it was red hot. And when he sighed, I knew the device was prepared.

"Deirdre?"

"Just do it. Now. Show no mercy."

I forced myself to lie still as he slid the heated poker over my bloodied skin. The smell of burning flesh permeated the flat and the pain was almost more than I could bear. Even in the midst of it, though, I thought I could feel the healing start.

"Enough," I gasped, opening my eyes when the heat subsided, watching the blackened patch begin to lighten and fill in the deep-chewed furrow of damaged flesh.

Mitch held his wrist next to my mouth then. "Drink," he said, "you need it more than I do right now."

"We haven't fed in weeks, Mitch. You cannot afford to give it." But even the mere thought of feeding brought a tingling response to my gums, my canines grew longer and sharper. He was right, fresh blood always sped the healing process.

"Just do it, Deirdre. Now. And show no mercy." He echoed my earlier words and I gave a low laugh.

"Thank you, my love." I breathed the words as my fangs came down on his wrist. The taste of that sweet blood, precious to me in more ways than one, blossomed in my mouth and surged through my body, eradicating the previous pain and the slow burn of poison. Three swallows, four, five—I could have taken it all and wanted more. But this was Mitch and I pulled my mouth away by force of will.

I smiled up at him as a huge wave of exhaustion overcame me. "Thank you," I murmured again as I fell into the dark abyss of sleep.

THREE

Mitch watched over me that day, not sleeping himself, but sitting by the bed most of the time. Periodically he would get up and turn on the small color television set to watch for any events about the war that had been declared on our kind.

Usually, in any given day, there were one or two vampire-sighting and/or killing reports. Although we suspected most of these were false, it made no difference to the general public. In addition to the television, he would also check, via the computer, for Internet reports.

At one point, early in the afternoon, he woke me.

"Deirdre, sweetheart," he said, "I hate to disturb your rest since you need some healing time, but I think you need to watch this."

I opened my eyes and sat up in bed, groaning slightly when I heard the horribly melodramatic organ music theme song to the show *Real-Life Vampires*—the program that had made the names Terri Hamilton and Bob Smith synonymous with that of Van Helsing. Their coverage of the bombing of Cadre headquarters and their startling revelation that vampires really did exist launched them almost instantly from their obscure jobs as local television reporters to national celebrity status. Over the past three years, I had grown to hate them on sight.

Terri seemed her usual perky self for this show, with her cropped, straight dark hair and simpering pasted-on smile. She wore white, as always, a statement of purity and innocence, while Bob wore his pinstriped Armani with dignity and authority.

"What you are about to see," he intoned, over the standard introductory shots of historical, literary and cinematic vampires, "is true. And none of the names have been changed, for there are no innocents to protect."

"Bullshit," Mitch said. "I wish to hell they'd get a new opening."

"I wish to hell they would drop back into obscurity." I shifted on the pillows, trying to get comfortable. My arm still ached slightly, but I said nothing about it, wanting to see whatever travesty our friends Terri and Bob had worked up this time. "I'm tired of having my name bandied about for public entertainment. This show is a good example of why I never went in for the watching of television."

"Tonight, Bob," Terri said, smirking into the camera, "we have some particularly vicious footage of a vampire attack on four of our heros in London. The film you are about to see is for mature audiences only; it contains graphic and disturbing events and should not be viewed certainly by children under the age of sixteen."

"That's right, Terri. I want everyone to keep in mind that the footage we're about to show is not cut or edited in any way; these are not actors, folks, they are Real-Life human beings being callously murdered by Real-Life monsters." The real-life phrase was obviously capitalized in his script and Bob milked it for all it was worth. "Because *we* believe *you* have the right to know."

"He's a Real-Life Ass," Mitch said with a small harsh laugh, when the show moved to a commercial break. "Notice that he's not out there fighting for the integrity and the safety of the human race. And I can't believe they're starting to film these encounters."

I sighed. "This is going to look bad, Mitch, I know it is. If only we had known that one of them had a camera hidden on him."

"It was an ambush, four of them against the two of us, and we barely escaped. We didn't have enough time to think, Deirdre, we were too busy protecting ourselves from heroes. And we didn't have time to search for hidden cameras."

The show continued finally with a plea for donations to the Real-Life Vampires Freedom Fighters Fund. I often wondered how much money was being made from this show—more than enough, unfortunately, to keep them on the air for three years.

"And we're back." Terri managed to don her serious face for this segment. "Once again, we suggest that children under the age of sixteen not be present for the viewing of this film footage. Are they out of the room?" She paused for a second. "Good. We will let the films speak for themselves."

The quality of the film was poor, grainy and underdeveloped, adding to the myth of its veracity. The camera must have been hidden in the lapel of one of the Others' coats, as at first nothing was seen but a bouncing version of the street they were walking down.

It was night, of course, and as in all Other attacks, the area was deserted. Neither Mitch nor I understood this phenomenon but had seen it too many times to question its reality. When the Others attacked, they attacked without audience or witness. We speculated that it was an effect much like the force field Eduard DeRouchard had demonstrated for us in a bar in New Orleans before he died. However, we had no evidence to back this speculation, nor did the current show offer any explanation. In truth, it made little difference why or how this worked; often the phenomenon was to our advantage as well as to theirs.

Voices had been dubbed over the film. I remembered these particular "heroes" quite well and like all of them, until this most current assassin, they did not speak.

The dialogue was surprisingly badly written; their chatter of wives and children and the trivial events in their lives belonged more properly in one of the old war films Mitch enjoyed watching, ones where men would reveal their plans to return home and marry their sweethearts seconds before they were shot and killed. Though banal and stereotypical, however, the words served their purpose admirably, making the four seem like nothing more than good friends, taking an evening stroll in the cool London air, instantly engaging a potential viewer's sympathy.

"Wait," one of them said, interrupting the talk of "Scott's" new car, "what was that?"

Suddenly the camera jumped and focused on two other people. At first I would not have recognized the blurred figures that sprang out at the camera as being Mitch and me, but they were obviously meant to be. The man had gray hair and intense blue eyes and the woman, long auburn hair and eyes that glowed like the red fires of hell. The astonished cries of the men were drowned out by the pair's loud growling and a very unflattering close-up of what was meant to be my face revealed yellowed, protruding fangs, positively dripping with gore.

Mitch gave a grunting laugh. "I guess we'd just come from dinner. How many times have I told you, Deirdre? Use your napkin."

I looked over at him, shaking my head and smiling, before turning my attention back to the television set. The colors for this segment had obviously been intensified and from my own first-hand perspective, I knew that they had done a great deal more than a little editing to make it seem as if we were the attackers. In fact, the whole sequence from this point on was mostly fabrication, with a few actual shots tucked in here and there. Gone were the weapons the men had carried, airbrushed or edited away. Two, I remembered, had in reality been armed with crossbows and the others had carried long, sharp knives that had claimed more than a small amount of our blood.

"We will drain you dry," a deep voice that could never have been mistaken for Mitch's boomed out into the night.

"And steal your immortal souls." The female vampire who was not me gloated over her victims before pouncing on one of them, knocking him down to the ground with a sickening crack of broken bones. She clawed open his throat and buried her mouth in the exposed flesh, making loud and grotesque sucking noises.

"Oh dear God," I said in disgust. "How could anyone think that this was real footage?"

The camera bent over her as she fed on this poor unfortunate; the audience was given a gratuitous glimpse of a demonic, blood-spattered face, a view of a creature from hell, reveling in the basest of appetites. Then, as if just becoming aware of scrutiny, she rose to her feet with a low, vicious growl, her lethal fangs bared and her clawed fingers crooked menacingly.

As she advanced, the vantage of the camera slowly retreated until it finally stopped. The female vampire also stopped, hesitating about a foot or two away, no doubt so that the next victim could say his lines.

"Scott's dead," he shouted right on cue.

"What a shame," Mitch commented dryly, "now he'll never get to drive that new car."

"Hush," I said, stifling a laugh, "this is serious business."

"Scott's dead and we can't help him now." The desperation in the man's voice rose as he came to the awful realization that he would soon be joining his friend. "And I'm trapped here, up against this wall. Save yourself."

The soundtrack included background noises of growling and fighting as, apparently, the male vampire gave the other two men the same treatment. Labored breathing was heard as the camera rose and fell.

Suddenly the female vampire made her move. The shot showed her clawed hands coming in, closer and closer, until they gripped the fabric of the man's coat. Then the viewpoint slowly rose, as, presumably, she picked up the man and held him up in the air over her head. Another close-up of her evil, laughing face ensued, followed quickly by the view of rushing pavement. The man had been tossed through the air and landed with a thud on the ground, obscuring the camera until she rolled him over.

"Mercy," the man whimpered, as her face moved closer and drool dripped from her mouth, "for the love of God, have some mercy."

She gloated and laughed again. "I have no mercy for scum like you. Humans are my food."

Apparently, though, in the end she did have some mercy, at least for those of us forced to watch this trash. Her hand came down, crushing the camera and ending the video portion of the film. The screen now contained nothing but darkness, but the microphone must have been concealed elsewhere, because the pained and agonized cries of the men continued for a full minute. And in the ominous minute of silence that followed, the audience was left to draw the conclusion that the heroes had fallen and that the villains lived in triumph.

Then the male vampire's voice rolled through the night air like thunder. "Come, wife," he said, "finish your feasting and get ready to fly. The sun will soon rise."

The next shot was of Terri, wiping away tears from her eyes with a lace-trimmed handkerchief. Bob had an arm around her shoulder and was patting her gently. The bottom of the screen proclaimed the current and rapidly rising amount of money in the Freedom Fighters fund, and the 800 number for donations flashed in bright red digits. "We'll go to a commercial break now," Bob said, "but stay tuned for more news and developments."

Both Mitch and I sat, stunned, staring at the screen.

"Unbelievable," he said finally. "I don't know whether to laugh or cry."

"It certainly won't be winning any awards at Cannes this year," I offered, shaking my head.

"But it's an effective piece of propaganda, anyway. Provided they can convince people that this whole thing is true. And based on the money they're collecting, I'd say that they've been successful."

"I don't understand. The whole thing was such

a blatant lie. How can they say it was not edited or cut? Wouldn't such tampering be obvious?"

Mitch shrugged. "People believe what they want to believe. And they all know that Terri and Bob would never lie."

The commercials were now replaced with Terri's face; her attempt at covering her tears with a sad smile would have been heartbreaking in any other context. As it was, I wanted to reach my hand through the screen and . . .

"Those two murderers are still at large, Bob," she said, sniffing slightly and squaring her shoulders. "And as the quality of our film was so bad, we are now showing another photograph of the two of them on the right hand of your screen. The woman is Deirdre Griffin-Greer, aka Dorothy Grey. And the man is Mitchell Greer, former NYPD police officer."

Somehow they had acquired a photo of the two of us at our wedding; *I wonder,* I thought, *if I could get a reprint of that.* All of our personal belongings were gone now, stolen from the storage unit into which Lily had them deposited.

"It is believed," Bob said, continuing the pitch, "that they are still residing somewhere in the United Kingdom. If seen, we advise you to approach them with extreme caution or not at all. And as always, donations can be made and sightings can be reported by calling 1-800 555-VAMPS or contact us at our e-mail address—tips@reallifevampires.com."

"I have a good idea." Mitch said, turning off the television as the theme music came back on, "let's send them an e-mail that says we moved to Iceland."

"If only it were that simple, my love. I wonder what the repercussions of this show will be."

He glanced at the clock. "No way to tell now and there's not much we can do about it in any event. Can you get back to sleep?"

I smiled at him, "I don't know, that was pretty frightening stuff. I might have nightmares."

He turned off the overhead light and the room darkened completely. "Come, wife," he said, lowering his voice to match the one on the show, "finish your speaking and get ready to sleep. The sun will set soon."

Giving a little giggle, I turned over onto my right side, adjusted the blankets and rolled myself into a little ball. Mitch slid into bed next to me and, avoiding my sore arm, wrapped his arms around my waist.

"I love you," he murmured, "even if your table manners are atrocious."

"Very funny, Mitch." I snuggled back into him, enjoying the feel of his solid body against mine. Sleep came quickly.

FOUR

When I woke at sundown I was alone in the bed and my arm was still sore. Not surprising, I supposed, it had been a particularly deep and brutal wound, but already a thin layer of new flesh was growing over the damaged area. I stretched, yawned and got out of bed, crossing the room and putting my arms around Mitch's neck while he sat at the desk, dressed only in a pair of jeans and reading something from the screen. "Couldn't sleep?" I asked, depositing a kiss on his dyed-black hair.

He shrugged his shoulders. "I wasn't all that tired. And I was restless. You, on the other hand, slept beautifully. I know, I watched."

I felt a huge rush of emotion for this man and hugged his neck tighter. "Have I told you lately how much I love you? In spite of everything that has happened and will keep happening, I wouldn't change a thing if this were the only way I could be with you. But"—I kissed his head again—"I think I liked you better with gray hair."

He gave a small grunt, reaching a hand up and running it over my hair, also dyed and cut shorter than his. "And I liked you better with long hair that wasn't bleached. But it will grow and your natural color reappear as will mine. The disguises are important. In the light of what we saw earlier, they turned out to be an excellent idea and just in time."

"Yes, you're right." Resting my chin on his shoulder I glanced at the screen. "Any more news?"

"No," he said, his voice sounding puzzled. "Not since this afternoon's show, which may well have been a repeat. No reaction to any of it—on the television or anywhere else."

"After that show, perhaps Terri and Bob have finally managed to stun the public with their appalling taste. No reaction is good, is it not?"

"Not necessarily. I'd prefer to hear their posturing; at least it gives me an idea of what they're up to. Silence is not always golden. Reminds me of when Chris was a boy—as long as he was making noise, I knew where he was and what he was doing. But when he got quiet, look out." He gave a small chuckle, then stopped and swallowed hard, sitting silent for a few seconds, his fingers resting motionless on the keyboard.

I had no words of comfort for him. Mitch's son had died a little over four years ago and anything I said or did now would not bring Chris back. So I kneaded Mitch's shoulders, trying to ease the tight muscles there, encouraging him to relax. Talking about it could only be beneficial; thus far he had managed to avoid the subject.

Finally he swiveled his chair around and pulled

me down to sit on his lap. "So how's my patient this evening?"

Sorry that he had changed the subject, I still smiled and held my arm out so he could admire the newly grown pale skin. "Much better; you did a wonderful job."

"Gave me a hell of a scare, though. You could have died. And then where would I be?"

I wanted to say that he'd have had a good life without me, one that made more sense and that caused less grief. A life in which he was not a criminal, one in which he could face the light of day, one in which his son would still be alive. I knew better, however, than to broach that subject. Instead I leaned over and kissed him, hard on the lips. "I am not dead right now," I purred into his ear.

He returned the kiss, his tongue lightly flicking over my lips. "So I see," he said, his voice hoarse. "You certainly feel right to me. But I don't know, in the excitement last night, there may be some wounds I missed examining."

"Oh," I breathed as he rose from the chair, holding me still in his arms, "I certainly hope so."

Mitch carried me over to the rug in front of the fireplace and gently set me down, unzipping and stepping out of his jeans. He straddled my legs, pounded his chest a bit and flexed his muscles.

I gave a small laugh. "Come here, you," I said, holding my arms out to him. He lay down next to me, not saying a word, his eyes burning into mine. He unfastened the bra that I'd slept in and threw it across the room, then slowly pulled my panties down.

I shivered from the feel of his hands brushing my thighs, my legs, my feet. "Everything looks fine from down here," he said with a long slow smile, "but I think I'd better keep on checking."

"Oh, yes." I moaned as his mouth touched my toes and he slowly kissed, licked and nibbled his way up my body. By the time he reached my mouth, I managed a gasping laugh. "So, will I survive?"

His voice was unsteady. "Unless you die from the loving I'm going to give you, yeah."

He entered me, thrusting deep inside, and I drifted away, abandoning my mind and my senses to our appetites.

Afterward, we lay quiet, breathing heavily.

"Mmmmm. That was worth getting hurt for, my love."

"Maybe," Mitch said, "but don't try it again, okay?"

I nodded, closing my eyes, basking in the warmth of the fire and his love. "I feel like I could stay here like this forever, Mitch. Not quite awake, not quite asleep. Floating."

He grunted, lightly gliding his fingertips over my arm.

"Forever," I said again, drifting into a delightful waking dream.

The languor, however, vanished with a loud knock on the pub door. The dogs outside the door began to growl, bark and then we heard them tear down the stairs.

"Damn it." Mitch jumped up and grabbed for his discarded clothing, hurriedly putting it on. "I completely forgot; we were supposed to open the pub tonight for Pete. He was heading out for some sort of event at the church." He slipped a black T-shirt over his head and stepped into his shoes. "I guess the regulars are getting restless."

He came back to the fire, and leaned over me, caressing my naked skin and giving me a long kiss. "Lock the door after me, sweetheart. And come down when you can."

I leaned back, closed my eyes again and sighed. We could not make love often enough to suit me. Every time was like the first time with Mitch. I wiggled my toes and gave a low laugh. "And to-night was even better than then," I said. "Must be something about living on the edge."

I might have drifted off to sleep again, but felt a touch of hot breath on my face and opened my eyes to a furry head and a cold nose.

"Which one are you?" I asked the dog, sitting up and holding my knees to my chest. "I know you're not Moe. So which is it? Curly or Larry?" He cocked his head at that last name so I repeated the word. "Larry?" The wag of his tail confirmed it. "And exactly what are you doing in here, Larry?"

The animal looked around a bit nervously, then walked over to the door and settled down in front of it. "Oh, I see." I laughed as I got up from the floor and walked over to throw the bolt. "Mitch let you in for a little more protection. That's a pretty funny little coincidence, you know." I looked down at him and smiled. "Not all that many years ago I needed protection from a Larry." The dog wagged his tail when I said his name, his eyes darting to my face and then back down to the floor. "And now here you are. He was not a nice man, that Larry. No, he was someone like Mitch's bad people. He smelled a lot better than you, though."

The animal sighed and I laughed. "Sorry, no offense meant. You be a good dog now and watch the door. I'm going to take a shower."

While I was upstairs, the pub had filled with more customers than normal for a weeknight and I felt guilty for the extra time I had taken for a shower. But Mitch seemed to be enjoying himself, talking up a young tourist couple. He winked at me as I came behind the bar and as I tied my apron around my waist he motioned for me to come over to him.

"Elise and Mark, meet my wife, Dottie."

I held out a hand and smiled at them. "Wonderful to see you here. Just visiting the town?"

Elise returned the smile, nodded and hugged Mark's arm closer to her. "It's our honeymoon," she gushed, "and we just got here this afternoon. Mark loved the name of this place so we had to come in."

Mitch came by and replaced their empty stout glasses with two full ones. "In fact, Dottie, Mark and Elise were the ones knocking on the door."

She gave a pretty little frown. "I know. And I'm

sorry I interrupted your nap. We didn't see the sign that said you were closed."

A flash of suspicion ran through me. Both of them wore turtleneck sweaters and Mark had not said a word. Could they be Others?

"It doesn't matter, my dear." I kept my smile cordial and welcoming. "So tell me, how are you enjoying Whitby? And do you like dogs?"

Mitch laughed. "Moe has already greeted the two of them and pronounced them acceptable people."

"Moe is adorable." She stopped midsentence and blinked when the absurdity of the remark hit her. Then she laughed. "Okay, maybe not adorable. But he's a sweet animal."

I nodded. "Smart, too. You would never know that he was a stray."

"Sometimes they make the best dogs," Mark said with little effort, and I relaxed fully. These two were just what they seemed: human tourists on their honeymoon. Perfect.

I caught Mitch's eye from where he stood at the other side of the bar. He gave a slight nod. Yes, perfect.

"Stay for a while." I turned back to them, staring first into her eyes, then into his. "And after we close up we'll take you for a walk in the abbey ruins. You can see them better, I suppose, in the daylight, but at night they're breathtaking."

Mitch agreed. "I guarantee you won't want to miss this sight-seeing opportunity. And afterward, Dottie, Moe and I will see you safely back to your hotel."

Elise giggled, reminding me briefly of Vivienne. "That'd be cool. Thanks." She hesitated a second, then continued. "So long as we don't see any ghosts or vampires or things like that."

"Well," I said with a low laugh, looking deeply into her eyes again and holding her attention, "there are more than a few ghosts, but they're shy and probably will not reveal themselves. As for the other, you can be sure there are no vampires in Whitby. Moe wouldn't permit it, for one thing. And for another, this would be rather an obvious place for them, don't you think?"

She giggled and nodded. "Yeah, but it's so perfect for them, too. All the old buildings and the ocean and all. I'd think a vampire would feel right at home here."

"Do you? I hadn't really thought of it in those terms, Elise, but I think you're right. If, that is, there were such things. But either way, this is a lovely little town."

She agreed and I smiled and moved over to the other end of the bar, putting a couple of stouts in front of some of our regulars.

Throughout the night, I saw Mitch continue to fill their glasses. He did not want to take the chance that they would leave; it had been a long time since we last fed.

Pete returned shortly before closing time, bursting with good news. You could almost read his excitement on his face, and the dogs milled around under his feet, catching the feeling.

"Hey, now, you mangy curs, give a man a little room, will you?" He took off his jacket and hung it on a post to one side of the bar. Picking up an apron, he fastened it around his waist, then stopped and looked around, hands on his hips and a grin so broad it threatened to split his head in two.

"So what's the news, Pete? I know you have some; it shows on every inch of you."

"I won, Mitch, my boy. A raffle at the church, can you believe it, Dottie darlin'? I won."

I smiled at his enthusiasm. For all of his years, he was still a child at heart. "And what did you win, Pete?"

"An all-expense-paid cruise. You should remember, I forced you to buy a few of the tickets. I leave in two weeks."

How would we manage to keep the pub open during the day with Pete gone? We needed this place for more than protection; it was also our only source of income since the Others had appropriated Cadre accounts. Pete's presence here was critical. I wanted to be happy for him, he was so very excited about the whole thing. But my face must have registered my distress.

He reached over and patted my cheek. "Not to worry, Dottie. I thought of you two and was going to turn it down, but then remembered I had a replacement. Not two weeks ago, I'd received a letter from my niece. She wanted to move out of London, she said, and wondered if I could find her employment here in Whitby. I told her to come on ahead and I'd find something for her. And so, I have."

He nodded his head, pleased over how neatly

the universe had expanded to meet his demands. "She and her son arrive in a day or two." He grinned broadly at me. "Must've slipped my mind, or I'd have been telling you before."

Mitch clapped him on the back. "Congratulations, Pete. And don't worry about us, we'll be fine."

"Maggie'll take good care of you and the pub. She's not exactly my niece, you see, but the daughter of a distant relative." Pete moved behind the bar and began washing glassware. He looked around and nodded. "Now our Maggie's a nice girl. Pretty as a princess. Two boys, she has, but the one is staying somewhere with his father's kin. She'll be bringing the little one with her. Can't be more than four or five years old. Haven't seen him since he was tiny. Cute little bug, he was, all blue-eyed and fuzzy-haired."

He pulled a few drafts and carried them down to the other end of the bar, greeting some of the customers by name. Then he returned to us and continued where he left off. "Had a spot of trouble right after he was born, though. A shame, it was. I'm remembering it was a tumor or such; they cut it out and he came through right as rain. He's a regular tiger now, or so she tells me, and being as I haven't seen him since, I'll have to take her word on it."

"Maggie Richards." Pete nodded again, happy in his good fortune and ours. "She's a fine girl and will do right by you both. Now why don't you run out for a little air? I'll manage things here."

FIVE

"Not much farther now." Mitch turned around from where he was leading the abbey expedition up the steep and narrow cobblestoned street. A very drunk and giggling Elise clung to him. Mark, equally as drunk, walked next to me, weaving from side to side every so often. The air blew cold and crisp in from the sea and our visitors shivered. Moe had declined the walk and stayed behind.

"Don't worry," I said, with a mock stumble, giving me a good reason to grab Mark's arm and pull him closer to me. "We can get out of the wind just as soon as we get there."

"That would be good," he said. "But," and he gave me a curious look, "you don't seem to mind the cold."

I shrugged, leaning farther into him, savoring his warm human scent. "I may have gotten used to it. And in any event"—we rounded the top of the hill—"here we are."

Elise gave a gasp of wonder. "Oh, you were right, Dottie. This is really cool. Can we go in?"

"You can dance on the grass, if you'd like, Elise," I said, "but stick close to Mitch if you want to do some exploring. He knows the place pretty well. We wouldn't want you to stumble into an open crypt, would we?"

She gave a practiced moan of delighted horror, tugged on his arm and off they went.

I turned to Mark. "You don't mind, I trust. She'll be quite safe."

"Funny," he said, staring off in the direction they'd gone, "you'd think I would. But no, I feel okay with it all."

"Good. So what would you like to do? Explore? Dance?"

He laughed. "What I'd really like to do is find a quiet place to sit and maybe watch the ocean. I had way too much to drink to go staggering off into the ruins."

"A quiet place to sit? This whole place is about as quiet as you could ever ask for." I took his hand and led him through the cemetery to where a bench rested, overlooking the ocean.

He glanced back over his shoulder only once. "Kind of spooky, isn't it? All those dead people just behind us."

I laughed. "I suppose it is. But somehow I don't think they'll be bothering us." Mark chuckled. "Nope. I gather you and Mitch are both Americans. What brings you to this area?"

I looked him in the eye. "It's a very long and unbelievable story, Mark. I doubt that it would be of interest to you. Tell me," I said, curious about the contemporary American's view of the Other situation, "does Elise really believe in vampires?"

He thought for a minute. "We've seen all the

shows, of course. And used to watch the one with those two newscasters, you know the ones I mean?"

"Terri and Bob." My voice tightened with disapproval.

"Yeah, them. What's it called?"

Real-Life Vampires."

"Yeah, that's it. We used to watch it all the time, but, you know, eventually it seemed like the whole deal was just a great big scam. They would rant and rave about this horrible threat to humanity and the American way of life, but never offered any proof, never gave anyone reason to believe it was a real danger. Lack of evidence sure didn't stop them from taking contributions from anyone with an open wallet, though. The show got boring and we stopped watching. Although I heard they had a real kick-ass one on not too long ago; we didn't see it, of course, being busy with the wedding and all."

"I saw it. The entire thing had to be faked."

"Probably was. You can do anything these days on film and make it look real. Anyway, I never knew anyone who's been killed or even threatened by a vampire. Have you?"

"No."

He tilted his head to one side. "It's a shame, really. I mean, it would be kind of neat to think that they existed, you know?"

I nodded. "Yes, it would be interesting, I suppose. As would meeting Santa Claus on Christmas Eve, but I don't think that's any more likely."

He laughed then. "It's a lot like that." He

rubbed his hands up and down his arms. "It's really getting cold here, you want to move someplace warmer?"

I turned to him, catching and holding his gaze. "No, I like it here. As do you."

"Yeah," he said reluctantly as my stare bored into him. "It's nice."

"Besides"—I pitched my voice lower, so that it was no more than a persuasive throb—"you're tired, I'm sure. Such a long flight here, and dealing with the airport lines and the customs checks, to say nothing of all the previous excitement of the wedding. Why don't you just close your eyes and rest for a while? You'll be safe, warm and I'll stay here with you. When Elise and Mitch are done exploring, you can go back to the hotel. Does that sound like a good idea to you?"

He muttered something and his eyes fluttered.

"Sleep, Mark."

He nodded once and gave a moan. His head rolled to rest on my shoulder and I hesitated. Putting him to sleep and then feeding on him felt unsporting, but I was so very hungry and the thoughts of the normal seduction that ordinarily preceded a feeding tired me more than I wanted to admit.

Somewhere from inside the ruins I could hear the echo of Mitch's voice and I smiled. Had Mark been awake, he would no doubt have been alarmed by the moon glinting off my fangs and there might have been a struggle. Instead, I gently pushed his head to one side and rolled his turtleneck down, making small comforting noises,

Easing my teeth into his neck, I drew on his blood slowly, delicately, holding him easily in my arms as if he were a child. He sighed in his sleep and his lips curled up in a half smile.

Time hung suspended as I drank, pulling in the richness of him, feeling it race through my body and warm me totally. *This,* I thought as I finally let go of him and swallowed the last precious mouthful, *this wonderful experience is worth all the danger, all the sorrow.*

I pulled his turtleneck back to its original position, folded it over neatly. "There you go, Mark," I murmured, smoothing back a lock of his dark hair, "good as new."

We sat for some time on the bench, Mark sleeping while I watched the sea roll under the light of the moon. Somewhere out there was the body of the young man who attacked us last night, somewhere out there were the answers we sought. But how would we recognize the answers, when even the questions evaded us? The only one I knew to ask was "why?" and I might as well have asked that of the ocean.

I heard Mitch's step behind me, and turned around on the bench. He was carrying Elise and she was still giggling softly to herself. "Ready to go?" he asked, nodding toward Mark.

I stood up and smoothed my sweater down over my jeans. "Absolutely. We'll just need to wake him up."

Elise scrambled down out of Mitch's arms and stood unsteadily on her feet. "Markie passed out already." She laughed, swaying. "We've only been married for two days. I guess the honeymoon is over."

"Not at all, my dear," I said, smiling up at Mitch. "Sometimes it can last forever. Now, let's get him up and walking; I don't want to carry him back down that hill."

It took us close to an hour to get them back to their hotel, Mitch supporting Mark with Elise and me walking behind, arm in arm.

After Mark stumbled and almost brought Mitch down with him, I expressed some worry. "Is he all right, do you think? He seems so unsteady."

Elise shook her head. "No, he's just like this. Once he falls asleep, you might as well forget him for a full seven hours. Chances are he won't remember a thing about this night when we get up tomorrow morning. Probably just as well, really, I don't know what I was thinking, going off with a total stranger." She gave me a glance out of the corner of her eyes. "No offense, Dottie."

"None taken. But you were always perfectly safe with either one of us."

"Yeah, well, I know that now." She rolled her eyes. "But what if you'd been, I don't know, psychos or something? Mark always says I'm too trusting. Was he mad?"

I laughed. "That you went off into the ruins with a total stranger, a potential psycho?"

She nodded, biting her lip. "Yeah."

"No, he's not angry. In fact, I think he was relieved he didn't have to go running through the abbey with you."

"Thanks. I'm glad to hear that. And I'm glad we met you guys. It was fun. Or at least I think it was fun." She put a hand up to her neck and sighed. "I guess I kind of passed out, too. But don't tell Mark, okay?"

I smiled. "Your secret is safe with me."

We walked the rest of the way in a comfortable silence, watching as Mitch half dragged, half carried Mark. Knowing that we were getting closer, Mitch picked up the pace. Finally, we escorted them into the lobby, waved as the elevator doors closed and practically ran out the door and into the night.

I paused and looked at the cabs waiting at the curb. "Should we take a cab back?" I asked.

He shook his head. "Can't really afford it. Besides, I didn't bring any cash with me."

I sighed, not so much for the lost cab ride, but for the state of our life. I'd once had millions stashed away before the Others appropriated it, and although money was not really necessary for our survival it certainly made everything much simpler.

On the other hand, it was a lovely night. Recent experience had taught us that it usually took one or two weeks to have another assassin dispatched, so it seemed unlikely we would run into anything more dangerous than a petty thief. Some nights we would welcome such trouble; on many occasions we sought it, leading an unsuspecting mugger into a blind alley. A human assailant could easily provide necessary sustenance, with little worry of the attack being reported. Especially now, when vampiric encounters with normal people might end up as front page news, the criminal element proved a mainstay of our diet and helped us hone survival skills.

We had, however, already fed well this evening, so there was no need to lure prey. Instead, we found ourselves free to simply exist in the moment, not driven by fear or hunger. We walked, arms twined around each other's waist, silent and secure in our relationship. Rarely did such moments exist and I savored them.

As we came within a block of the Black Rose, a large dark form ran out of the shadows heading straight into our path. I tensed, preparing myself for combat until I recognized the creature as it barreled toward us and flung himself at us.

"You missed a good walk, Moe, old man," Mitch said, "and a good dinner although we didn't save any leftover scraps for you."

I shook my head and laughed. "He far prefers solid food, Mitch." Eying the dog's size and bulk, I added to the thought. "And we certainly don't want him ever to get a taste for blood. None of us would be safe."

"Not fair," Mitch said, scratching the dog's ears. "Moe's nothing but a pussy cat." At that statement the animal turned his head to me. With his tongue lolling out of his mouth, and Mitch's vigorous attention, the dog looked as if he were nodding and smiling in agreement.

I shook my head again and grinned in response. "Fine. I give up. No one should ever try to come between a vampire and his hellhound."

"A good theory, Mrs. Greer. But in reality, he's more yours than mine, although I don't know why. I pay him more attention."

"Perhaps he's just a ladies' man."

"Or maybe he's got a thing for cats. We should take him out for a run some night and find out."

"I think not, Mitch, thank you very much." I eyed the dog. "He's friendly enough when we are in human form, but I don't think I would care to tangle with him. Cat or no."

We started walking back toward the pub, the dog between us, my hand resting gently on his head. I found his presence reassuring, somehow, if only for his value as a warning device. Or perhaps it was more than that. The addition of another living creature into our lives made us into a family.

Mitch unlocked the door to the pub and the dog walked right in, bounding up the stairs to lie by our door. I hesitated outside, not wishing to confine myself again, within the pub or even within our cozy lair. There were hours remaining before dawn; the feeding rejuvenated me and I had energy to spare.

Mitch looked at me questioningly.

"Now that you've mentioned it, Mitch, I think a run would be a wonderful idea. Without the dog, of course."

"Do you think that's wise after last night?"

"No. Probably not. Although we're not likely to meet another assassin so soon after that last."

I paused. "And if we do, so be it. We manage their attacks well enough."

"Brave words from a woman who could have been killed last night."

I touched his arm. "But I was not killed. And don't you see, Mitch? That's an even better reason for going. If life is short, then let us enjoy what pleasures we can."

"Deirdre?" He put his hand on my forehead as if taking my temperature. "Are you sure you're okay?" Then he laughed. "Maybe a better question is, are you sure you're you? Normally you're the one who wants to play it safe."

"Of course I am myself. I have never felt better. And we are never safe, not now. So the hell with all of it, I say." I touched his face, enjoying the roughness of his cheek on my hand. "Let's run, my love. It will be just you and I and the night."

He shrugged and smiled. "You know, now that you mention it, it does sound like a good idea. Back to the abbey?"

I pulled the pub door shut and he locked it up again. "Yes, back to the abbey."

SIX

The walk to the abbey was much quicker with just the two of us. Once there, we went into the inside of the building and into an area we knew was sheltered from watching eyes. We stripped off our clothing and hid it in a niche we'd discovered on a previous trip.

Then we began to change, Mitch to a large silver-gray wolf and I to a tawny-haired lynx. As always, Mitch completed his metamorphosis quicker and more effortlessly than I ever had been able to. For years, I had fought against the trappings and powers of vampiric life, staying as close to my human origins as was possible, considering the way I had to live. That was why I refused to sleep in a coffin and why I was still considered a rogue by the rest of the Cadre.

With time, though, I had learned to accept the Cat and had finally come to terms with her appetites and instincts. Yet, even with that acceptance, I still felt reticent about forsaking my human form. To be trapped in that body or any body, living merely on instincts and appetites, without emotions or memories, was one of my worst fears.

The Wolf nudged at my still human-formed

hand and nipped gently at my fingers. His eyes glowed with the thrill of transformation and I gave a low laugh. "Yes, I know, Mitch, this was my idea, so I should just get on with it."

Shivering slightly in the night air, I curled up on myself and summoned the image and the soul of the creature that lurked beneath my human surface, the creature that begged constantly for release. My limbs stretched and reshaped themselves, the fine hairs on my body coarsened and lengthened. There was pain, yes, but it was a familiar pain, and one that was almost instantly paid for by the absolute freedom that followed.

And then it was completed and I was the Cat. As always she roared defiance to the being that kept her caged. *Free,* she cried, *we are free.*

Mitch gave a howl, I gave a rumbling growl and we began to run, loping off into the night, no destination and no purpose, just the sheer exhilaration of perfect bodies and powerful muscles, leaping through the barren and empty countryside.

Behind the abbey were miles and miles of nothing but sparse grass and hills and rocks—the perfect hunting ground for us, or would have been, had there been anything out here large enough on which to feed. But we had fed well enough earlier to satisfy even the Cat's appetite.

I glanced over at the Wolf, running next to me, his mouth open to catch the wind, his eyes still the eyes of the one I loved. The Cat had learned to accept his presence in our lives just as I had learned to accept hers. He pulled ahead of us and the Cat growled.

Come, she said, *give up these foreign thoughts and just run. The door of the night is opened for us.*

Abandoning the human emotions that had been holding me back in this race, I allowed the Cat to take full control. With a burst of speed we drew up next to the Wolf and matched him, step for step.

When we had run for about a mile, we slowed and stopped, taking shelter in a spotty clump of shrubs. Not another soul, human or animal, was in sight; we shifted back into our natural form and made love, quickly and violently—a human response to the sheer excitement of the night. It was different than the love we had made earlier in the flat, dictated by animal instincts and the beauty of the night sky rolling overhead. Different, but no less better.

When we had finished, he rolled from me and we lay in silence for a while, side by side, both staring up at the clear night sky. "About an hour to dawn," I whispered, tugging teasingly on his earlobe with my teeth. "We should probably be going back soon."

He grunted his agreement and I closed my eyes, leaned over to kiss him and ended up kissing the cold wet end of the Wolf's nose.

He smiled at me, tongue lolling, eyes glowing, looking so much like Moe that I laughed, shaking my head. "I think you and that dog must be brothers under the skin," I said, starting my own transformation.

We were about five hundred yards from the abbey when the Wolf stopped short, sniffed the air and began to growl. The hackles on the back of his neck rose. I moved forward a step or two and stopped, pacing, catching the scent as well. My tail twitched wildly.

The scent of man, the scent of Other. The Cat gave a low rumbling sound.

And yes, there, up against one of the crumbling walls near the niche where we'd hidden our clothes, stood a man. Dressed all in black as he was, we might have missed him had we been in our human forms, but we were still Wolf and Cat and the Other reek of him was strong.

He held my shirt in one hand and was idly slashing it with the large knife he held in the other, looking more bored than alert. But that was just an act, I knew, for when he looked up and in our direction, I saw the glint in his eye.

I began to advance on him, my tail still whipping in the air. Slowly and cautiously, I padded toward him, my quiet paws making no noise on the grass. The Wolf circled back to come up behind him.

Foolish man, the Cat growled, *you should have chosen a better place to hunt.*

One step and then another I took, moving like a shadow in the night. He stood, still looking unconcerned. He dropped my ripped shirt on the ground and began to clean his nails with the tip of his knife.

Seeing that the Wolf was in position, I gave a

loud roar and the man looked up at me, smiled and nodded.

Bare your teeth all you like, Man, it will do you no good. For you are the hunted now and soon you will be dead.

I do not think he knew that there were two of us. Perhaps he had not burrowed deep enough into our hiding spot to find the other set of human clothing, perhaps he thought that we ran separately.

Or perhaps, the Cat interjected, *he is just a stupid man. The scar on the neck grants long life, not cunning.*

In a blur of motion the Wolf struck, hitting him from behind and knocking him to the ground. The man, however, managed to retain his grip on the knife and he slashed at the Wolf. The scent of blood splashed into the air, the Wolf growled in pain and anger and I sprang forward, fangs bared, biting deeply into the wrist of the hand that held the knife.

The man made no sound, neither of pain, nor of surprise. He did, however, drop the knife and within seconds the Wolf had ripped his throat wide open.

The man is dead.

I loosened my grip on his wrist and licked the blood from my mouth, then transformed back into my human shape. I knelt next to where Mitch crouched over the dead body, still in wolf form. His breathing was quick and the silver fur on his right shoulder was tinged with red as was his muzzle and neck.

I touched a finger in the Wolf's blood and brought it to my lips, tasting and testing.

"Not poisoned," I said, "so it should heal." I licked my lips. "And the man's blood itself tastes pure. I wonder what this means. Was it possible that last night's poison was a onetime attempt?"

Mitch began to pull back into his human self. As the fur covering his body disappeared, the cut on his shoulder became more obvious. It did not look deep and the bleeding had already ceased.

He looked up at the sky. "I don't know, but we have no time to discuss it. And no time to dispose of the body. I'll go through his pockets and you gather up our clothes. Make sure you don't leave anything behind. We're going to have to just leave him here and run for home. No doubt he was waiting, hoping to detain us until dawn."

I did as Mitch instructed and we hastily dressed and hurried down the dark streets to the pub. Mitch unlocked the door, and we ascended the stairs and made it inside with just minutes to spare, stopping for one second to reopen the door to let Moe inside.

Mitch closed and bolted the door then, turning to me and giving me a twisted smile. "Is this living close enough on the edge for you?"

"Oh, love, I am so sorry. You were right, we should not have gone. I never wanted you to get hurt."

He slipped off his shirt and I saw that the place where he'd been stabbed was completely healed. "No harm done," he said. "And I'm not at all sorry we went. In fact"—he gave me a mischievous smile—"until we met up with our friend, the evening was perfect. Running free and making love—nothing wrong with that at all."

I nodded and he continued.

"But this incident makes me wonder what the Others are up to, even more than I normally wonder. It can't have escaped their notice that none of their assassins ever come back."

He crossed the room and sat down at the computer desk, turned the machine on and swiveled his chair around to face me while waiting for it to warm up.

"Early on, that may not have been true," I said, "but at this time, yes, you're right. Terri and Bob proved that the other day; this was the first show they didn't brag about the vampire kill statistics."

Mitch typed a few commands into the computer, then spun back around. "The whole situation is damned odd. This most recent one didn't even put up a fight. He could have slit my throat easily and instead chose to stab me in the shoulder. Had the knife been poisoned, that kind of action would have been understandable. But a clean blade? It makes no sense. Do they all have a death wish? Who is in charge and why does he keep sending them after us, knowing they'll never return?"

"Perhaps he thinks that eventually one of them will get through."

"And what does he do to demand such dedication? The fact that their souls can be transferred doesn't do some of them much good. Our friend floating in the North Sea, for example, will get no rebirth. He is truly dead. They've got to know the risks and still they come."

I shook my head. "It all begins when they are babies, so perhaps they are trained from childhood to hate us. To believe that the extermination of the vampire menace is greater than individual purpose. And maybe they are told that their success will be rewarded with renewed life."

"Who knows? It's utterly futile to try to second-guess an organization filled with murderers and maniacs." He turned back to the computer and began his regular news search.

I took off my clothes, examining my shredded shirt. "This is one for the garbage now," I said, not expecting Mitch to hear or to answer. "Too bad, it was one of my favorites."

"I'll buy you a new one. While you were gathering the clothes I found a couple thousand pounds in his pockets. No identification and no credit cards, but plenty of cold, hard cash."

I chuckled as I put on my nightgown and crawled into bed. "Nice of them to subsidize us, isn't it?"

He nodded and turned back to the computer. "Sleep well; I won't be too much longer."

I smiled and turned off the light, so that the room was illuminated only by the glow of the computer screen. I knew he would be at least another hour or two, longer if he found something of interest.

I fell asleep, feeling safe and secure with the sound of the keyboard tapping and the quiet snore of the dog guarding the door.

* * *

To sleep, perchance to dream. The tapping sound follows me as I run along, run along, run along. The Cat knows nothing of poetry, of human fears. She is tireless and so am I. Immortal and free. We do not run to, nor do we run from. We have nowhere to go, no goal in mind. The running is the goal. The running and the sweet freedom. Our feet and our paws carry us far away, far away, over hills and rocks, out of the concrete and hard stone of the cities.

But we cannot go fast or far enough to please ourselves. We race up another hill, panting slightly, and stop at the top of it. Gazing up at the sky, thinking, yes, that would be a good place to run.

And we wish for wings. Silken and feathered, strong enough to kiss the fiercest wind. Yes, wings.

We curl down into ourselves and pull up that winged creature that has been lurking, that has been held captive, hooded and jessed—waiting and longing for so many years. Waiting for this night. Longing for this dream to give it release.

She bursts free, free of Cat, free of human form; this great and magnificent bird with feathers of velvet, brown and white and red. Pushing off from the ground, she spreads her wings, leaving the earth for the first time with a cry of triumph and defiance.

And we fly. Far and fast and free with no boundaries and no limits. Others now fly with us, we see. An eagle with silvered head, his strong wings carving out pieces of the sky. A swan with feathers black as midnight, her neck graceful and elegant even in flight. They call to us, swooping in lazy circles, but we push our new wings to their limits and fly beyond them, above them, higher now and faster than we would ever have imagined.

And then I see a black shadow, flying right next to us, pacing us, watching us, matching each of our movements. The Cat takes no notice of the shadow, nor does the Hawk, glorifying the use of her wings for the first time.

But I see him, he who is the shadow, and the form causes some spark of recognition deep inside me. I know him.

How did he find me, I wonder, *from so far away?*

And with the human thought, I falter. The Cat disappears and the Hawk is gone. My wings fail me and I drop to the earth.

SEVEN

I woke with a quiet gasp. Mitch lay next to me, sound asleep as was the dog by the door. I slid out of bed, walked across the room and built up a fire, then sat down on one of the small sofas in our sitting area, curling my legs up underneath me and watching the flames rise. Moe woke with my movements, he yawned and stretched, then came over to me, laying his massive head on my knee.

Idly stroking his ears, I remembered the dream and wondered why I had never attempted to transform to a winged creature. That the possibility existed was certain: I knew that Mitch and Vivienne had mastered the form, presumed that other vampires also had winged counterparts. Often difficult to know, since many kept their animal forms secret. And no wonder, they seemed to be a reflection of our inner selves—not something one wishes to share with the world at large.

Max, I felt sure, would have been a raven or a crow, black, glossy, beautiful and totally evil. Larry Martin had been a vulture, ugly and vile. And Victor? I pictured him with a soft chuckle; Victor could be nothing other than a giant bat.

I had been a hawk in the dream. Could I change into one in reality? Glancing at the clock, I saw that it was almost sunset.

After last night, of course, it would be folly to go out, especially alone. But I felt different now than I had before. My flesh had been pierced with poisoned wood and it was not healing. This small taste of mortality and pain made me restless, as if the very blood in my veins had been set on fire. I grew more foolhardy, perhaps, but also more free, more willing to take a risk.

What the hell, I thought, *there's no benefit in living forever, if one must hide away to continue such a life.*

I got up from the couch, signaled the dog to stay. Keeping an eye on Mitch's sleeping form, I dressed quickly and slipped out the door.

"Dottie!" Pete spotted me at the bottom of the stairs. "You're up and about early. Going out?"

"Yes, for a little bit, Pete. If Mitch comes looking for me, tell him I am fine and that I will be right back. I just have an errand to run."

He nodded. "Did a bit of that myself this afternoon. Don't you be stayin' out too late, now; I'll have a hard time holding that husband of yours back if you're late."

"I'll only be gone for an hour or so, Pete, no more than that." I smiled at him. "See if you can manage to hold him back at least that long."

That what I was doing was a mistake, I had no doubt. I lectured myself about it all the way to the abbey. And turned away several times, starting back for home. But something drove me onward, some longing that I did not fully understand. I should not have been out here by myself, I knew this more certainly with each and every step I took. I should have stayed in the flat with Mitch where I was safe.

At least by the time I arrived at the ruins, I had managed to talk myself out of attempting the transformation this evening. Instead, I walked through the graveyard and sat on the same bench Mark and I had sat on the other night, listening to the sea and the sounds of the night, watching dark clouds roll across the sky.

As it was early after sunset, there were a few other people around. Their presence reassured me; if humans were about, then there probably would not be Others. And while it was true that humans represented a different sort of threat, I felt capable of handling the situation, even when, after hearing a step behind me, I turned to see an unknown man approaching me through the graveyard. He was dressed in a pair of dark slacks, a white shirt and a brown corduroy blazer.

"Excuse me, miss," he said in a voice that sounded calm and harmless. "I don't want to disturb you, but I wondered if I could share your view."

I gave a low laugh. "Help yourself. The view is free."

He did not attempt to share the bench with me; instead he sat down on the ground, his knees cracked as he lowered himself and he gave a small grunt of pain as he settled himself in, legs stretched out in front of him and arms straight behind him, propping him up, hands resting in clear view on the ground. I gave him a glance out of the side of my eyes. Definitely not an Other. He spoke too easily for one thing and for the second, he looked to be in his late fifties to mid-sixties. Others tended to opt out of a body before it became damaged with wrinkles and the approach of old age. *Not much of a threat,* I decided, *at least not at this very moment,* and relaxed slightly.

"Nice night, isn't it?" His accent was not local, he sounded more urban, more sophisticated, upperclass. Most likely a tourist, out of season, searching for peace and solitude. Whitby provided both beautifully, as long as you were not being pursued by immortal assassins.

"Yes, lovely. But then it always is here. The ocean and the ruins so close by make for a peaceful combination."

"American?"

"Pardon me?"

He laughed. "I was commenting on your accent. You're American, aren't you?"

"Yes." The caution in my voice was apparent. I did not like people asking questions.

"Just making an observation, miss, no need to be defensive about it. I suppose it would be totally inappropriate if I asked what brought you to this part of the world."

"Yes, it would be." But I smiled to soften my words. "Would the same be true of asking you?"

"No." He smiled and turned his body slightly so that he was facing me. "I don't mind at all.

But I fear that I am here for nothing more exciting than business. I would hope that a woman as attractive as you would have a more interesting tale to tell."

I looked at him and began to laugh. Having been chased for years by predators who desired my life, I had apparently forgotten that there were other kinds.

"I seem to have missed part of this conversation," he said. "Was my last comment that humorous?"

"Yes."

"Oh." He paused for a bit, staring at my face. "May I ask why?"

"No, you may not."

"Then what shall we talk about?"

"Is there a need to talk at all? Why can't we just sit here in perfect silence and watch the ocean?"

He laughed. "I fear that talking is a prerequisite with me. I've been cooped up in a stuffy hotel room all this week, with nothing but a computer and a half-written article to keep me company. A nice young couple, American also as a matter of fact, recommended that I visit this site at night. I must say that they are right in their assessment; it is most interesting."

I tensed. "Article?"

"Yes, I'm a reporter. Which, of course, explains my need to talk." He gave a self-deprecating laugh. "As well as the half-written article. I've been meeting more dead ends than deadlines, I fear. None of the locals are particularly chatty, you see, at least not about what I wish to discuss. They'll discuss the weather and the latest football match, but on some subjects, they are as quiet as the locals represented here." He waved a hand at the gravestones and I smiled despite my tension.

"Perhaps you're not listening closely enough."

"Perhaps," he said, narrowing his eyes and focusing on my face, "but I have an odd feeling that my luck is changing, even as we speak. And that I will soon be blinded by a flash of inspiration."

He chuckled and stood up, grunting just a bit from the effort and brushing off the seat and legs of his trousers. "Hopefully it won't strike me dead in the process. However, I believe in playing hunches." He took a deep breath. "So here goes. Your name wouldn't happen to be Deirdre, would it?"

In the split second of indecision on how to answer this question, my eyes darted up to his. And that was all the confirmation he needed.

"So it is true. Despite the hair, I thought the face looked familiar."

With a quick movement I sprang up off the bench and into a defensive position. "I didn't say that it was."

"You didn't have to. But listen to me." He held his hands up in front of him, palms facing me. "I mean you no harm. Truly, I don't. Would I have come here, alone and unarmed, to face you if I were a threat?"

"You would be surprised, I think, at how many come alone. And as far as unarmed, I only have your word on that." I spun around behind him and grabbed his arms roughly, stretching them behind his back. "Put your head up," I said.

"So that you can rip my throat out? I think not."

"Well," I said with a laugh, "I believe that statement is obvious. Think, man, think. If your death had been my intention, I would have killed you already and your lifeless body would be on the ground." I pulled on his arms to emphasize the threat. "Now, do as I say and put your head up."

He complied and I stared at his neck. No visible scar. I reached a hand up to touch the area. He flinched as my finger ran over the whole length of his throat, but he stood stock-still and made no further move. I breathed a sigh of relief—no traces of a scar—his skin was smooth and unmarred.

"For what are you searching?"

I let go of his arms. "If you truly do not know, then perhaps you have a chance of leaving here alive."

"And then again," a familiar voice sounded through the cemetery, accompanied by a deep-seated growl, "maybe not. None of your kind can stand up to both of us together."

The reporter showed an admirable and surprising courage. The giant black dog skirted past him, still snarling, on his way to my side, but the man remained calm and stood still. When it appeared Moe was not going to attack or kill, the man straightened out his suit jacket and stepped forward slowly, his hand extended.

"I presume you are Mitchell Greer," he said. "Pleased to make your acquaintance. I'm with the *London Profile*. He paused for a second to see if we recognized the name. We did not. "And the name's George Montgomery."

"What's it to me who the hell you work for or what your name is?" Mitch's eyes glowed with anger. "When I find you up here threatening my wife, your name is more likely to be dog meat."

Moe growled and Mr. Montgomery gave him a glance out of the side of his eyes. "Please, Mr. Greer, I'm not threatening anyone, least of all your lovely wife. And while I understand your hesitancy to speak and your paranoia, I promise you I mean no harm. All I wish to do is set the story straight."

"There is no story," Mitch said, "and there never will be. Anything that is printed from this encounter will be dealt with swiftly."

"You'll sue me?"

Mitch threw his head back and laughed unpleasantly. "The correct response from a civilized man. Too bad for you that I'm not a civilized man, Mr. Montgomery, not now. Maybe I never was. I don't know anymore. But I do know that if you know who we are, then you know more than is safe for you. And there'll be no story."

"I don't understand, Mr. Greer. After that hideous television show, one would think that you'd be grateful to have your side known. It's a travesty of the worst kind, sensational and instigating; they don't even attempt to make it appear real now. It's all blood and guts and murder and, most importantly, contributions." George's eyes darted back and forth between the two of us, pleading. "If you trust me, I can help you; it's perfectly obvious to me that the two of you, indeed, all of the other 'vampires' featured"—he implied the quotes with a raised eyebrow—"are being unjustly persecuted. Isn't that the sort of thing for which you Americans fight?"

I caught Mitch's eye and he nodded. This man was telling the truth; in his mind I suppose he really did mean us no harm. But any publicity was bad publicity and must be stopped.

I moved in front of him this time, reaching up and holding his face between my hands, staring deeply into his eyes.

"We do not need your help, Mr. Montgomery. We merely wish to be left alone. There will be no story. And no blinding flash of inspiration either, I fear." I smiled and he gasped slightly at the sight of my fangs.

"So," he said, squaring his shoulders against the fear that entered his eyes. "I see. It's like that, is it? Everything they say is true. And now you're going to kill me."

"Kill you? No. We are just going to relieve you of the burden of this memory. It may be slightly painful, but I assure you that you will awaken tomorrow morning with no lasting harm. Relax now and it will hurt less."

I twisted his head down and bit his neck, sinking my fangs in deeply and taking his blood swiftly and effortlessly. After I estimated that I had taken enough, I pulled my mouth away. His eyes glazed over and he stared at me vacantly.

"You do not know me. You do not remember meeting me here." I led him back to the bench on which I'd been sitting and sat him down. "You met no one here. No one."

"No one," he murmured back to me.

"Yes," my voice low and soothing, "that's right. You met no one here. And you fell asleep, watching the ocean. The ocean is very peaceful, is it not? So calm. So soothing. You are tired, are you not, Mr. Montgomery? And sleep would be good, so good, would it not?"

He nodded and closed his eyes. I stood over him for a while to make sure that he actually was sleeping. Then I looked up at Mitch. "He's out." I mouthed the words.

Mitch came over to me and took my arm. "Let's go home," he said in an angry whisper, "and then you can explain to me what the hell you were doing out here all by yourself."

I shook my head. "I don't actually know, Mitch. And I don't want to explain, nor am I sure if I could. It all seemed the continuation of a dream. I dreamt that I could fly and I wanted to see if it was true."

"A dream? You came out here tonight and put your life in danger for the sake of a dream?"

"Mitch." I stopped in the middle of the street and looked over at him. "My only love, you know I adore you. And I love the way you protect me and care for me."

"But?"

I sighed. "There are times when I feel that I am suffocating in this stuffy little town, in that tiny little apartment. I don't know why. Cabin fever, perhaps. Or just the stress of dealing night after night with a death sentence. All I know is that when I feel that way, I must go out. And you must learn to accept that fact."

"I can understand that, Deirdre. Just let me know next time, okay?"

"You were sleeping."

"Well, wake me up next time. You might have been able to sneak past Pete without too much notice, but the dog went crazy almost as soon as you walked out the door. He woke me up and he led me here. Not that I couldn't have guessed where you'd gone."

He pulled me close to him, whistling for the dog, and we continued walking.

After a while he chuckled. "At least you got an extra meal out of the encounter. And Mr. Montgomery is none the wiser, I hope. But I really do wish you'd quit picking up strange men in cemeteries."

EIGHT

We arrived back at the Black Rose with no new incidents. Outside, at least, all was peaceful and calm. From a block away, however, we could hear belligerent voices and hurried to see what was happening.

"I'll not be servin' you more, mister." Pete's voice carried out into the street. "You've had more than enough for one night, more than enough for two. And it may just be the drink talkin', but I'll thank you to keep a civil tongue in your head when discussin' friends of mine."

"Yeah," a voice from the end of the bar chimed in. "Nothing wrong with Dottie and Mitch. In spite of their being from the States and all."

"Is 'at so?"

We walked into the pub as the man in question stood up from his bar stool, swaying slightly on his feet. Moving up behind him, we stood there, silent. Moe kept next to my side, whining quietly.

Too drunk to notice us or even to sense our presence, the man continued. "Nothing wrong with 'em, eh? Well, I'm tellin' you I saw 'em on telly t' other day and they seemed all wrong to me. We don't need their kind here in Whitby. Never have and never will."

A snicker ran through the regular customers. There was nothing they liked better than a confrontation, provided they were not directly involved. How we handled this would be talked about in many a home tomorrow.

"Wha?" The man leaned on the stool for support with one hand while banging the other down on the bar. "You think this is funny, don't you? Damn stupid twits. You think lettin' their kind in our town is a joke? Nah, I'm dead serious. I saw 'em on that Terri and Bob show and I'm tellin' you it's the truth."

With that comment, Mitch cleared his throat and tapped the man on the shoulder. "Excuse me, sir. I believe it's time for you to leave."

"I ain' goin' nowhere until I get another drink. Nowhere near closin' time." He staggered and turned around to face us.

The pub fell silent. The man looked at Mitch and gulped. He looked away and saw me with over two hundred pounds of dog by my side. I smiled pleasantly, but touched Moe on the back of his neck, giving him the signal to bare his impressive teeth.

The blood drained out of the man's face. But he kept up his aggressive actions, putting up his fists and jabbing them at Mitch, giving the dog wary glances every now and then. "You think you can take me? Come on, I'm ready for you."

Mitch did not move, did not say a word.

"See?" the man said, dancing around a bit.

"He's not that scary, all you need to do is stand up to him." He pulled his right arm back and aimed a punch right for Mitch's jaw.

It never connected. Mitch caught his fist in mid-air, held on to it tightly and squeezed. The man's eyes rolled and seemed about ready to pop out of his head. He whimpered and the regulars at the bar laughed out loud.

"That'll show him who's a damned stupid twit, Greer," one of them shouted encouragingly. "You go get him."

Mitch caught Pete's eye. "Is this guy paid up," he asked, "or do I need to collect on his tab."

Pete laughed. "You know better than that, Mitch, my boy. I don't run tabs for the likes of him."

"Ah, too bad," Mitch said, hustling the drunk toward the door. "I'd have liked to make him pay."

The bell on the front door jangled as Mitch escorted the man outside. Once there, I knew, he would send him on his way with the suggestion that he forget all about what just happened. Drunk as the man was, the suggestion would work fine even without the taking of blood. He would wake up tomorrow morning with a bad hangover, a sore right arm and hand and a few missing minutes.

"Last call," Pete announced, and the regulars turned back to the bar and their own drinking.

After closing, we washed up, Pete still chuckling over the drunk. "The look on his face, Dottie, when he saw that dog standin' next to you—he must've turned a hundred shades of white. And Mitch, catching that punch and dragging the idiot out of the pub? I guess that'll teach him to mouth off in the Black Rose."

"Or anywhere else for that matter, Pete," I said, with a smile, stowing away the clean glassware. "I wonder what brought it on."

"Too much drink in his gullet and too much time on his hands." He reached over and patted my cheek. "Don't you be worryin' yourself about it, Dot. He won't be comin' in here again any time soon, if I have anything to say about it. And I do, bein' the owner and all." He chuckled again as he took off his apron. "And that'll be it for me tonight. Have a lovely evenin', the both of you."

He headed back to his room and Mitch came up next to me, wrapping an arm around my neck. "Never a dull moment," he said, kissing my shoulder.

"Not lately, at least. I rather miss them, to be honest."

Mitch laughed. "Pardon me, but aren't you the woman who was craving excitement so much earlier this evening that she snuck off all alone and worried her husband half to death?"

"Guilty as charged, Detective. I think what bothers me the most is them finding us and naming us, Mitch. Outside, we are on their turf. But it should not be that way here, not in our home."

"You're not still worried about that jerk from the pub, are you, sweetheart?"

I nodded.

"He wasn't a threat, Deirdre," Mitch said, tightening his hold on my shoulders. "He wasn't anything more than a belligerent drunk. And I took care of him. So come on, let's go upstairs. And I'll teach you to fly if you want."

I smiled. "There's not much room up there to soar, is there?"

"You forget," he said with a playful grin, "the windows do open. And maybe it's time to let a little fresh air in."

He whistled for Moe and the other dogs and they came, padding out from the kitchen, licking their lips. "Okay, you lazy mutts," he said to them, pointing his arm to the stairs, "get upstairs now. For once you hellhounds are going to earn your keep."

They ran up the stairs and we followed. Mitch unlocked the door and let all three of them enter.

He answered my questioning look. "If we're going to leave the windows open, and go outside flying around, we'll need a guard posted. I don't much want to return and find an unwanted visitor. And I doubt anyone is going to break in here with all of them raising the alarm."

Locking and bolting the door, Mitch turned to the dogs. "Stay," he said, staring into the eyes of each of them in turn. "Lie down and stay." Curly and Larry obeyed instantly, but Moe gave a little whine and looked to me.

"Stay, Moe." I chuckled as Mitch gave him a dirty look. The dog sat at my command and then lay down, his eyes never leaving mine. "What a good boy," I said, then smiled. "Well, he is my dog, after all."

Mitch snorted. "I guess I hadn't realized how much. No problem. Are you ready?"

With my nod, he started to take off his clothes and I did the same as he began his tutorial. "I'll be honest, Deirdre, this form may be a problem for you. True, the transformation is not really all that much different from taking on the Cat. And it's much simpler than mist. The biggest problem with flying is that the process is completely foreign to us at first."

I nodded, understanding completely. Running as a cat or a wolf was similar to running as a human; one merely needed to get accustomed to the two extra legs. Flying, on the other hand, would involve a whole new set of rules.

"It's too easy," Mitch continued, "to get yourself lost in the experience. In fact, it's necessary. You must bury your true self deep in the instincts of the bird. It's dangerous if you think too much and it's dangerous if you abandon yourself completely. In short, it's a highly complicated balancing act. But," and his eyes glowed, "if you think the freedom of the Cat is exhilarating, you will love this. And I'll fly close if you get into trouble."

I remembered the dream and how I fell at the end of it, remembered the pain of transformation and the difficulty I'd initially had in adjusting to it all. "You know," I started, "none of this seems like such a good idea right now."

Mitch looked at me. "Are you sure? This was something you said you wanted."

I bit my lip. "And I think I've changed my mind. There will be plenty of time for the experience later. Right at this particular moment, I find I have no desire to lose myself. But," and my voice acquired a wistful note, "we could still turn out all the lights and open the windows, couldn't we?"

He smiled. "But of course, Mrs. Greer. Your wish is my command."

We spent the rest of the night sitting together on one of the sofas, watching the night sky rush past our open windows. When the sky began to lighten with the dawn, though, we closed them again, bolted the shutters closed and went to bed.

"Son of a bitch. I don't believe this."

I woke up to Mitch's voice, swearing. I sat up in bed and looked over to where he was sitting at the computer.

"What is it, love?"

"An e-mail from George Montgomery."

"Really? I erased his memory of us."

"Yeah, you did. But like any good reporter, he keeps notes. Somehow, he found our names again. And figured out how to contact us."

I got up out of bed and read the e-mail over Mitch's shoulder.

Dear Mr. Greer,

You don't know me. My name is George Montgomery and I have been a reporter for the London Profile *for over thirty years.*

I have reason to believe that you and your wife are being unjustly persecuted by an international group known as the Others. If this is the case, I would most sincerely like to help clear your names of the ridiculous charges being leveled against you by the show Real-Life Vampires.

While I can certainly understand hesitation on your part to meet with any reporter, no matter what his credentials, I'd like you to know that I have your best interests at heart and plan to write an article that once and for all sets the record, put forth by the most exploitative show of this century, straight.

I am most eager to arrange an interview with you and/or your wife at your earliest convenience. A meeting would prove beneficial to all of us and I would be honored if you would grant me one.

Please, Mr. Greer, let me help you. You may contact me by replying to this e-mail or by calling me at the Hotel Whitby Arms. Thank you for your time and consideration.

Sincerely,

George Montgomery

The London Profile

http://www.londonprofile.co.uk

"This is the same story he gave us at the abbey last night. Are you sure he sent this after we met him?"

"Positive," Mitch said. "The e-mail is date-stamped as having been sent today, not yesterday."

"So what should we do? Ignore him and hope that he'll go away?"

Mitch laughed and picked up the phone. "We can ignore him all we like, but I suspect it won't make any difference. He has a lead and he seems determined to follow it, at least for now. So we meet with him tonight and erase his memory again. And we do that every time we run across him. Eventually, he'll have to leave the area; he can't stay here indefinitely, following a lead that goes nowhere." He dialed the operator.

"Yes," he said when he received an answer, "I'd like the phone number for the Hotel Whitby Arms."

Mr. Montgomery was waiting for us by the hotel's front door right on time, in compliance with Mitch's telephoned instructions. From there we shook hands and exchanged pleasantries, a vast improvement over last night's hostile and threatening proceedings. We walked for a time, chatting about nothing in particular, until he cleared his throat and began his spiel.

"I hope you've had a chance, Mr. Greer, to check out my credentials and verify that I am, indeed, who and what I say I am. As I mentioned in my e-mail, I believe a great wrong has been done to you, your wife and many other people who have been branded as vampires, for what reason I cannot even fathom. But an article stating your side of the story could go a long way to dispelling these rumors and allegations."

I nearly laughed out loud, having now heard these same sentiments three times, twice in person and once in writing. After sneaking a glance at Mitch and receiving his slight nod of agreement, I turned to him.

"Mr. Montgomery," I said, with a sympathetic smile, "this is all well and good. If the rumors and allegations, as you put it, were not true, we would be most happy to provide you with the information you seek. However," and I put a hand on his arm and looked into his eyes, "we really are vampires. I do not think that is a story you wish to print."

"Excuse me?" His eyes, still held captive in my gaze, showed surprise and confusion. "I must not have heard you correctly. I thought I heard you say you were vampires. And what you must have meant, of course, was that you were not."

"No, Mr. Montgomery. The former is true."

"But I don't understand—" he started and I interrupted him.

"Yes, I know you don't. But it is all quite simple and just a moment of your time will suffice to explain."

I gripped him in my arms and my mouth came down on his neck for the second night in a row. He struggled for just a minute, then relaxed, permitting me to draw the blood I needed. Then I pulled away and planted the same suggestion as I had last night.

"You do not know us, Mr. Montgomery. You will forget everything about this meeting, you will only remember that pursuing this particular subject is futile. Futile, do you understand?"

He nodded and murmured something vague.

"Mr. Montgomery?"

"Hmmm?"

"You do not know me, you do not know Mitch Greer, you have never met us and you have no need to contact us in the future. No need, Mr. Montgomery, because vampires do not exist. There are no vampires, not in Whitby, not anywhere else. No vampires, Mr. Montgomery. Do you understand?"

"Yes."

"Good. Now go back to your hotel room, Mr. Montgomery, pack your bags and arrange to leave Whitby as soon as possible."

I turned him around and gave him a small push in the general direction of his hotel. He walked slowly at first, and then with more purpose, not once turning back.

Shaking my head, I turned to Mitch and sighed. "Let us hope that suggestion takes hold and stays with him. He seems so sincere that he almost had me persuaded to give him that interview this time."

"Yeah," Mitch said with a glance at his retreating figure, "he seems a decent sort. Too bad he's as persistent as he is; if he doesn't leave Whitby soon, he's going to suffer from an inexplicable case of anemia."

I laughed and linked my arm in his and we headed back home.

NINE

When we arrived, we saw Moe, waiting outside the pub for us, pacing back and forth in agitation. That he was happy to see us was an unmistakable fact, as he bounded over to us, tail wagging and tongue lolling. "Sorry to have left you behind, big fellow," I said to him, placing a hand on his head, "but we didn't need to intimidate Mr. Montgomery that much."

Mitch opened the front door and gestured for the dog to go inside, but the animal hesitated slightly and whined, lowering his head submissively and tucking his tail between his legs.

"It's okay, boy," Mitch encouraged him. "What's wrong with you? We're home. Come on, get in." Reluctantly the dog entered ahead of us.

"Oh, so you're back?" An unfamiliar female voice asked the question and I tensed. We'd had more than our share of unwelcome visitors and surprises these past few days; I did not feel up to dealing with another.

So, I put a hand on Mitch's arm, holding him back, wanting to ascertain who this new person was before entering.

The voice was low and sultry, containing just

enough of an edge to make you stop and listen, pleasant in tone, but mildly threatening overall. *A potent combination,* I thought, and one that I had used myself many times in the past. *Very effective. Sex and power.*

The woman stepped into our view and I saw that she matched the voice perfectly. At least as tall as Mitch, she stood slender but solid, glaring down at the animal. Thick curly jet-black hair fell down to her waist, her black jeans were skintight, her white cotton blouse had ruffles around the neck and dropped over one shoulder, exposing a lacy bra strap and a provocative glimpse of flawless skin. The hands resting on her hips looked strong and purposeful.

Then she smiled, exposing even, startlingly white teeth and a pair of dimples. With the dim bar lights shining behind her she looked like an angel. One who was, perhaps, not above a bit of vengeance.

"You may stay, dog," she said, a touch of laughter in the words, "but mind your manners."

Mitch stepped out of the shadowed doorway. "Thanks for the welcome. But I assure you, I always mind my manners."

The woman jumped slightly and it seemed that every muscle in her body tensed for just a second. "Oh," she said, relaxing and flashing him that sweet angelic smile. "It's you."

"That it is, my girl." Pete came up behind her. "This would be the very same Mitch and Dottie I'm always telling you about."

I did not need Pete's subsequent introduction

to realize with a sinking of my heart that this woman must be our new guardian, our female Renfield, the one who would, in Pete's words, do right by us and manage the daytime pub business in his absence.

Maggie Richards had arrived.

We spent the rest of the night in the pub, lingering long after the private members left. Maggie's son, who went by the improbable nickname of Phoenix and who had turned out to be substantially older than Pete remembered, had been put to sleep in Pete's bed as soon as they'd arrived.

"Poor little tyke," Pete had said, after the pub had closed and we were seated around one of the tables. "The train ride just tired him out."

"No so little, Uncle Pete." Maggie gave him a fond smile. "I can't believe you thought he was only four."

Mitch laughed, got up and brought a bottle of wine to the table. He moved around and poured us each a glass, pausing by Pete and putting a hand on his shoulder. "And I can't believe you don't know this old man better than that. He's rarely gotten a year or a name right since I've known him."

"Old?" Pete took a mock punch at him. "I'll give you an old man, Greer. You should be knowin' that most folks my age are already dead." Then he stopped and a broad grin crossed his face. "Oh. I don't imagine that makes my case any better, does it?"

They all laughed, Mitch sat down between Maggie and me, and raised his glass. "To family," he said, reaching down with his free hand and clasping mine, "old and new."

"Cheers." I clicked my glass with theirs and took a sip. As I set the wine down on the table my elbow rubbed on something warm and furry and I looked down to see Moe, sitting by my side. I looked at him, making full eye contact, expecting him to look away, but instead he sighed and whined quietly, eventually resting his head on my knee.

"Mitch?" I interrupted the story he was starting to tell Maggie, something about a particularly funny case he'd solved before we met. "I think something is wrong with the dog."

Mitch looked around the barroom. "I don't see him."

"That's because he's here, sitting next to me."

Mitch leaned over and the dog looked up at him nervously. "So he is. And what's wrong with him?"

"Well, for one thing, he's shaking like a leaf and whining."

Maggie laughed and I felt the dog tremble again. I put a hand on his head and he calmed. "I can explain that, at least, Dottie," she said. "He carried on so much when we came in, I had to chase him out with the broom. Cracked him right on the nose, I did."

"You did that?" Mitch turned to Maggie, astonished. "He might have ripped you to shreds, you know."

Maggie gave another laugh, but it had a heavy sound as if filled with darkness, not mirth. She tossed her head and the action caused her thick black hair to sweep in ripples across her back. "Not me. No dog will ever get the better of Maggie Richards."

I took another swallow of my wine, nodded, then drained the glass. "This is nice, Mitch," I said, getting up from my seat, and walking toward the bar, trailed by the dejected dog, "but I think I would like something a bit stronger. Port? Or whiskey?"

"Whiskey for me, Dot." Pete sounded tired and old. I looked at him and saw new signs of aging I was sure had not been there before. Feeling a flash of anger for the shortness of human life, and realizing with a twist of my heart that I truly cared for him, I gave him a broad smile. Then I poured a shot of whiskey, set it on the table before him and deposited a quick kiss on his cheek.

Even in the dim light of the bar, I saw him blush. "Thanks, Dottie. What say you and me take that cruise together? You can leave that Greer fellow behind."

"I doubt that, Pete. He's probably a very good swimmer." I walked back to the bar. "Mitch?"

"Damn straight."

"No, I wanted to know if you would like something else to drink. Maggie, how about you?"

"Whiskey," she said, giving Mitch a confident glance. "For both of us."

Mitch shrugged. "Sure, why not?" He turned around in his chair, his back to me, and started into the telling of his story. Why not, indeed.

I poured two glasses for them and carried them over. "Here you are," I said. "Can I get you anything else?"

"Thank you, Dottie," Maggie said. "Aren't you nice?"

"No," I said, my voice flat, "not particularly."

She sat there, drinking her whiskey and looking so absolutely beautiful that I felt, for a second, small and homely and totally undesirable.

Mitch gave me an odd look. "Are you okay, sweetheart?"

I leaned over and gave him a kiss, full on the lips, felt his arms rise up around me, felt the wave of his passion, knew that I could not doubt his love for me. I pulled away and smiled. "I'm fine, my love. Just tired. I think I need some air."

Mitch started to get up from his chair. "No, absolutely not. We were just out."

I shot him a warning look. "And I plan to go out again." I pitched my voice low enough so that only he could hear. "You are not my jailor, Mitch."

Pete leaned over drunkenly and put a restraining hand on Mitch's arm. "If the lady wants to be goin', she'll go. No one in the town would harm our Dottie, no, not even one hair on her funny yellow head."

"Thanks, Pete."

"No problem, Dottie darlin'."

Mitch twisted his mouth in a grimace. "Fine. Then I'll go with you."

"No." I kissed him again, a short one this time. "Don't be silly, you should stay and talk. I may not go any farther than the back of the pub. But I'm sure it's a lovely night and I cannot bear the walls around me."

He nodded reluctantly, understanding. "Just out back shouldn't be a problem. But take the dog with you. And if you do go somewhere, don't go too far."

I kissed him again. "Thanks, love." Then I turned to the dog. "Come on, you." Moe jumped up from where he'd been cowering and instantly came to my side anxious to leave the room and the strange woman.

We went out through the door in the little kitchen, leaving it unlatched so we could return. Pete had equipped the small porch outside with two wrought-iron chairs and a small table on which rested a pack of Players, a pack of matches and an ashtray. I laughed to myself, remembering that when Pete's wife was alive, she wouldn't allow him to smoke in the house. Apparently he still followed that restriction. "Old habits do die hard," I said and the dog wagged his tail briefly, then lay down with a sigh, facing the door.

I took one of the cigarettes, lit it and inhaled deeply. "Speaking of old habits," I said softly, "here is one of the oldest. Did you know, Moe, I began smoking when it was something that helped one fit in? Now it only ostracizes one and I'm still doing it."

He wiggled and whined, still staring at the door. "Yes, I know. I don't like her much either and she didn't even hit me with a broom. I wonder what her sons are like. Or more importantly, what Phoenix is like. What sort of name is that for a little boy? And why on earth am I asking you? Your name is Moe." I laughed then and the dog sat up. "Come on," I said, crushing the half-smoked cigarette into the ashtray. "Let's walk for a bit."

We crossed some of the other backyards and ducked through a narrow alley to the main street, joined there by the other two dogs. At first, they shied away from me, but since it seemed that I had their leader's endorsement, they followed as I made my way down to the river.

"I feel like the Pied Piper, somehow. I hope you boys can put up a fight if we run into any of Mitch's bad people."

The night, palely lit by a cloud-enshrouded moon, was peaceful and quiet. I'd found I never tired of watching the water, seeing the ships bobbing and weaving in the harbor, listening to the waves lap up against the stone walls. Off in the distance, I thought I saw the dim shape of a swan, an early riser, apparently, gliding like a feathered ghost over the water's surface.

"I suppose," I said softly, smiling to myself, "that life is not all that bad. If it were not for someone trying to kill us every so often, I might be able to adopt Vivienne's positive attitude."

One of the dogs gave a quick low growl and I heard the sound of footsteps on the pavement behind me. Much too late to change form, I gripped the railing as I braced myself for the sound of a gun or crossbow, held my breath, waiting for the burning pain of the poisoned wood.

When it didn't come, I spun around to face the intruder, with a growl of my own.

A boy stood there, staring. Dressed in pajamas and barefooted, he was not much of a threat.

"Hello there," I said, and relaxed and smiled, hoping that my fangs would not show. "Should you be out of bed? Should you be out here at all?"

He did not answer me. His eyes, shining blue in the moonlight, stared off into the distance, unfocused and vague.

"Sleepwalking?" No response. "And what am I to do with you? Leave you here? Find your house? Call the police?"

I walked over and knelt in front of him. "Hello? Boy? Can you hear me?"

His eyes never wavered, never moved to my face. The child unnerved me, his hair so blond it was almost silver in the moonlight, his body so slight and so thin that a strong wind could have knocked him over.

I touched his shoulders and he shivered violently. His small hands came up, gripping my arms tightly. A sudden pain shot through my left side, then subsided as quickly as it came. As I looked down at his quiet little face, I saw that his eyes were still unfocused, but his mouth had stretched into a tight-lipped grin. He shivered again and I moved my hands away.

The dogs came over and sniffed at him, warily at first, then with more enthusiasm, wagging their tails and putting their noses against his hands. But nothing they did seemed to register with the boy and eventually the dogs moved off in confusion at his lack of response.

I sighed and stood, gently removing myself from his hold, wincing from the pain his touch had caused. "Well, I certainly cannot leave you out here dressed like this. And on such a chilly night. What must your mother be thinking?"

I hesitated and permitted myself a twisted smile. Maternal instinct was hardly one of my better virtues. My own daughter, Lily, had walked the earth for over a century before I even knew of her existence; I was most certainly not a good one to make judgments in matters of children. I decided to take the boy back to the pub with me; Mitch would know what to do.

"Come with me," I said, reaching down and taking his cold hand in mine. Except for one tremor that seemed to shake his whole body, he gave no resistance and walked beside me, silent and grim.

When we arrived at the Black Rose, I opened the front door. "Look what I found by the river," I said.

Maggie turned away from where she and Mitch were still deep in conversation.

All of the blood washed out of her face; she rushed over and gathered up the boy, tearing his hand away from mine and holding him tightly to her.

"He's cold as death," she said, glaring at me, then looked back at the boy, her eyes searching. Her voice rose and contained a note of panic. "What the hell did you do to him?"

"I did nothing to him, Maggie, but bring him back here with me when I found him. I don't even know who he is."

She crooned something to the boy and smoothed back his short blond hair. His eyes were closed now and his face peaceful, innocent. It was almost a scene from some medieval mural, the beautiful woman, the lovely child. A mother's love. Why did I not know the boy instantly?

She looked up from her examination. "No harm done." She smiled, then said quite unnecessarily, "This is my son Phoenix."

TEN

Maggie tucked Phoenix back into bed and came out of the room with a rueful smile. "I'm so sorry, Dot. I didn't mean to jump all over you like that. I got a scare, is all, seeing him there with you when I thought he was safe in bed. Thank you for bringing him back."

"I trust he's all right?"

"Oh," she said, with a bit of a shrug, cavalier now that the shock had worn off, "you know how kids are. I'm sure he'll be fine after a few more hours of sleep. But he was chilled to the bone, going out as he did in just his pajamas, no coat or shoes. You wouldn't happen to have an extra blanket or two lying around that we could use, would you? That would seem to be all that Phoenix needs right now."

"Absolutely," Mitch said, "I'll go up and get some."

As he started up the stairs, Maggie came over and put a hand on my arm, gentle but firm.

I tried to suppress the slight shiver her contact caused and must have succeeded, or else she was too polite to mention the fact.

"You and I haven't exactly gotten off to a great

start," Maggie said, her voice hushed and urgent, "have we? First I terrorize your dog; then I monopolize your husband, and finally I completely lose my cool and scream at you for no reason at all. When I should have been thanking you." She glanced down at her feet, seemingly embarrassed, and a slight blush rose to her cheeks.

I had a difficult time focusing on her words, distracted by the heat of her skin through my heavy sweater—so lovely, so human.

I cleared my throat. "Thanks are not necessary, Maggie. I found the boy and brought him back, without even knowing who he was."

"But you're wrong," she insisted. "Thanks are necessary." She gave me a shy glance. "You know, before I arrived I had this picture in my mind that we would become friends. Because Uncle Pete thinks of you as his daughter, and that makes us family in a way. And because I'd heard so much about you and Mitch from him that I felt I already knew the both of you. Then I go and ruin everything with my quick temper."

"Nothing has been ruined."

"Good," she said, smiling, hitting me with the full impact of her beautiful face. "I hope you'll forgive me, Dot. Please say that you can."

I studied her; she seemed totally sincere and open, even down to the tears collecting in the corner of her eyes. I wanted to believe her, I wanted a friend, but over the years I had discovered that friendship was as great a risk as love. And something did not ring true about Maggie Richards; underneath that angelic exterior lay something dark, something she may not have known existed.

She inspired emotions in me that I did not understand and she frightened me. As did her son.

On the other hand, it was more than possible that three years of being hunted by seemingly innocuous killers had made me paranoid and untrusting. Perhaps the darkness I feared in her was merely a reflection of myself, a reflection of the fear and desperation that had driven me for so long.

I could not say any of this to her, however, so instead I gave her a slow, reluctant smile and nodded. "I can certainly try, Maggie."

"Fair enough," she nodded, smiling, pleased with my answer. She removed her hand from my arm and I breathed a silent sigh of relief.

"I guess," she continued, "we'll start here and see where it goes." Before I could protest or back away, she reached her arms out and enveloped me in a hug. "Thank you."

Her warmth and vibrance took me by surprise, and the musky scent of her hair and her flesh made me hunger as if I had not fed for centuries. My gums tingled, my fangs grew and I gave a low moan, struggling against her, trying to push her away from me, to a safe distance.

Her arms, though, held me tightly. It was almost a lover's embrace and awakened in me an instant and overwhelming desire. A desire for her blood, yes. But it was more than that. So much more.

I wanted to possess her in every way possible. I wanted to drink her deep into my soul and keep her captive there forever. I wanted to utterly consume her, remake her and consume her once more.

At that moment nothing else mattered. No one else existed; the entire universe consisted only of Maggie, this intoxicating morsel of flesh and blood.

My mind filled and overflowed with images of this woman: Maggie, smiling a welcome in the darkness of the bar, a halo of light surrounding her. Maggie, with her flawless skin, her perfect teeth, her full lips pressed to me in an eternal kiss. I could taste her sharp tongue darting against mine. I could taste her flesh, strong and vibrant, every inch alive and vital.

Time stopped. I could not breathe. Each gasping breath only served to pull in more of her heady fragrance, dropping me deeper into my fantasies.

I envisioned her naked, now, and the sight flooded my senses. Her beautiful ripe body lay before me, exposed for tasting and exploring, opened for my tongue and my teeth and my hands. Her sultry laugh rang in my ears, her deep and lovely voice whispered in my mind, and my desire for her quickened.

I moaned softly. Oh, the heat of her and the feel of her body pressed up against mine—this was surely heaven. My skin tingled from our contact, from the inner fires burning unbridled inside her. She enveloped me with those flames, searing my skin more surely than sunlight. And burn I did, delightfully, unquenchably, longing for more.

Somewhere, far in the recesses of my mind, a thousand warnings flashed. This union was forbidden, I knew with certainty. This union was fatal. One taste of her blood and I surely would be lost forever. She was tainted in some way I could not understand, she was a trap, she was the lure on the hook.

Still, fully knowing this, I took the bait offered. I could not resist, though all of my soul and all of my self denied the urge, though all of the people I loved cried out for me. Her presence drowned out their calls, her voice silenced the alarms, and the air around me hung heavy with the scent of her, soft and wild.

I hovered on the edge, it seemed, teetering between the safe ground of past life and the abyss of hidden passion and fires that opened invitingly before me.

I cannot resist, I thought, as I swayed and shook under her touch. *God help me, I cannot resist.*

And the thought became action. With blessed release, my mouth opened and my teeth pierced her skin. I drew her essence into me and her blood, so sweet and so spicy, exploded deep inside me. No other blood had ever been as rich, as fulfilling; the red flood of it raged through my veins, setting my entire being on fire. It fed my darkest hunger and filled the empty recesses of my soul.

There could never be enough of this, never be enough of her. I could drink forever, hold her forever and still be left unsatisfied and desiring more.

Swallow after swallow, I drained her. Her pulse slowed against my lips and still her hot rich blood flowed into my mouth.

How long, I thought, *can this ecstasy continue? How much more blood can she have, can she give? How much more can I drink?*

As if the thought broke a spell, my world suddenly spun back into motion; the split second of time that had held me frozen and rapt in her embrace began to move once more. I heard her laugh echoing through my mind, found myself in her arms again as if nothing had happened. Finding the strength this time to deny my appetites, I managed to push her away.

"Have I offended you again, Dot?" Was there just a small note of laughter in her voice? Was she taunting me, teasing me? Had my instant attraction been a deliberate attempt on her part? Had it been real? I could not tell, my senses were still reeling. I was dazed, confused.

Had I imagined all of it? I must have imagined it, I decided; she would be a bloodless husk otherwise, I had taken that much from her. But the taste of blood lingered on my tongue. The taste of her blood, for it could be from no other.

I shook my head, fighting the dizziness, attempting to calm the tremors that shook me.

"No, you have not offended me, Maggie," I said, turning away so that she could not see my growing bewilderment, "not one bit. It is nothing you have done. I find myself out of sorts this evening, I fear. It has been a busy evening for all of us and I am so very tired."

I had meant it for an excuse only, but when the words crossed my lips, I realized it was true. I was bone weary and felt ready to drop. "Once you get Phoenix settled in and we lock the doors, I believe I will retire for the night."

She peered out the front window of the pub. "Retire for the day, is more like it." She laughed. "The sun will be up soon."

"Even so."

Mitch came back down the stairs. For one small panicked moment I did not recognize him, he had been gone from my mind for so long.

"Here we go," he said, "extra blankets, as requested." He handed them over to Maggie and looked at me as I stared at him.

"Mitch?"

"Deirdre? Sweetheart, are you okay?"

I opened my mouth to speak but no words came.

Maggie answered for me. "She's completely done in, Mitch. All this business with my arrival and Phoenix's sleepwalking." She turned to me then and I stepped back. An amused knowledge bloomed in her eyes. "Dot, why don't you go upstairs and sleep now? Mitch and I will take care of the boy and lock up. Can't be too much left to do and there's no time like the present to start learning my new job."

I nodded and started up the stairs, hearing their quiet voices as they walked down the hall and into Pete's room. I wondered where Pete would be sleeping this evening, I wondered if Maggie would have the same effect on Mitch as she did on me, but I suddenly found myself too exhausted to care about any of the answers.

My arm ached and I felt the approaching dawn weigh me down with each step. Finally, after what seemed ages, I reached the top of the stairs. I opened our door, vaguely registering the fact that one of the dogs came inside with me, while the other two settled down outside. Not even bothering to slip out of my clothes or under the covers, I fell on the bed and slept.

I wander through the ruined abbey, happy in my solitude, enjoying the gleam of the moon reflecting in the fallen stones. I have no worries, no fears. The night is beautiful, sacred and silent.

Running underneath the silence, though, I notice now the sound of breathing. I stop and hold my own breath. As I listen the noise grows louder and louder, until it seems that the very walls surrounding me echo the sound. Louder and faster the breathing progresses and I catch low moans of pain mixed in with the steady inhaling and exhaling.

Following the sound, I see movement in the cemetery, a rising and falling of the earth itself, it seems. But as I draw closer, I see that it is a woman. Naked, she lies on the cold ground, her pregnant stomach heaving with each contraction. Her eyes catch my movement and she holds a hand out to me.

"Help me," she gasps, "help me."

I take her hand and look down at her. I know her, know the scent of her flesh and the taste of her blood. She cries out from the pain and I drop to my knees next to her, brushing her long dark hair out of her eyes.

"Hush," I whisper to her, a comforting lullaby. "I am here now and I will help you."

I put my free hand down gently on her rolling stomach. Her skin is stretched so taut and thin that I can see the movement of the child in her womb. More than that, I realize, I can see the face of the child, pushing out against the skin, fighting for its release.

It must be a trick of the moonlight, I think, that causes me to see the face of her unborn child in her skin. But I can also feel the face beneath my fingers, his eyes, nose and chin, the opening of his mouth in a silent scream of pain. Not the face of a child anymore, but that of a full-grown man. It smiles at me through the skin of her belly and the lips move, saying my name.

I try to jump up, but her hand still clasps mine. She gives a great cry of pain and the child is born. *See?* I say to myself. *It is only a child and nothing to fear.* I pick up the boy and hold him close to me, wrapping my shirt around him for warmth.

"It is a boy," I say to her, "a fine healthy boy."

"There is another," she gasps, still caught in the grips of birth contractions. I look at her stomach and see that she is right, there is another face, a different face, trying to find its way through her flesh. She gives another call of pain and another push and the second child is born. I put him into her arms and she begins to cry. Thinking she wants her other son, I hold him out to her, but she shakes her head. "No," she says between her tears and labored breathing, "that one is for you."

Well, I think, *why not? I helped him to be born, after all.*

The baby moves underneath my shirt, squirming over my naked flesh until it finds my nipple. Its mouth closes around my breast and its teeth dig deep into the skin. The woman laughs and I scream.

ELEVEN

"Evening, sweetheart. Did you sleep well?"

The dream faded into nothingness as soon as I opened my eyes to Mitch's face. He gave me a kiss and I smiled at him. "I think so," I said, faintly puzzled. "I can barely remember getting into bed at all."

"I'm not surprised, you were completely out of it last night. I tried to talk to you a little when I came up, but you were dead to the world. Worried me, so I tucked you in, all nice and cozy, and Moe and I sat watch all day."

I reached up and touched his cheek. "That wasn't necessary, Mitch, my love. I was tired, true, but nothing more than that. You should have slept."

He ran his fingers through his hair. "I wasn't really tired. And you shouldn't have been either. We had just fed. Was it the arm?"

I thought for a moment. "It did ache some as I came up the stairs."

"And now?"

"Fine." It was a lie, of course, one I did not even know why I would want to tell. "Perhaps it took a while for the poison to work its way out?"

He shook his head. "I don't like this, not one bit. There should be no pain, no aches and no aftereffects." He sat down on the edge of the bed. "Let me see it, sweetheart. Roll up your sleeve."

Reluctantly, I did so.

The skin in the area had completely regenerated; only a faint tinge of darker red tissue underneath indicated that I'd even been hurt. As we looked at it, though, there seemed to be a fluttering under the surface.

"What was that?" Mitch jumped slightly and reached out to touch the spot.

"A twinge?" I suggested. "My cells moving around trying to repair the deeper damage? I have never sustained a wound of this sort, so I'm just as confused as you. But it doesn't burn anymore and it doesn't really hurt at this moment. There are no striations and it hasn't swelled. Honestly, Mitch, I feel sure it will heal, given enough time. Can we not obsess about it anymore?"

"I'm sorry my concern for you has fallen into the obsession category." He sounded hurt.

"Oh no, Mitch, my love, I don't mean it that way." I wrapped my arms around his neck and kissed him long and hard on the lips. "But I'm not used to having something physically wrong with me. And I think I would feel better not talking about it."

"But—"

I let go of his neck and laid a finger over his lips. "Moe listens better than you, did you know that?"

He laughed at that, as I had intended him to

do. Rolling my sleeve down, I stretched and sat up in bed. "What time is it?"

"About an hour before sunset. We'll need to be down in the pub soon to get Maggie acclimatized."

"Maggie?" My voice sounded unsure. There was something about Maggie that I needed to remember. Something vital. Something that caused my pulse to race and a flush to rise in my cheeks.

Mitch laughed. "Yes, Maggie. I know you weren't yourself last night, but you can't possibly have forgotten her. She's much too overwhelming to forget." He tilted his head to one side. "So, tell me, what do you think of our newest addition to the family?"

"Family is probably stretching the concept, Mitch. She seems capable, I suppose, but I'm not sure I trust her." *Or trust myself in her presence,* I added mentally.

"She'll only be here for two weeks, Deirdre. We can manage that long. And"—he gave me a mischievous smile—"you have to admit, she's easy on the eyes."

I shook my head. "Handsome is as handsome does. She is easy on your eyes, perhaps, but she makes me nervous."

"Ridiculous. I think she makes you jealous."

I thought about that for a moment. "No," I said finally, shaking my head, "not really jealous per se, although she does make me feel small and plain. In the same way that Victor always makes me feel uncouth. She is so vibrant and warm and so very much alive. Her smell alone . . ." My voice trailed off. Her scent had been bewitching, mesmerizing, confusing. And her blood and the taste of her skin . . .

Mitch laughed. "Now you're saying she doesn't smell good? Deirdre, I think you just got off on the wrong foot with her last night. She seemed perfectly fine to me; maybe you just need to give her a chance."

I did not want to talk about how I felt about Maggie; I did not know how I felt about her. So I shrugged and moved to a different subject. "And the son? He frightens me. If you could have seen him last night, Mitch, standing there in the dark. Silent and staring. He doesn't seem right."

"He's just a kid, Deirdre," Mitch said. "I remember Chris at that age, walking in his sleep. It's something they do and while, yeah, it can be creepy, it's nothing to get upset about. Believe me on this, you're not used to kids."

"I do have to admit that you're right about that, Mitch." My own daughter could barely stand to be in the same room with me. What did I know of children?

"Then quit worrying. And prepare yourself. There's a repeat of the very first *Real-Life Vampires* show airing in a few minutes and I thought we should both see it, if only to compare then and now."

I groaned and pulled the covers up over my head. "Not another Terri and Bob show, Mitch, please. Anything but that."

"Sorry, babe." He yanked the covers off the bed. "If I'm going to watch it, you have to too."

The introduction was the same, the same melodramatic organ theme and the still photos of vampires. Bob made his remark about there being no names changed and no innocents. But they both seemed inordinately nervous, which, since this was their first national broadcast, should not have been unusual. Except that their level of anxiety was so high and so obvious, I started feeling nervous myself.

Perhaps that was the attempt they were after. If so, they succeeded admirably: a paranoid edge sharpened every word. Terri's eyes kept darting off camera, and flitting back and forth. She had not worn virginal white for the first show, I was surprised to see. Instead she dressed in a suit of pale variegated coral that under the cameras ended up looking as if it had been dipped in blood and then hurriedly bleached. Her hair was a bit long, also, and her smile seemed less practiced.

Their lead story was the bombing of Cadre headquarters, with a repeat of the original footage that shockingly revealed the existence of vampires to the general public. Following that was a lengthy obituary on Eduard DeRouchard, lauding him as a praiseworthy man of business and philanthropy.

"Doctor DeRouchard," Terri said, while behind her rolled collected films of Eduard, "was a pillar of the community and a prince among men, as well as a devoted family man." The photo behind her changed now to a casual family shot, the proud father with his two young sons. "Brutally murdered, incinerated alive by vampires of the

Cadre, he will be sorely missed by the world in general and this reporter in particular."

Mitch scoffed. "Not a surprise, Terri, considering he single-handedly jump-started your dead-end career."

"Good-looking boys, although neither of them look like him," I said. "I wonder who the mother was."

Mitch shrugged. "Could have been any of his various breeders, I suppose. Victor never said anything specific about the process, but I always got the impression that they bred these children like prize cattle, with the high-ranking Other officials serving as studs."

"That is a particularly nasty interpretation, Mitch."

He laughed. "These are particularly nasty people, Deirdre."

"Yes, I know that, but what an awful life for the children and their mothers."

"I'm sure there must be compensations. Don't get all soft on me, sweetheart. We're not watching this to acquire sympathy for the bastards."

I shrugged and the show returned from a commercial break. Bob introduced their newly opened Web site and the toll-free telephone number for contributions. At the bottom of the screen the dollars were already accumulating at an amazing rate.

"And now," Terri said, smugly now, as if she was over her stage fright and had warmed to the show, "it's time for *Real-Life Vampires'* frequently asked questions. Each week we'll be taking one question each from three of our viewers and if we use your question on the air we will send you a free *Real-Life Vampires* coffee mug."

"That's right, Terri," Bob said. "Our first question today comes from a viewer in Laurel, Maryland. Brian asks: 'How do I spot a real-life vampire?' "

Terri smirked. "That's an excellent question, Brian, and one that is often difficult to answer. Some signs to look for are abnormally pale skin, sharpened canine teeth and discomfort when exposed to sunlight."

"That's useful information, Terri," Mitch said, tossing a pair of his dirty socks at the television. "Thanks so much."

"Our second question," Bob continued, "comes from a viewer in Pittsburgh, Pennsylvania. Will writes: 'I think I've been bitten by a vampire. What do I do now?' "

"I can understand your distress, Will." Terri smiled reassuringly at the camera. "First of all, don't panic. Just one bite will not have any harmful effects. But be sure to call our toll-free number at 1-800-555-VAMP to report this attack. Or contact us from our Website at reallifevampires.com. It is true that a vampire living in your neighborhood can drastically reduce property values and the quality of your life."

I groaned. "Did she really say that?"

"I'm afraid so."

"Our final question," Bob intoned, "comes from Sue in Burbank, California. Sue asks: 'Is it true that vampires don't have reflections in mirrors?' "

"Thank you for writing, Sue. And the answer to your question is sadly, no, that particular myth is not true. Vampires have reflections in mirrors just the same as you and I. Another popular myth that vampires are unable to cross a stream of flowing water has also been proven as untrue."

"And that's all the time we have tonight, Terri," Bob said, "so until next week, we urge you to be vigilant and be strong. We will be here to give you the truth, because *we* believe *you* have the right to know."

"So much for that," Mitch said, turning off the television set. "That's probably got to be the biggest load of misdirected bullshit I've ever seen. It's hard to believe that even Terri and Bob could have been that melodramatic or that they've actually improved over the years." He leaned over and gave me a kiss on the tip of my nose. "I'm going to go downstairs now and get the evening started. Get up when you feel like it, then get dressed and meet me down at the bar. But don't be too long, or I might have to get friendly with our new guardian angel."

Even that threat was not enough to hurry me through the shower. The water was as hot as it could be and I stood for a very long time just letting it cascade over my cold skin. I laughed to myself, thinking how glad I was that Terri was right at least about one thing. Certain mythical restrictions of vampiric life *were* wrong. Life would not be worth living without flowing water.

When the water finally cooled, I turned it off, took a towel from the rack and dried myself. Looking in the mirror was still a shock for me; I had cut my long auburn hair very short and bleached it blond shortly before moving here to Whitby. And while I was glad now that I had, I still felt that the woman looking out from the mirror at me was someone different.

I finished up with a little bit of makeup, a few passes of a towel over my hair and walked out into the bedroom to get my clothes from a small wooden dresser. *At least,* I thought as I pulled on my last pair of clean jeans and a heavy black sweatshirt, *I don't have to worry about wardrobe choices these days.* Every article of clothing I currently owned was made of dark material to better blend into the night. In addition, everything could also be rolled up and crammed into a small backpack. When we traveled now, we traveled light and in a hurry.

I began to gather all of the clothing strewn around the apartment and stuffed it all into a large canvas bag, except for the black sweater I'd worn the night of the attack.

Inspecting the tear in the sleeve, I determined that I might be able to fix it, and set it aside for repair. It was a favorite of mine and I did not want to discard it. Carefully folding it, I put it back into one of the dresser drawers. Then I topped off the bag with the wet towels from the bathroom and sat down on the bed to lace up my black hiking boots.

"A fine thing, Moe," I said to the dog by the door when I stood up. At the mention of his name, he jumped to his feet and wagged his tail; I lifted the bag and settled it over my right shoulder. "Who ever heard of a vampire having to do her own laundry? Picking up dirty underwear? Buying fabric softener? I know. Perhaps Terri and Bob could do a special show on that topic. *'Real-Life Vampire* Laundry: How to Tell if Those Dirty Clothes Have Been Worn by a Bloodsucking Creature of the Night.' " I laughed at the ridiculousness of the thought as I opened the door.

I had to set the bag down to turn the key in both locks, and then slipped the key into the back pocket of my jeans. Shifting around, I started forward and almost ran right into the boy standing there.

I jumped, surprised at his presence. Then I smiled. "Hello," I said. "You frightened me. I'm Dottie."

He nodded sullenly.

"And you must be Phoenix. I met you last night but I feel sure you don't remember. You should not be up here, I think."

He reached up to touch my left arm, shook his head, then pointed down to the laundry bag.

"It's our laundry."

He nodded more enthusiastically this time, gave me a small grin that lit up his entire face. Then he picked up the bag and started down the stairs, dragging our dirty clothes behind him.

I watched him struggle with the load and shook my head. Mitch was right, I did not understand children.

"Come on, Moe," I said to the dog, hesitating at the top of the stairs, "let's go down."

TWELVE

Mitch stood behind the bar with Maggie; my entrance interrupted their quiet conversation and he looked up and smiled.

"Did you," I said, walking over to him and giving him a kiss, "happen to see a boy come through carrying our dirty laundry? And would you happen to know where he went with it? I won't even ask why."

Maggie laughed. "Isn't that lovely? He's such a good boy. You see, that's always been his chore, Dot, carrying the laundry for me. It's nice that he did it for you. It means he likes you. I think he must have heard us talking about your sore arm and decided you needed help."

"My sore arm? Why were you talking about my arm?" I gave Mitch a sharp glance.

"Yes, your arm, Deirdre. You do remember that, don't you?" Mitch looked at me, faintly puzzled.

"Yes. But my arm is fine."

Maggie's eyes swept over my face and I felt myself blush, remembering what had transpired between us the previous evening. She gave no sign of embarrassment. "That's not what Mitch says. Maybe you should see a doctor?"

"My arm is fine," I repeated and headed toward the small laundry area located off the kitchen. The boy was already there, sitting in a little chair next to the washing machine, kicking his feet against the bag of laundry.

"Hello again," I said to him, offering him a smile as I pulled out clothes and put them into the washer. "Thank you for carrying the laundry down the stairs and into here for me. That was a very nice thing to do."

He shrugged his shoulders and kept staring at me with his pale blue eyes.

"Your mother says that you help her a lot. It's a good thing for a child to help his parents, don't you think?" I spun the dial to the proper setting, added detergent and glanced at him again. "You don't talk much, do you, Phoenix?"

I waited for a response. When none came, I sighed, closed the lid and started the machine. Turning and leaning back against the washer, I met his direct stare. "Do you even talk at all?"

Phoenix gave his head a violent shake, jumped up from the chair and ran out of the room.

"No, I suppose not," I said. "Or at least you don't seem to want to speak to me."

I heard laughter come from the bar: Pete's deep rumble, Mitch's hearty bass and Maggie's sexy contralto. Suddenly I felt very much an outsider—a feeling I knew all too well.

It didn't help knowing that there was no need to feel this way. All I needed to do was enter into the bar and I would be included into the group. Pete treated me as his daughter. Maggie wanted me to be her friend and sister. And Mitch loved me and only me; all I had to do was look into his eyes to know that truth.

Knowing all of this did not help. At that moment in time, as they laughed and talked, I felt desperately alone, more than I had ever been, more than I had ever expected to be again.

Quietly, I opened the back door and slipped outside into the night. I stopped by the wrought-iron table, picked up a cigarette and lit it, staring off into the darkness. Moe came up beside me, eagerly anticipating another walk, perhaps. "You cannot come with me tonight, old boy," I said softly, shaking my head and motioning for him to sit and stay. "You would not be able to keep up."

Crushing the cigarette out, I moved away quickly, heading back out an alleyway and onto the steep street that led to the abbey. The sky was cloudy, overcast with more than enough moisture in the air to bring a fog up from the water. A perfect night for a run.

Ordinarily, Mitch would be by my side. And although I knew he would be angry again at my going off alone, I needed solitude for reasons I could not put into words.

All I knew was that something was wrong. With me. With the world around me. With Maggie and with her son. With how I reacted to her. All of it was wrong, dead wrong. The situation's evilness hit me in the pit of my stomach and turned me inside out. And I did not know why.

My mind was as hazy as the sky, my thoughts as restless as the sea. A run would clear this, it always had before.

I stumbled over something as I entered the ruins. Looking down at my feet, I saw that it was a dead swan. "Oh, you poor thing," I whispered and reached down to touch its feathers. The lifeless body was still warm and its neck had been broken and crushed. It rested in a little pool of its own blood, coming from, I thought, the abrasions on its neck. It bore no other marks of violence. *How strange,* I thought, *that whatever animal killed it didn't carry it off somewhere to finish its feast.*

Perhaps my arrival had spooked the killer. And it didn't matter, the poor swan was beyond any help I could have given it. I left it lying there, thinking that I would bury it when I returned.

Finding a sheltered corner in the ruins, I removed my clothes and folded them neatly, tucking them into the niche we always used. Then I stood and took in a deep breath, preparing myself for what awaited.

I knew that the Cat would run the restlessness out of my bones, the uneasiness out of my heart, and that I would return from my run refreshed and released of fear and doubt.

A growl started deep within the center of my body, and I felt the transformation begin, the exhilaration of the Cat being released.

Free, she rejoiced, *I will be free.*

Suddenly, though, the normal pain of change became worse: an excruciating burning that started in what I thought was the fully healed wound on my left arm, a torture that spread to every inch of my body.

"No," I screamed out in the darkness, my need for secrecy supplanted by the severe pain. My voice sounded both human and bestial, my body caught between the human form and the feline.

"No!" I screamed again. "I cannot." The Cat howled in frustration and pain at being denied its freedom and retreated once again.

I fell to the ground, panting and sweating and shivering. The pain was more severe than any I had ever experienced or imagined. I longed to just close my eyes and drift away from it, but I knew that I must return to my natural form. With a tremendous effort of will, I kept my mind focused on the change back to human.

Finally, when my limbs returned to frail-seeming humanity, I curled up upon myself again and closed my eyes. The pain subsided as quickly as it had arrived, but I wanted to rest, just for a little bit of time, before returning to the pub. Something large and warm nestled down next to me, whining softly and offering comfort as it could. I wrapped my arms around him and smiled. "I thought I told you to stay," I said to Moe. "But you are a good dog for finding me. We'll go back home in a moment." My eyes closed and I slept.

I rise up from the cozy little nest I'd made for myself, laughing at how the pain was gone. I dress in the clothes I'd left stashed away: black leather jeans and a red silk shirt; slip my feet into black high-heeled pumps. I brush my hair out of my eyes, throwing it back over my shoulders, and look around. The city streets are quiet and empty. That does not matter. Nothing matters now. Although I do not know where I am or why I am here, I know that I am home.

My feet find their own way and I arrive outside the door of a building—a club, it seems. A young and handsome blond-haired doorman with insane eyes smiles and lets me enter. Inside, everything is strange but comfortably familiar. A band is playing and I watch the people on the dance floor. A tall gray-haired man dances with an equally tall black-haired woman; his eyes meet mine as he turns in the dance and I gasp. They are beautiful, blue and glowing. I know him. My heart aches with love for him and the knowledge of him. Why is he here? Why is he dancing? His name is—

He turns away and the thought is gone. Another dancing couple catches my eye. In this one the woman is small, frail and impossibly blond with keen gray eyes and an impish smile. The man she is with is young, much younger than she, with eyes similar to the gray-haired man's, but not as piercing or as familiar. He bends his mouth to her and drinks from her, draining her until her long slender neck falls limp and her feet falter in the dance. Like a swan, I think, a dead swan I saw somewhere, not here, but far away and so very long ago.

The crowd closes around them and they are gone, replaced by a woman, no, a girl, with short red hair. I feel as if I know her better than any of the rest and yet at the same time, I do not know her at all. Her partner seems to flicker in and out of existence. He is dark and elegant and carries the weight of many years in his body. I know him too.

There are more, dancing there. I know them all. But I cannot remember the names. I cannot remember how I met them or what importance they held in my life prior to this moment. And I realize it does not matter.

For, now, in the center of the dance floor, a lone man stands, beckoning to me. The knowledge of this man runs deep in my veins. I fear him. I hate him.

I love him.

He reaches his hand out to take mine and I marvel at his finely chiseled features, his dark hair streaked with gray, his twisted smile. I had thought never to see him again.

"Welcome home, little one," he says. "It has been a long time." Pulled into his arms, I cannot resist. I relax in his embrace. His mouth brushes my ear and he whispers a name—

"Deirdre?" I opened my eyes to an angry male face leaning over me. Disoriented as I was from the aborted transformation and the dream, it took more than a few seconds to recognize him.

"Mitch?" My voice sounded small and frightened.

"What the hell are you doing here? Naked and

sleeping in the ruins? Have you lost your mind? What if one of the Others had come across you?"

"Oh, Mitch." I held back a sob. "I have never . . . changing into the Cat hurt so badly that I couldn't do it . . . and then I dreamt that . . ." But the dream escaped me, as if it had swirled off, dancing into the fog. Perhaps it had.

"Well," he said, looking down at me, still angry, "get dressed and let's go home. We can talk about it later. At least you had the good sense to bring Moe with you this time. He was standing over you, growling and snarling, when I arrived. He didn't even want to let me near you, until I convinced him otherwise."

I stood up unsteadily and began to dress myself. "Really? I didn't hear him. What time is it?"

"Almost dawn, love."

"Ah. Almost dawn." The dream languor continued; somewhere in the back of my mind I remembered the importance of dawn. I slipped into my sweatshirt, pulled up the jeans and zipped them, tucking my panties and bra into the back pocket. I picked up one of my heavy hiking boots and leaned against the wall, trying to support myself and put on the boot at the same time.

"Forget this." His voice now held more laughter than anger and he walked over to me quickly, picking me up, cradling me in his arms. "We don't have time to struggle with your boots. I'll carry you home."

Home? But I was home, in the dream. And I no longer dreamed. "Home?" I said, my voice bouncing from the ruined stones and returning to my ears as if from faraway. "I have no home."

His blue eyes stared down at me. "Why would you say that, Deirdre? You know that your home is with me and it will always be."

I took in a deep breath of air, shivering slightly. "I'm frightened, Mitch. What's happening to me?"

He did not give me an answer, just held me close to him and started out of the ruins. I clung to him and cried.

THIRTEEN

"Good." Maggie's brisk voice greeted us at the back door of the pub. "You found her. Two lost people in two nights are two too many."

"Lost?" From the shelter of Mitch's arms, I looked up at her in confusion. "I wasn't lost."

Maggie shook her head. "I'm not sure what else you'd call it, Dot. When Phoenix told us you'd gone out, we figured you'd be back in a little bit. But you've been out all night. If that's not lost, I don't know what is."

"Phoenix told you I went out? But he doesn't speak, as far as I can tell. How did he know? And how could he have told you anything?"

A mixture of sadness and anger entered her eyes. She moved in toward me, opened her mouth to speak, but Mitch shifted his weight, pulling me in closer to him, away from her, and interrupted. "Look, Maggie, I need to get her to bed now, I think. And try to get some rest myself. We can continue the discussion tomorrow sometime. I can explain to Deirdre about Phoenix, if you'd like."

"Yes, of course," she said, her expression softening. She patted me on the arm, surprising me once again with the heat of her touch. "I wasn't thinking. It's been another bad night, hasn't it? This keeps up and before you know it you'll begin to think it's all my fault."

He leaned over and gave her a quick kiss on the cheek. "I promise you, Maggie, no one thinks that. And don't worry; it's nothing we won't survive. Thanks, though, for caring. We'll both see you tomorrow night."

Once we had entered the apartment and locked the door, Mitch set me down gently on the bed. "Take your shirt off."

Something in the peremptory tone of his voice angered me. "Do not treat me as if I were your child, Mitch. I am perfectly capable of taking care of myself."

"Are you? I'd have said so until just recently. Now? I wonder. What the hell were you thinking? Going off alone like that again, without a word to me that you were going? You promised not to do that."

I shrugged. "I knew what I was doing. And I didn't think you would notice since I only planned to be out for a short run. Besides, you were completely preoccupied with Maggie."

His eyes narrowed and his mouth drew into a frown. "Exactly what's that supposed to mean?"

"Nothing. Just that you were busy." I could have stopped with that statement, but I was frightened and hurt and angry. "Apparently," I continued, the words spilling out, "you were so busy that you didn't even realize I was missing until it was almost dawn."

Mitch sighed, still frowning. "The pub was crowded, Deirdre, someone had to tend to business. We need this money, you know that as well as I do. We need to make a success of this place."

"And after the pub closed? What were you doing then?"

He ran his hand through his hair and shook his head, his eyes glinting at me. "Jesus, I can't win. You complain when I look after you and now you're complaining because I didn't." His eyes shifted away from mine. "As far as what I was doing, well, you know, I don't like what you're implying."

"And I don't like implying it. But it is an interesting question, don't you think?" I stopped for a minute and heard the words I had just spoken, seeing their meaning clearly as if they hovered in the air above us.

What was I doing? I loved this man more than life itself and I knew he felt the same about me. If I could trust no one else in the world, still I knew I could trust Mitch. Pain was only pain and the dream was only a dream and both could be ignored. But this moment was real and words could be said that we both would regret. I sighed and swallowed my anger. Smiling up at him, I touched a hand to his cheek.

"What am I saying? I'm so sorry, Mitch. I don't mean to imply anything about you. And I don't want to fight with you. Not about this, not about anything. Not for as long as I live. I love you."

"And I love you, even if you are an idiot at

times. Now be a good girl and take off your shirt so that I can see your arm."

I nodded and pulled off the sweatshirt, wincing slightly, more from anticipation of what I might see than from the brushing of the fabric against my skin. I squeezed my eyes shut; I did not want to look.

"Interesting." Mitch gingerly touched the flesh. "Does this hurt?"

"No. It should, I suppose, considering how badly it did earlier. But no," I said in amazement, "it doesn't hurt."

He gave a low whistle. "And it's completely healed. Look for yourself."

I turned my head, opened my eyes and saw that Mitch was right. There was no mark, no scar remaining to show that I had ever been wounded there. Just as it should be.

"Then what's wrong with me?"

"Maybe nothing." He touched my skin again. "Unless . . ."

"Unless?" I bit my lip. "What are you thinking?"

"It doesn't necessarily have to be something bad, sweetheart. Why do you always think the worst? Maybe the poison has been dispersed through your body or maybe it's been neutralized by your metabolism. That process may just have taken longer than normal. I wish Sam were here. He could take a blood sample and find out for sure."

"Or you could sample my blood yourself."

"True enough." He smiled at me. "I know the

taste of you better than anything else in the world."

"Do me a favor, my love?"

"Anything for you."

"Make love to me first."

"Why, Mrs. Greer." His eyes glinted at me as he turned out the light. "I thought you'd never ask."

His arms went around me, his mouth came down on top of mine, and all thoughts of the world outside disappeared. There, in the total darkness of our room, in the ruins of our life, we made love. Slowly and delicately, Mitch covered every inch of my body with his hands and his mouth until I grew wild with hunger and desire for him. He coaxed me to climax twice and I cried out with passion, thrashing and moaning.

"There," he said, when I had quieted and lay breathing heavily, "isn't that better than fighting?"

"Oh, yes, absolutely." I inhaled deeply. "Much better. Now I want you to lie still and let me love you."

He gave a little laugh, which turned to a low moan as I began kissing him, starting with his eyelids and his cheekbones and his bristly chin. Playfully I bit at his earlobes and his lips, nibbling my way down his body, hands trailing in the wake of my mouth. I loved the feel of him, loved the scent of him, loved the taste of him.

He gasped when I took him into my mouth completely, gave another moan and began to rise and fall with me in perfect rhythm. His hands

touched my head and he laughed when he could
not grasp my hair. It didn't matter, nothing mattered but my mouth and his body and the love
between us. My teeth grazed the taut skin of his
penis, drawing off a drop of his precious blood.

His muscles tensed and he growled, thrusting
himself deeper into my mouth. I sucked on him
deeply, savoring this fluid as much as I savored
his blood, swallowing each and every drop.

Then it was over and he gave a loud sigh, reaching down and pulling me up to lie next to him.
I smiled and snuggled into his side, my hand lazily
brushing over his chest.

When his breathing returned to normal, he
bent his head down and sank his fangs into the
tender flesh over my right nipple. I felt the soft
suction of his mouth on my skin. He took no
more than a small taste before he stopped, his
body going totally still. He choked and pulled his
mouth away from me.

"I'm sorry, love." His voice was filled with anger, not directed at me this time. "The poison is
still there. Those damn bastards; they'll pay for
this. But first . . ." he gave me a quick kiss, got
up from the bed, turned on the light and walked
to the phone. "First, I'm going to call Sam.
There's no way we can treat this ourselves. And
you're more important than—"

"No, Mitch," I interrupted, my voice small and
frightened, yet determined. "I am not more important than the continuation of our friends and
our family. This must be what they've been planning: to force us out of hiding, to cause us to

reveal the locations of those remaining. They know you apparently and they know how you think. How are they able to know so much about us when we know nothing about them?"

"You're right, of course." He set the receiver down. "But what am I supposed to do, Deirdre? Just stand around and watch you die?"

I forced a laugh. "I don't think I will die any time soon, my love. For one thing, you won't permit it. So," and I stretched my arms out to him, "come back to bed. You have had no sleep for two days now while I seem to have done nothing but."

He hesitated.

"Mitch, my love, there is nothing you can do right now. Come. Sleep. I'll watch and wake you if there is any change. Things may seem different after a good sleep."

He nodded, crossed the room and lay down next to me. I stroked his hair; he relaxed and slept.

The day passed slowly for me, with nothing to do but lie still, stare at the ceiling and think. My thoughts, however, were disturbing and always came to the same dead end. We did not know who and we did not know why.

I concentrated for a while on the feel of poisoned blood rushing through my veins. By filtering out all outside noise and distractions, I could hear the thrum of movement, the pounding of my heart and I could feel the slow burn spreading; not particularly unpleasant or painful, the feeling was just different.

I wondered if there was a cure, wondered what sort of progression the poisoning would follow, wondered why they had arranged it this way. I was not an important person in Cadre politics; Mitch would have been a more obvious target. Even had they chosen to poison Victor, that would have made more sense than inflicting it upon me.

To keep away from the dead ends, I began to run through my life, replaying important memories, calling to mind faces of those I had loved and lost.

They were not that many, especially considering the many years I had lived. I had always structured my life to avoid involvement whenever possible, but there were still a few dear ones who managed entrance.

Gwen, my sometimes silly but always endearing secretary when I owned Griffin Designs—dead at the hands of Larry Martin. Chris, Mitch's son, murdered also by Larry. Elly, our next-door neighbor when we lived in our cabin in Maine—not dead, perhaps, but certainly lost to me. There would be no return to that place.

One by one, I worked my way through the list, replaying important events, summoning up very real emotions until I made it down through the past and into the years of my humanity.

There I stopped with a shock as if I'd hit a brick wall. And try as I might, I could not get beyond it. Objectively, of course, I knew that something existed on the other side of that wall. But I could not even summon up the barest trace of what had been.

Gone were the memories of that time: the rich emotional warmth of recollection, the love I must have felt with people that I knew then, the laughter and the tears, even the process of becoming what I was now—all of this was gone, all of this that helped to make me who I was, violently ripped from me with no notice and no purpose.

"Bastards." I whispered the word so that I would not wake Mitch. "Goddamned bastards." Would it continue, I wondered, this loss of memory, until I became nothing more than a shell of the creature I was now? An undead machine, emotionless and cold. Was this the cost of the poison that even now I could feel filtering through my body?

I crawled out of bed carefully, and, finding the laundry that I had started earlier, now dried, folded neatly and stacked on the sofa, I dressed in black jeans, a black tank top under a red plaid flannel shirt and a pair of thick black socks. *Quite a change from the elegant costume of the dream,* I thought, and gave a small bitter laugh.

Not distracted by thoughts of clothes, though, I felt my mind still reeling with the implications of the memory loss and I sat down at the small computer desk, staring at the blank screen. "Is that what you want, you bastards? To drain me of everything that makes me what I am now? What possible use does that serve?"

"Deirdre?" The sleepy voice from the bed startled me. I had forgotten how lightly Mitch slept these past few years. "What time is it?"

I checked the clock on the mantelpiece.

"About an hour to sunset, my love, go back to sleep."

"No." He yawned loudly and sat up. "I can't now, I'm awake. I'll make some coffee." He came over to me, looked at the blank screen and laughed. "I should have known you weren't using that," he said, "but you really should learn."

"Yes, I suppose I should." My voice sounded flat and emotionless.

"Something's wrong. Is it the arm?"

I laughed. "No, nothing that simple, Mitch, or that easily observable. I cannot remember."

He shook his head. "Maybe I'm just fuzzy from sleep, but I don't understand what you're talking about. Did you say that you can't remember what's wrong?"

"No." I sighed, leaned my head against the back of the chair, closed my eyes and tested the memories again. "Yes, they are gone, not even a trace. And although I know those times happened and I know I must have lived them, I cannot remember my human years."

FOURTEEN

"So what do you think, Sam?"

I could not stop Mitch from making the call. In all honesty, I didn't try very hard. I was more shaken than I had ever been; the prospect of death was not nearly as frightening as the thoughts of having to live eternally yet without memory.

I could hear Sam's response, I could have guessed what he would say.

"I don't know, Mitch, there's no way I can tell anything over the phone. I'll need to see her. And soon. Should I come there?"

"If you would, yeah. Consider this our scheduled meeting, just a little bit earlier than intended. This is something we all should know. And I think it's time we fought back."

"I'll be there as soon as I can make travel arrangements." Sam's voice, even from such a long distance, was calm and reassuring. "Should I bring Viv along?"

I smiled, hearing her frantic answer in the background.

"Try to keep me away, Sam, *mon cher,* and you will find an angry vampire in your bed."

Mitch laughed. "God forbid, Sam. As someone who speaks from experience, an angry vampire in one's bed should be avoided at all costs." He sobered. "Look, the two of you be careful when you're traveling, okay? These guys aren't pulling their punches. They're using wooden bullets, apparently, tipped with the same poison."

"What is this all about, Mitch? Eduard is dead." Sam was still talking, but in the background I heard a few vehement words from Vivienne. I did not need to speak the language to get their meaning and I smiled again. "And if he's dead," Sam continued, "his resentments should have died with him."

"We'll find out, Sam. We have to." Mitch paused and ran his fingers through his hair in the tired gesture I knew too well. "You do know where we're located, right?"

"I'll find you. Are we contacting the others? Cadre members, I mean. Damn, I wish these bastards had used another name for themselves. It gets too confusing."

"Yeah," Mitch agreed. "And yeah, I'm officially activating the call list. Get as many of them together as you can; this sort of situation doesn't just affect one of us. It's something they should all be aware of, whether they can attend the meeting or not."

"Okay. I'll start the calls. You tell Deirdre to hold on for me. We'll be there as soon as we can. Wait, Viv wants to talk to Deirdre."

Mitch handed me the phone and I put the receiver to my ear. "I just wanted to ask, *mon chou,* what sort of clothes I should bring." She laughed, realizing the frivolity of her question. "And you are by the sea, are you not? Should I bring a bathing costume?"

I smiled. "You never change, do you, Vivienne? Even when the whole world is falling down around our ears, you are the same and you are wonderful, precisely the way you are. Thank God for that."

Her high-pitched metallic giggle warmed my heart, even through the phone lines. If I closed my eyes, I could picture her face, the dimples forming with her smile, the glint of innocent mischief in her eyes.

"I fear, Deirdre," she said, "that God has very little to do with it. But you must know that I love you, *ma chere*. And do not worry, sweet sister. Even if my Sam cannot work his normal miracle, I have the perfect solution to your problems. If you lose any more memories, I will simply share with you some of mine. I certainly have more than my share, and some of them? Oh la, yes, they are very interesting."

"I can believe that. And thank you, Vivienne. Walk softly this night and stay well."

I hung up the phone before she could hear the tears in my voice.

"Feel better?"

I wrapped my arms around Mitch's waist and buried my head in his chest. "Yes. But I hope they get here before I forget who they are."

"It's not going to get that bad, Deirdre. I promise."

Grateful for his confidence where I had none of my own, I nevertheless changed the subject. "I think I'll make us some coffee."

"Oh, yeah, I'm sorry, I was going to do that, wasn't I?"

I laughed on the way to the kitchen. "Until I dropped this bomb on you, yes, you were." I measured the water, put the coffee into the filter and set the machine to start. Reaching up into the cupboard for two mugs, I called out to him. "Did I tell you that I found the body of a dead swan in the ruins last night?"

"We didn't talk about last night at all." He came over and leaned on the door frame. "So tell me."

I set out the sugar and the creamer, along with a spoon. "I wanted to go for a run—you know how it always calms me down. I was feeling left out. Alone. And I knew the Cat would help."

"Left out? You're jealous of Maggie, aren't you?"

"No. Not jealous. She and her son make me nervous. There is something that does not ring true about the two of them. Does the boy talk?"

Mitch shook his head. "No. But it's not what you think. He can't talk. That tumor Pete was telling us about had grown around Phoenix's vocal cords and when they removed it, well, something went wrong."

"Surely they could do something to remedy that now?" I poured two mugs of coffee and slid one over to him.

Mitch shrugged as he spooned sugar and

creamer into his cup, taking less of both now than he did when he was human. "I get the impression that Maggie distrusts the whole medical profession. She clams up completely when the situation is mentioned. And maybe there *is* nothing they can do. The boy seems healthy enough otherwise. But we were talking about you and the abbey."

"Yes, we were. Although, there's not that much more to tell, actually. I attempted to change into the Cat, but the pain of transformation was so severe she refused to come out. For a while I seemed caught midway between human form and animal, but I forced the change back. Moe found me then, he had not been with me initially, and I just wanted to close my eyes and rest for a minute before returning home. I dreamed, I think, but I don't recall about what. And then you were there and you carried me home."

"Did you try any other transformations? To mist, maybe. Or did you try your winged form?"

Shaking my head, I took a long drink of my own black coffee, savoring as always the warmth of it filtering through my body. When I opened my mouth to reply, I managed only a gasp, as a sudden wave of nausea overwhelmed me.

Quickly, I leaned over the sink and vomited up the little bit of coffee I had just drunk along with a small residue of blood. The sour smell from the sink wafted up to me and I vomited again and again until nothing was left.

"Deirdre?"

I held up a hand to hold him off, turned on the water and washed the vileness down the drain.

Then I splashed my face with some cool water and dried myself with a paper towel.

I looked up.

"Deirdre, are you okay? What's wrong?"

He had never seen me sick before. *Hell,* I thought, *I should not be sick. I am a vampire, eternal health and youth are supposed to be my birthright.* I had never before been sick, except perhaps during my human years, and those now I did not remember.

"Are you okay?"

My teeth began to chatter as I realized that I was cold, deathly cold. "No, I am not, Mitch." I groaned a bit and shivered. "I don't think I will ever be right again."

He came over to me and wrapped his arms around me. "Jesus, Deirdre," he said, "you're burning up. It's like you have a fever. But how the hell can you have a fever?"

I gave him a confused look, but could not find the words to say. My mind was hazy, my whole body shook and I felt waves of hot and cold along with the continued nausea.

"Never mind that," he said briskly, "let's get you into bed and warmed up. Or cooled down. Damn it, I wish Sam were here."

Mitch undressed me like a child, his hands gentle and strong. He helped me into a nightgown and settled me into bed, piling blankets over me. Laying a cool hand onto my hot forehead, he shook his head. "It's hard for me to tell, love, but your body temperature is certainly higher than our normal, maybe even higher than human normal."

Then he pulled all the blankets from me and I shivered violently in the open air.

"Mitch?" I asked, my teeth chattering together. "No blankets? But I'm so very cold."

"Best not to be covered, I think. I'll start up a fire, though, and that should help. I'd go downstairs and find some aspirin for you, but I have no idea what they would do to you. We'll just have to wait this out."

I curled up on my side as he stacked wood in the fireplace. "Perhaps," I said, my words muffled by the pillow and by my shivers, "the poison is working its way out of my system."

"Maybe," he said, his voice grim and dark. "Or maybe it's working its way deeper."

I felt a flash of heat as he got the fire started, heard the warm crackle of flames. But I experienced it all as if from a distance. Nothing outside of me seemed important. Pain was the only reality. My head ached, my limbs ached and pain shot through every portion of my body. Nothing in my previous vampiric life had caused such distress.

Over the long years, I'd been beaten, stabbed, shot. I'd had a bullet cut out of my shoulder with no anesthetic. I'd suffered horrible pangs of hunger, burns from careless exposure to the sun, my skin had been slit open with glass and metal and wood. Through it all, though, I managed to completely ignore the ravages of pain, knowing that they were only temporary conditions. But this pain was different in that it seemed endless. And ultimately, fatal.

"What is happening?" I whispered the tearful words and fell into a state of unconsciousness.

The fever and the pain are gone, as quickly as they came. I get up from the bed quietly so as not to disturb the man sleeping in the chair next to the bed. I look at him fondly, wishing that I did not have to leave him behind, but knowing that I must. My desire for flight is a compulsion I cannot deny.

The windows open onto the night air and the crisp ocean breeze energizes me. I slip out of my nightgown and perch briefly on the windowsill, listening to the call of the night.

With a sudden forward movement, I launch myself out of the window, sprouting feathers and wings before I hit the ground, catching a wind current and soaring high into the sky.

My wings are strong and my heart is free and I fly tirelessly and quickly, crossing the ocean in just a matter of seconds, eventually touching down in a city of concrete, steel and glass. Home.

I search the streets for the place I want, for the place I need. Everything looks different from the air, even the scents of the city have changed. But still I know this place and know that this is my destination. I have been called, summoned to this place and I must obey.

There, I say to myself, as I dip lower and spot a familiar building, *there is where I am going.*

His window is open and I fly in. He is waiting, I recognize him from the other dreams. He is the man from the dance floor, he is the black shadow that paced me while I flew.

Laughing, he holds out his arm and I go to him, perching on his wrist, digging in with my talons.

But he does not seem to notice the pain. No, more than that, it is as if he welcomes it. He smiles and strokes my head, smoothing my feathers and whispering words of calm. Drops of blood, like crimson beads, roll from the wounds I have made and fall hissing onto the floor.

"Here, little one," he says, dabbing his finger in the blood and putting it up to my beak so that I can drink. "Remember this. Here is where you belong. Look around you and engrave it on your soul. You must remember this place, you must remember me, for when all else is gone from you, I will still remain."

I do as he commands. I will remember.

As if he had heard my thoughts, he nods. "Good. And now sleep." He fits a leather hood over my eyes and tenderly places me into a small silver cage.

"You will stay safe here, little one. Remember."

FIFTEEN

The dream ended abruptly, long before I could grasp the significance of the man's words. And soon, after waking, they melted away into nothing as dreams often do. Like the memories I had lost.

I tested the edges of my mind, but try as I might, I could not bring back the past. More of it now was gone, but the pain of the loss seemed lessened, softened somehow by dream words of comfort that I could not recall.

I did, however, remember the sickness. Unfortunately it had not disappeared with the other portions of my mind. I moaned softly, slowly becoming aware of the activity around me: a soft knock on the door, and a whispered exchange between Mitch and Maggie.

"I've brought this for her," Maggie said, "nothing much, just some herbal tea and a bowl of broth. She might feel better if you could get her to drink some of it."

"Thanks, Maggie. I appreciate your help."

"And don't worry about the pub, Mitch. We're having a slow night anyway and it's nothing I can't handle."

There was a pause and then Maggie's voice

again, still pitched low but with that threatening edge. "Hey, you dog, you can't come in here."

I heard a low rumbling growl that ended in a whine.

"He'll be fine in here, Maggie. Go ahead, Moe, find a place to sit." I heard the clack of his nails on the floor, felt his heavy body lie down on the floor next to my side of the bed, heard his sigh. *Not such a bad protector,* I thought, and reached down and weakly patted his head, grateful for his presence.

"Now," Mitch said, "since you are here, why don't you come in too? And please, set the tray down." There was a pause and I could hear him clearing things from the computer desk. "Here will be fine."

I opened my eyes and looked around. Maggie stood in the small sitting room and surveyed the flat; she looked beautiful as usual, wearing a lacy white blouse and a full denim skirt, with a wide black leather belt cinched around her tiny waist. Even in my weakened state, I could scent her strong human aroma from across the room. Licking my dry lips, I realized that I was famished, longing for another drink, another taste of her richness.

"Very cozy," she said, "just like a little love nest." Then she laughed and pointed to the windows. "Steel shutters? Are you expecting to be bombed?"

Mitch shrugged. "Keeps the sun out, mostly. Deirdre is very sensitive to sunlight."

"As she should be, most people of her kind are."

"Her kind?" I heard the threat in Mitch's voice, felt the tensing of the dog next to me.

"Of course, she's a redhead, isn't she? The bad bleach job doesn't really fool anyone, especially another woman. She has a redhead's complexion. Why, what did you think I meant?" Her voice shook with hidden laughter.

"Nothing. I'm just worried about her. She's never been sick before."

"Never? Imagine that, never been sick before. Poor baby." Maggie looked over at me and our eyes met. "She's awake now, though." She picked up the cup of tea from the tray and brought it over to me. "Here, Dot, drink this."

"What is it?" I leaned into her, sniffing, feeling my mouth begin to water and not for the tea. I licked my lips again, then wiped my mouth with my hand.

"Chamomile, mostly. It will help calm your stomach."

I had drunk chamomile tea before; it was something Elly always served me. I had not appreciated the taste then and probably would not now. *But hell,* I thought, *I am already poisoned. What harm can a little tea do?*

I nodded, and Maggie put an arm behind my back and lifted me up, pulling me close to her and holding the cup to my lips. My fangs clicked on the ceramic mug. "Careful now, don't want to chip a tooth."

She laughed as I sipped at the tea. "That's

right," she said in the condescending exchange usually reserved for nurses and their patients, "just take a little bit at a time. We don't want it coming right back up, now, do we? I'll put it down on the nightstand here and you can have more when you feel up to it."

She laid me back down on the bed. "You're such a little thing, Dot. A strong wind could blow you away." Maggie laughed briefly, then put a cool hand on my forehead. "Still feverish, I see."

There was an awkward pause. I closed my eyes and settled back into the pillows.

Maggie pulled a blanket up over me, brushed my forehead briefly and stood up. "Well," she said, "I need to get back downstairs. I left Phoenix to watch the cash drawer. Get better soon, Dot. We need to get better acquainted and we can't do that with you sequestered up here, cozy though it is."

Mitch escorted her to the door. "Thanks again, Maggie."

"No problem," she said, "we're almost family. You've taken me and my son in, and that's reason enough for me to want to help."

I heard the door close, heard Mitch set the locks and relaxed.

"Deirdre?" He sat down on the bed next to me. "Are you feeling better?"

"Some," I said softly. "I think now I just need rest. And blood. I am so very hungry. Had I not been so weak, Maggie would have found out what my kind is capable of."

Mitch laughed. "Probably not a good idea, although she is tempting."

"Yes. Very tempting." It did not seem a good time to reveal to Mitch that I may already have drunk from Maggie. And that if what I remembered was true, her blood was as intoxicating as she was herself. I was uneasy about the incident, feeling guilty about that transgression and for not being able to confess to Mitch what had happened. That is, *if* it had actually occurred. Maggie herself seemed oblivious of that particular interaction between us and she had never given me any indication that what I remembered was true.

"As your waiter, madam, I fear I must warn you that the dinner specials are scarce this evening. You only have the choice of me"—he made a broad flourish of his arm and bowed, causing me to giggle a bit, as he had intended—"or"—he pointed down to the side of the bed—"the dog. And in this case," and Mitch grew serious, "I would advise you to choose me. You need the extra strength."

"Mitch, you cannot keep offering yourself like this to me. You need your strength just as much as I do."

"No, Deirdre," he said, "no protests. After I get you taken care of, I can always go out and find something. Here."

Once again he offered me his wrist, and once again I accepted, sinking my fangs into him and pulling on his rich blood. I felt it rush through my body, a comfortable warmth, unlike the progression of the poison. I started to pull away when

I felt I'd taken enough. "No," he said, his voice stern, "take more. I'll be fine."

I drank fully then, abandoning myself to the sensations, to the sweet wild taste of him. He stroked my hair as I drank, until finally he pushed me away. "We won't tell Maggie," he said with a glint in his eye, "but I'll bet that'll help more than a thousand cups of chamomile tea."

I looked up at him and smiled. "Thank you, love." Then I closed my eyes and slept.

At some point during the day, I heard Mitch turn the television on. He turned the sound down quite low, but still I managed to make out what he was watching, another repeat of the *Real-Life Vampires* show. I listened for a while, without bothering to open my eyes to watch, drifting in and out of sleep.

"That's right, Bob," Terri was saying. "And this next question comes from Meg in Madison, Wisconsin. Meg writes: 'Dear Terri and Bob, is it true that vampires can change shape?' "

I answered for Terri on this one. "Provided they are not poisoned by the helpful *Real-Life Vampires* team, Meg, yes, they most certainly can."

Mitch looked over at me and smiled. "Sorry, Deirdre, I'll turn it down a bit more if you'd like."

"Just turn it off instead." I groaned, pulled a pillow over my head and fell back to sleep.

When I woke with the next sunset, I felt fine. No traces of pain or fever. Mitch was sleeping in a chair next to the bed where he'd kept vigil during the long-seeming day. I sat up, the bed creaked slightly and he woke.

I smiled at him. "All better," I said. "Thank you for taking such good care of me."

"What else could I do, sweetheart? You are my life."

"Did you manage to feed last night?"

He nodded. "Yeah, I did, indeed. You and Moe were all snuggled up safe and sound, so I took a little walk on the bad side of town looking for trouble. Fortunately, I found some. So I feel good about that. And then when I came back, Moe and I switched places." He gave a little laugh. "Took some convincing to get him to leave the room, but I managed. That creature is devoted to you, Deirdre. You seem to have that effect on us canine types. So tell me, do you feel like getting up?"

He turned grim and seemed anxious about something. "Yes, I would like to get up. What are you suggesting?"

He looked away from me. "I'd like to do something for Phoenix, maybe get Sam to look at him while he's here. I can't believe that his situation is irreversible. But Maggie doesn't seem to want to talk about it much. Maybe she would with you."

"Why get involved, Mitch?"

"Because, damn it, I like having the boy around. I don't think you've ever understood what Chris's death meant to me."

"How could I," I said softly, "when you won't talk about it?"

"How can I talk about it with you? Do you think I don't know that you blame yourself for his death? Guilt gets us nowhere on this, Deirdre, and it solves nothing. Chris is dead and although I'd give my right arm to get him back again, it's not going to happen. But this boy? He reminds me of Chris, not so much in looks, but in the way his eyes follow me, the way his face seems to light up when he sees me. It's like life has given me a second chance. If it weren't for you, I'd marry Maggie Richards just to have responsibility for the child."

"Oh." I could not hide the hurt in my voice.

"Shit." He ran his fingers through his hair. "That didn't come out quite the way I'd intended. I don't want Maggie, not like that, not ever like that. In fact, I can't imagine being with anyone other than you. An eternity with you is more than I'd ever hoped for. But the boy has gotten under my skin, somehow. I think about him all the time, even though the time we've spent together has been brief."

While he talked, I got out of bed, slipped off the nightgown he had dressed me in last night and put on the clothes I'd worn before.

"I don't understand any of this," Mitch continued. "I used to feel like I could rule the world. But now I feel so helpless, what with you, sick as you are, with that bloody poison eating its way through you and your memories. And I can't do a damn thing to stop it. But maybe I can do something for Phoenix. He's lost in a nightmare of silence."

"And you want me to talk Maggie into letting Sam examine him?"

"Exactly." He smiled at me and put his hand

out. I went to him where he sat in the chair and kissed the top of his head.

"Done."

"I've been thinking anyway that I should stay up here for the night, check around a bit on the Internet for news and be available for any Cadre members who call. So this is a perfect opportunity for the two of you to get better acquainted."

"I can hardly wait."

"Be nice, Deirdre. She means no harm. If you gave her a chance, you might even find that you like her. You could use a friend, I think. Maybe the two of you could—"

I interrupted him with a laugh. "Go shopping together? Or maybe pub crawling? I know, we could exchange recipes. That would certainly be amusing. However," I said quickly when I saw that I had angered him, "you are right. I haven't given her a chance. I'll try to make amends this evening."

"Good." He stood up and gave me a brief hug. "Now what's this about a dead swan?"

"Dead swan?"

"Back before you got sick, remember? You said you found a dead swan in the ruins."

"Oh. Yes. There was a dead swan there. Didn't you see it?"

"I was looking for you, sweetheart. I doubt if I'd have seen a swan if it jumped up and bit me."

"Its neck had been broken, Mitch. Twisted and gnawed; then whatever did that just left it there."

"Maybe one of the dogs did it. It needn't be any more sinister than that."

I nodded and bit my lip. "Yes, I realize that. But it was just so sad. And I dreamt about it, I think." The whole incident seemed to me to be a long time ago. "But I don't remember for sure. And it was only a dream, after all. So for now, I'll follow your instructions and go down to help Maggie."

"Deirdre?"

"Yes, my love?"

"How are the memories?"

I sighed. "I was hoping you wouldn't ask. As far as I can tell, another twenty years are gone." I laughed humorlessly. "It is rather difficult to keep track of what is gone."

His blue eyes narrowed with worry. "Do me another favor?"

"Anything for you, Mitch."

"No matter what happens, don't ever forget me."

I smiled and taking his face between my hands, kissed him again, full on the lips. "You foolish man. As if I could."

I walked to the door and opened it, stepped over the dogs sleeping in front of it and went downstairs.

SIXTEEN

Maggie and I worked side by side until the pub closed. She proved Mitch right; she was more than competent and certainly as friendly as one might ever want. I watched her interaction with the customers; her easy confidence and ready smile won their hearts and their attention. She seemed larger than life, somehow. Her laugh was infectious and overflowing with humor, her eyes flirtatious and flattering. Man or woman, it made no difference, Maggie Richards charmed them all.

By the time we had shown the door to the last of the regulars, she had charmed me as well and I found myself almost ready to admit she was nothing more than she seemed: a beautiful, good-natured and high-spirited woman with a flair for pleasing others. Pete chose well when he picked his temporary replacement.

As for what had transpired between the two of us on her first night here, I was by now more than half convinced that the whole incident was imagined, a by-product of my sickness and the poison.

After we cleaned the tables and swept the floor

I started for the stairs, but she laid a hand on my arm.

"Don't go yet, Dot. Please. We need to have a heart-to-heart. Sit." She pointed to a chair. "And I will wait on you."

I hesitated, giving her a doubtful look.

"Please," she repeated. "You seem to be feeling better now, and I thought, or rather hoped, you might enjoy my company a little while longer." She walked over to the bar. "Port?"

I sighed and settled into the chair she had indicated. "Yes, thank you, that would be fine."

"And I'll join you." She grabbed two glasses and a bottle of our best tawny port. "The good stuff," she said with a flourish as she sat next to me, "not the stuff we serve the customers."

I laughed. "Mitch has been teaching you well."

She looked up at me briefly as she poured, her eyes glittered. "He's a good man, Dot. You should be proud."

"I am." I took a drink of the wine. "You do know that my name is not Dot or Dottie, don't you?"

She chuckled. "Dot is what Uncle Pete has always called you and I'm not sure I can do otherwise. But yes, I do know it's not your real name. And I know that the two of you're in some sort of trouble."

I started to protest, but she reached over and touched a finger to my lips. "It's okay. Life is trouble, most of the time. And when it catches up to us, sometimes we just need to take a break from it all. No one in these parts cares in the least who you are or why you are here. And Uncle Pete would defend you to the death."

"There should be no need for that." I looked around. "Where is Pete?" I asked, suddenly realizing I had not seen him since the night Maggie arrived.

"He left a bit early for the cruise," she said, "so that he could visit with his daughter in London for a day or two. He wanted to say good-bye last night but didn't want to disturb you. Nothing will suffer for his absence, though. I'm here and I'll take good care of the both of you and the pub."

"And would you defend me to the death?"

"Of course." Maggie gave a delightful laugh. "I'm quite the fighter with a broom. Just ask Moe."

"And where is he? I tripped over Larry and Curly to get down here, but don't see him around. He's been constantly at my side for days, now."

"Moe? He's sleeping with Phoenix right now," she said with a sigh. "I'm sure you gathered that I don't particularly like dogs. But I've never been able to deny either of my sons anything."

She gave me a hard, cold look. "Can you understand that? Loving someone that much? Of course you do," she continued, giving me no opportunity to answer. "It's that way with you and Mitch, isn't it? Anyone with eyes to see can tell that. Watching the two of you together is just lovely; you are so in tune with each other."

I reached for the bottle of port. "Oh, no," Maggie said, pushing my hand out of the way, "tonight I said I was going to wait on you. And so I will." She filled my glass and sighed.

"Yes, you and Mitch are quite the couple," Maggie continued. "I can well imagine that you'll stay together forever. I wish it had been that way with me and the boys' father. For a while, I thought it might be. And then . . ." Her voice trailed away.

"And then?" I prompted.

"He died. I mean, he was a lot older than me, but I never expected him to die." She gave me a twisted little smile, "Funny, that. I mean, everyone dies, don't they? But he, oh, I don't know, he seemed too grand to die. Too large and too powerful to ever be subjected to death. Still, he gave me the children, my boys. And now that Eddie is gone, they make all the difference. Mitch says you have a grown daughter?"

"Yes, I do." I was unable to control the stiff tone of my voice. "Lily. She lives in New Orleans. She's a beautiful girl, but I don't hear from her much."

"Like that, is it?"

I gave Maggie a questioning look. "Excuse me?"

"The two of you don't get along, is all I meant. It happens. Take my oldest, for instance. He's living with his father's kin now. And seems more than pleased with the arrangement. I hardly ever hear from him either, not a word for months sometimes, and then when he does contact me, it's only because he wants something." She lifted her glass to her lips and drained it, scowling briefly.

"Well," I started, "perhaps he's just busy."

Maggie nodded. "He is that, yes. He's learning a trade, though, and that's something. They own a chain of funeral homes in the States, you see."

"Ah." I took a sip of my wine.

"What do your people do?"

I stifled a laugh. "For the most part, they run bars and clubs and restaurants." I could hardly tell her the full truth; that the only people I had were vampires, related to me by breed and blood.

She nodded and poured us each another glass of wine. "It's a good business. People always need food and drink. The way they always need burial. What did your father do? The same thing?"

"My father? Why, he—" I hesitated, sipping the wine to stall for time. What *did* my father do? I searched my memory frantically and came up with nothing. "He owned a bar." I smiled to smooth over the lie. "Family tradition, I suppose." For some strange reason, I felt driven to say more—something interesting, something that might impress her. "Before that, though, he was a priest." It could have been true; it was true of Max and he was almost a father to me.

"No, go on. A priest?"

"Really. I could never see it, myself. But that's what he said."

She chuckled a bit. "I guess he wanted to serve them wine, one way or another."

"Yes, I suppose that's true."

"We have much more in common than you'd

think, Dottie. Take my oldest, he once wanted to be a priest, but life had different plans for him. Now, I fear, he is too solidly ensconced in the world of flesh." She laughed her low, charming laugh. "Both dead and alive."

"And what about Phoenix? What does he want to be?"

"Grown up." Maggie smiled sadly. "It seems to me that if I look hard enough I can see him grow a little bit every day. His brother was the same. They stay little for such a short time."

I thought of Lily's extended childhood, a childhood that, even though it had been spread out over a century, I had missed completely. I knew nothing of children or motherhood, as my own daughter constantly reminded me. I sighed and nodded as if in agreement. "So, why do you call him Phoenix? I assume that's not his real name."

She laughed. "Might as well be—it's the only one he'll answer to. When he was born, you see, he had a tumor and they all said that he would die. But the doctors operated anyway and miraculously he lived and thrived. Rising from the ashes, so to speak."

"And he can't talk at all?"

She dropped her eyes, her sooty black lashes covering any expression they might have held. "He makes sounds, sometimes. Grunts, moans, that sort of thing. And I have heard him laugh, once or twice."

"Mitch and I have a friend. A psychiatrist, really, but still a medical doctor. He will be visiting us in the next day or two. Would you like him to examine Phoenix? Perhaps he could help?"

Maggie gave me a curious look. "Somehow I suspect that it's really Mitch doing the asking on this." She laughed. "If it makes him feel better, yes, certainly. I just don't think it will do much good. We've seen more doctors than I care to remember. Some of them think that eventually the vocal cords will heal. I'd like to hope that, for his sake. He never learned sign language but he's smart as a whip. Reads and writes years beyond his age. I've taught him myself. I was a teacher at a private boys' school before I met his father."

I smiled. "I'm sure all the students were in love with you."

"What a lovely thing to say, Dot." She reached over and touched my hand. I stiffened as, once again, I felt that surge of warmth wash over me. *Damn it,* I thought, *why does she have to be so attractive? So alive? So human?*

Her voice continued, droning on and on, spinning its tale, until it became nothing more than an insistent, seductive whisper. I was not listening to her words; all I could concentrate on was the burning of her flesh against mine. She loomed very close to me, so close that I could scent the aroma of her skin, her hair, her blood. I wanted to taste her again, wanted to explore and pierce that perfect body with fang and claw, to drink in her incredible life force. Slowly. Savoring her flavor, basking in her heat.

"Yes." Her answer was not communicated by voice, she was still telling me stories about the school at which she'd met Phoenix's father. Instead the unspoken word seemed to fly through my veins and shout in my head, "Yes, please, let's do that again."

I leaned in close to her; her hair, soft as a cloud, brushed my cheek. My fangs began to grow and I licked my lips in anticipation of the feast. Luscious and ripe, Maggie's neck loomed in front of my eyes. I felt hypnotized by the faint beat of her pulse visible through her skin. *Lovely, she is so lovely,* I thought. And *I must have her again.*

Once more I bent my mouth to her neck, once more I drew in her blood and vitality. Before I could completely abandon myself to the experience, though, I caught a glimpse of Phoenix, standing as I'd first seen him, barefooted and dressed in pajamas. But this time his eyes were focused and on me. He smiled, nodded and his frail body shook with silent laughter. One hand pointed at me and in the other he held a long white feather tinged bloodred.

I blinked and when I looked again, he was gone. Had he ever been there? What was happening to me?

I swallowed hard and shivered, pulling away from Maggie and forcing myself to concentrate. I needed to remember that I had come down to the pub to learn what I could of this woman. Not to feed, and certainly not to abandon myself to instincts and emotions that normally I kept under better control.

You are not hungry, I told myself, *and you do not want this woman, sexually or any other way.*

Biting my lip so hard it drew my own blood, I roughly removed my hand from her grasp.

"Oh," she said, her voice shaking. *With laughter,* I wondered, *or a sense of shared passion?* "I'm sorry."

"What?" In my dazed state it was all I could say.

"I forgot, you don't like to be touched, dear, do you? I could tell that, the first night I was here, by the way you instantly drew back when I hugged you." From across the table, Maggie inspected the hand she had touched. "No harm done, though. And I will try not to remember not to invade your personal space, Deirdre. It won't be easy; I'm a naturally demonstrative person, I fear."

"No, no, it's not that. Or rather, it is. But the fault is not yours, it is mine."

She smiled at me, baring her teeth in the perfect example of angelic innocence.

I glanced at the clock over the bar, then gave it a second look. "How did it get to be so late?" I could not believe I had spent the entire evening talking to Maggie without realizing the time that passed. Was this why Mitch didn't come to find me that night? Did she have the same effect on him as she did on me?

Maggie nodded, rather smugly, I thought. "Yes, you're right, it's late. Near dawn. But you know, I have this strange desire to go out and watch the sunrise over the abbey. Care to join me?"

"The abbey? It must be beautiful at sunrise."

"Yes, it is. Join me?"

For one small second of time I almost agreed,

even knowing that such an expedition would mean certain death for me. What power this woman had to exert such a strong pull. Our evening together did nothing to make me her friend; it merely made me fear and desire her more. *And still, the abbey would be beautiful,* I thought, *I should go with her.*

"No." With great reluctance and greater resistance, I shook my head. "No, thank you, Maggie. Some other time perhaps. For now, I think I had better go upstairs now and see how Mitch is doing."

"Suit yourself. And good night, Dot. Pleasant dreams. Give my regards to that handsome dog of a husband and tell him I hope to see him again soon."

The sound of Maggie's laughter lingered in my ears as I mounted the stairs. The remembrance of her touch burned, very much like the poison in my blood. And I felt wearier than I had ever felt in my life.

SEVENTEEN

"Maggie must leave. Both she and her son. Soon. I don't care about the pub or who takes care of it during daylight hours. We could just close it until Pete returns. But, no matter what else we might do, one thing is quite certain in my mind. They have to go."

I had not even greeted Mitch on entering, but closed the door and leaned up against it, out of breath as if I had been running for miles.

"Leave?" Mitch looked up at me from where he sat at the computer, wearing only a pair of jeans. "Why the hell would we want her to leave? She's here to help us, remember?"

"Help? She is dangerous and I want her out. Jesus, Mitch, she almost talked me into going for a sunrise walk with her in the abbey ruins."

He laughed. "She did? She's quite a persuasive person, isn't she?"

"No, Mitch, you don't understand. There is something not right about that woman. And Phoenix? I know you like him, Mitch, and that you feel drawn to him, because he reminds you of Chris and gives you a second chance to be a father. But I'm sorry, I cannot agree. I think he is the one who killed that swan. The boy is a monster."

"A monster? That sweet child? You must be joking, Deirdre. One only needs to look in his eyes to realize what kind of boy he is."

"I am not joking, Mitch. Phoenix is an evil boy. Disturbed. And frightening."

Mitch laughed again and I grew angry.

"You may find it all amusing, Mitchell Greer, but I still say that he is not quite right."

He sobered. "I'm sorry, I'm just having a little fun with you. God knows we get precious little opportunity for that. And I'm in a good mood; I'm rested, you're obviously feeling better, I didn't have to deal with Maggie or the pub and I had a remarkably good night of research on the computer. Amazing what one can find out with just a little bit of information and a lot of time."

Didn't have to deal with Maggie? "I thought you liked Maggie."

"I did. And on the record, of course, I still do. Or at least I want everyone to think I do. Nothing like a little good cop/bad cop to throw someone off guard."

"You *don't* like her?" I felt as if I had walked into the middle of a story.

"I might still like her, Deirdre, her charm is irrepressible. But after what I've found out about her today, I wouldn't trust her any farther than I could throw her. I'm ashamed to admit that I was taken in by her act at first and completely charmed by the son."

"I don't understand, Mitch, what could you

have found out tonight to make you change your mind so completely?"

"I found out the name of Maggie Richards's husband."

"And?"

"And if you are right about Phoenix being a little monster, and I still can't agree with that, it's hardly his fault. Heredity and environment play a huge role in forming the personality of a child. And with his parents? I'm surprised he turned out as well as he did." He smiled at me, drawing out the news.

"You have been around Pete entirely too much, Mitch," I said, giving him a fond smile. "Now, quit dancing around the subject and tell me what you've learned."

He laughed again. "Evil, like beauty, is in the eye of the beholder. If, as you say, the boy is evil, then it's for a good reason. I suspect that's just the way he is. What else would one expect of a DeRouchard?"

I took a deep breath. "DeRouchard? Eduard? But Eduard is dead. They could not have transferred his soul or his consciousness. We saw him die. Burned beyond belief, beyond revival or resurrection."

"But his sons live on, Deirdre. And his deep hatred of vampires continues in them. We needn't look any further for our persecutors."

I felt my legs weaken and I slid down the door, landing on the floor in front of it. "His sons." My voice was flat as the realization sunk in. His sons. "And Maggie's. Oh, dear God. And two of them are living here? Protecting us? Do you suppose they know who we are?"

Mitch looked at me and raised an eyebrow. "What do you think?"

"Then she knows we had a part in killing her husband?" I stopped for a moment. "Of course she does. Hell, even Terri and Bob knew that he was dead and knew who killed him."

Mitch tensed for a second. "Come to think of it, how *did* they know about his death? Or how he died? That show can't have been taped much more than a week after he died. Unlike bloody *Real-Life Vampires,* we don't gloat over our kills. We don't publicize them. And in Eduard's case, there wasn't even a body to discover and identify. All that was left of him was a pile of ashes."

"What difference does that make, Mitch?"

"It makes a difference, Deirdre. A big difference. It means that either someone observed that confrontation or that one of those present for the occasion talked. Neither is a good alternative, but you're right, it has no relevance to the matter at hand. Which is, what do we do with his widow and son?"

"Sons, Mitch, don't forget that there is another one out there. Living with Eduard's relatives. And still, I'm not sure. If neither of these children is carrying Eduard's soul, then why has the persecution continued? It should have died out when he did."

"Deirdre, sweetheart, I think that fever must have addled your brain. Revenge for a beloved husband's murder? Or for a father's life? Vendettas have been waged for far less important reasons."

"So what are we to do? Stay here and accept their presence as if we had no idea who and what they are?"

"Well, not hardly, considering that we know what they are now. But that seemed to have been their plan. Gain our trust and our friendship. And then hit us when we least suspect it."

"But now that we know, we can get rid of them." He looked over at me. "Right?"

"A good plan, Deirdre. But exactly how do you propose to do that?"

I shrugged, sighed and got up from the floor, brushing dog hair from my pants. "I don't know, Mitch. Kill them both and drop them into the North Sea?"

"Could you? Could you kill that beautiful woman and her angelic son?"

I thought for a moment. I feared her, mistrusted her, while at the same time desiring her more than I'd ever have thought possible. And her son made me shiver, arousing both disgust and sympathy. I thought of how I might kill them. Would I slit their throats, suffocate them as they slept, rip open their chests and tear our their still-beating hearts? Just the thoughts alone brought tears to my eyes and made my stomach roll over inside me.

"Could you?" Mitch repeated.

"No," I said, a defeated tone to my voice, "I don't think I could."

He shook his head and ran his fingers through

his hair. He smiled at me, his blue eyes shining with love. "That's not saying much, though. You're not the murdering kind, we both know that. God, woman, you've got more humanity than most humans. That's not the issue, really. We're talking about Maggie Richards and her bloody little mute son—hell, I don't think I could kill either of them. And we both know it's not because I'm incapable of murder. I'd gladly wipe anybody off the face of the earth if he threatened a hair on your head, or," and he winked at me, "even Viv's head. In the abstract.

"But the reality of the situation, I suspect, is that none of us are going to prove capable of killing our Maggie. She's good, damned good. In fact I suspect she is one of the best breeders those bastard Others have ever had. She has layer upon layer of protective covering and she's the perfect vampire bait. Remember what Vivienne told us about Monique? How she could not forsake her or abandon her no matter what the circumstances were?"

I nodded.

"Maggie," he continued, "seems to have developed that quality a hundred times over. Have you noticed that the scent of her skin alone can put you into a feeding frenzy? I'm a happily married man and I love you more than I'd ever dreamed possible, but the touch of her hand makes me forget all of that. She arouses emotions in me I've never felt before."

"You're not the only one, Mitch. But I attributed it to my poisoned condition. And I think I may have fed on her." I looked down at the floor and began to cry softly. "Twice. But I don't quite remember; since I have been sick it feels as if everything now is a dream. I don't know what is real and what is remembered."

"Oh, baby." He pulled me into a tight embrace and stood there for a long time, holding me and rocking slightly from side to side. I pressed my head against the smooth skin of his chest. "It'll be okay, Deirdre. I promise you," he whispered into my hair, "I'll make it right."

"Then we will have to kill them somehow, all of them."

"No." He pushed back so he could look into my face. "Don't you see? There's no value in their deaths right now. Alive, though, they provide a nice little bargaining chip. We will trade Eduard DeRouchard's son for the poison antidote."

"What if there is no antidote? We don't really know what this poison is supposed to be doing."

"Sam and Viv will be here soon, possibly even tonight." He moved away from me and headed back to the computer desk. "You and Sam can work together on analyzing and, I hope, counteracting the poison. Vivienne and I will keep an eye on Maggie and Phoenix. And the rest of the Cadre will begin arriving in a week." He sat back down in the chair. "Damn. We'll have to give some thought on where to put them all, since they'll all be arriving now too early for the Goth Festival. I'd counted on that to help camouflage all of them."

I nodded and began to strip off my clothes. "How many have you heard from, Mitch?"

"Forty-three have been accounted for. Not that many will be coming, though. I suspect we won't have more than fifteen or twenty once they all get here. But that number includes Vivienne and Victor, the two oldest surviving house leaders, so we're likely to get agreement in whatever we decide to do." He shrugged. "Not that it really matters at this point, the Cadre has outlived its usefulness. Hell, let's be honest—the organization was outdated years ago and has just sort of been running out of habit. And personally, I don't give a damn whether they approve of my actions or not."

I gave a grim little laugh, wiping away the rest of my tears. "Most of them will never agree on anything, except that none of them have ever liked either one of us. There are still some major grudges being held because I killed Max. So if you can get fifteen to come, that is a major accomplishment."

"If it were just for you, Deirdre, that would be true. We need to face the facts. This may be our last stand before total extinction. You have been poisoned and although we don't know what that will eventually do to you, I'm sure it won't be good. At the very least, the remaining Cadre members must be warned. And at the very worst, who's to say that you aren't just one of many?"

"On that cheerful note, my love, I think I will take a shower. Would you like to join me?"

"You start without me; I'll catch up later. I still

have a few e-mails to answer and reservations to tend to."

"Suit yourself, but if you wait too long I'll use all the hot water."

"You wouldn't do that to me, Deirdre, would you? You wouldn't use up all the hot water and make the man who loves you more than life itself take a cold shower, would you?"

I smiled at him and shrugged. "I might," I said. "It could be that a cold shower would do you some good."

"Is that what you think?" Mitch got up from the desk and slowly removed his jeans and advanced on me in a mock-threatening pose, backing me into the tiny bathroom and closing the door behind us.

I put my arms around his neck and whispered in his ear, "So now I'm to understand that you want to take a shower?"

"Not exactly." He reached around me and through the curtain, turning on the water. "I want to take you, in the shower."

I laughed softly as he picked me up and I wrapped my legs around his waist. "Here is a question for that stupid show. 'Mitch from Whitby, England, asks: Why do vampires engage in sexual intercourse as often as they do?' "

"That's an easy one," Mitch said in his best Bob Smith imitation. "Because they can. And because they never know if this time will be their last. Now quit asking these silly questions, Deirdre, and kiss me."

EIGHTEEN

I hummed a little song to myself in the shower, loving the feel of the water on my body, amazed at how well I felt, compared to that one period of being ill. "You know," I said to Mitch as he soaped my back, "I don't think we fully appreciate the perfection of our bodies."

He laughed. "Funny," he said, "I vaguely remember doing just that not all that long ago."

"No, you know what I mean. After being sick, I realize what a gift it is to be immune to human illnesses, to be ageless and immortal. I used to hate what I was; every waking moment was spent in self-loathing for the monster I was. But now, I feel enriched, enlightened."

"That's good, sweetheart. But I feel cold. Is the hot water running out?"

"No, I turned it down a touch."

"You what?" He sounded shocked. "Since when did you start taking cold showers?"

"It's a far cry from cold, Mitch." Turning around to let the water rinse my back, I gave him a quick kiss. "However"—I shrugged, stepped out of the shower, and reached back in, turning up

the hot water to full force—"I was finished anyway. Enjoy."

I dried myself, still humming the song I had
been singing in the shower. I wrapped another
towel around my body, tucking the top of it in
above my breasts, and wiped the steam off of the
mirror with my hand. I turned my head from side
to side, looking at my hair. "Now that they've
managed to find us, and plant their agents in our
home, there's probably no good reason for me to
stay a blonde. What do you think? Should I dye
it back to the original color, or just let it grow out
on its own?"

"It's up to you, Deirdre," he called to me over
the running water. "It looks fine now the way it
is, and it looked fine before."

I made a face at him. "Some help you are. I
think the color is horrible with my complexion,
makes me look even paler than I am." I leaned
farther in toward the mirror. "And shows up the
dark circles under my eyes. I should not have dark
circles."

Mitch made some noncommittal grunt when I
heard a crash in the apartment. I ran out into
the hallway.

"Mitch!"

In the time we had been in the shower, what
Maggie had called our cozy little nest had been
vandalized. The computer had been knocked off
the table, the television overturned, the phone
had been ripped out of the wall and tossed into
the fireplace. The cushions on the furniture had

been torn off and one had been shredded, bits of fluff and stuffing were spread across the floor.

And from underneath one of the cushions, I saw the tip of a dog's nose, a large black nose. My first thought was that Moe had done this damage and then had tried to hide.

Then I realized that he was not moving, that there was no way his massive body could have been hidden under the pillow. I held my breath and walked slowly to the middle of the room. A large butcher knife, one I recognized from the pub's kitchen, was driven down into the floor next to the dog's lifeless and bodiless head. The open eyes stared up at me, a sad parody of his attentiveness in life.

I knelt down and patted it. "Poor thing," I said, starting to cry, "you were such a good dog. Who did this to you?" Tears were now streaming down my face and I made no attempt to stop them. "Oh, God, Moe, you certainly did not deserve this. I am so sorry."

"Deirdre?" Mitch came out of the shower, a towel wrapped around his waist. "What the hell happened?"

I stood up, holding a hand over my mouth while my other arm cradled my stomach. I sniffed, choking back a hysterical sob. "Someone broke in, the goddamned bastards. And left me a little present."

"Break in? That's a solid steel door, how the hell can somebody just break in? A present? What do you mean, a present?" Then his eyes focused.

"Oh, bloody fucking hell. Why on earth would anyone do such a thing?"

With that statement, the door swung inward slowly and both Mitch and I turned with a growl.

"Mitch? Dottie? Are you okay?" Maggie stood on the threshold, staring in shock. "I just came back from the market"—she held up a bag filled with groceries to illustrate her alibi—"and noticed that the door was open."

"We had a small intruder problem, Maggie," I said.

"Someone's broken in? Who would do such a thing?"

"I wish I knew," Mitch said, "and I'm sure we'll eventually find out. But for now . . ." He shrugged.

"We should call the police and report this." Maggie's eyes widened as she saw the dog's head. "What is that? Is that . . ." Her voice trailed off and her eyes seemed to glaze over, frozen to the sight. "Oh, dear sweet heavens, yes, it is. Have you called the police?" Not waiting for an answer, she continued. "We should call the police, you know. They'll take care of it."

"No," Mitch said, "no police. We'll deal with this ourselves. Just close the door, Maggie, and go about your business. There's nothing you can do in this situation. Please leave us alone."

"But the dog." She stared at the mess on the floor. "He's dead. And where's"—Maggie gulped. "Where's the rest of him?"

"I'll find him. And bury him myself." Mitch's

voice was cold and hard. "Tonight. It's no concern of yours."

"Phoenix will be heartbroken, though. I won't let him up here until it's all over."

"That would be a good idea, Maggie." I walked over to her, adjusting my wrap, noticing that my hands were shaking and that there was a smear of blood across the towel. "Now, you should go back downstairs."

She looked into my eyes and backed away from me, and for the first time since we met I noticed a trace of fear in her face.

Good, I thought, *you should be afraid, you goddamned bitch. Hold on to that fear, remember it. Perhaps it will make you think twice about doing something like this.*

But I said nothing; instead, I closed the door on her stunned expression and set the locks.

"No one broke in that door," Mitch said, "not without major explosives. We may have been preoccupied when it happened, but we'd have heard something. No, that door had to be opened with a key."

I agreed. "And we know that there are only two other people besides us with access to that key."

He knelt down next to the dog's head. "Maggie does seem like the obvious suspect, doesn't she? Even so, I think we need to look elsewhere. She certainly seemed genuinely shocked, more than enough to give me reasonable doubt. For what it's worth, my gut feeling is that she would never have killed the dog, no matter how much she disliked him. And she's not here to kill us, I'm sure of that. She's had ample opportunity to finish off either one of us."

"Perhaps it wasn't her. I don't remember if I locked the door when I came upstairs. If I didn't lock it and you didn't, then this could have been done by anybody."

Mitch gave a short laugh. "I don't know which is worse—to think that Maggie did this, or to think that a total stranger was here. Either way, they've left us quite a mess to clean up."

I sighed, dropped the towel from me and tossed it over to Mitch. "We might as well start there," I said, pointing and choking back a sob. "Poor dog."

"Yeah." He mopped up the small sticky pool of blood as I pulled on a heavy flannel nightgown. "I wonder how anyone managed to do this to him. I'd think he'd have put up more of a fight."

I had a sudden vision of the boy, bending over the dog he'd befriended, sitting down next to him. The dog would look up and wag his tail and the boy would hug him around the neck before quietly and happily slitting his throat and carving off the head. It was a particularly revolting image and kept replaying itself over and over in my mind.

My stomach rolled. I swallowed to keep down the bile that rose in my throat, but it did no good. Clapping a hand over my mouth, I quickly turned and ran for the bathroom.

When I had finished vomiting up the remains of what I had drunk earlier, I washed my face and hands. "Fine vampire I make these days," I said with a small laugh. "Apparently I can no longer stand the sight of blood."

"Are you okay?" Mitch had finished mopping up the blood and had wrapped the head up in one of the blankets from our bed. He picked up the bundle now and gently carried it to the front door, laying it down to one side.

"Fine." I pulled the phone out of the fireplace and set it back on the small computer desk. "At least the fire had gone out," I said, bending down to plug the cord back in. "This might still work—wait. What is this?"

The computer was still operating, apparently, resting on its side. The screen had not broken and the machine was turned on. A message ran across the screen in big black letters.

NOT HIS SON.

I tilted my head to read it. "This says *Not his son*. Is this something you were working on earlier, Mitch?"

"No. Before I was so rudely interrupted by my overly amorous wife, the screen was displaying the marriage data I'd found for Maggie and Eduard." He dropped the towel from his waist and pulled on a pair of briefs, then his jeans. "I may not have logged off and I may not have closed down the screen; I was distracted, as you should well recall."

"We're getting careless, Mitch. First, I don't lock the door and second, you leave the computer running. What do you think it means?"

He picked up the television and put it back on its stand. "It means we're letting ourselves get overwhelmed with all of it. It means that I can't think straight for worry over you, wondering if I'm the memory you'll lose next. Worried that no one will be able to stop the progression of whatever goddamned poison these bastards put into you, sick to death at the thoughts of you being left only a hollow shell."

I went over to him and held him close to me. "I know, my love, I worry about the same things. Promise me." I reached up and touched his cheek gently, enjoying the rough texture of his beard against my skin, inhaling deeply, savoring the scent of him. "If the worst happens, if I become a mindless creature with no memory of who I really am, promise me, Mitch, that you will let me go."

"Deirdre." His voice was almost a moan. "It's not going to get to that point."

"But if it does, you must promise me."

His eyes did not meet mine. "I can't."

I sighed. "But you must, Mitch. And you will, my love. You will remember this discussion and you will let me go. It would be a blessing then, Mitch. And a sweet relief. But that isn't what I wanted to ask, really. I wanted to know what you thought the message on the computer meant."

"I assume it means that despite the marriage certificate, Phoenix is not Eduard's son."

"But that makes no sense. Even if it were true, why would whoever did this want to tell us? Maggie certainly wouldn't admit to that, she loved Eduard. I could feel it when she spoke of him last night. And if Phoenix did this," and once again

I flashed on the image of the boy with the knife and shivered, "why would he deny his own father?"

Mitch shook his head. "I don't know, Deirdre. And with the exception of the dog, who wasn't even killed here, there's been no real damage done."

I sighed. "Then this was just malicious mischief for no reason at all?"

"There's a reason, there always is. Why they killed the dog, of course, is obvious. You have been specifically targeted by these people, singled out for some purpose. And now you have lost your protector. Moe"—his eyes darted to the door—"had been your constant companion pretty much ever since we've been here. He was a good deterrent for humans and Others alike. That night in the abbey, when he was guarding your sleeping body?"

I nodded.

"Well, he was acting up so much, snarling and growling, that even I was afraid to approach him. God only knows what might have happened to you already if it hadn't been for him."

"He was a good dog," I said, starting to cry again.

Mitch came over and held me in his arms. "Yeah, he was. And we'll find the person responsible and he will pay for it. But you know, I can't seem to think clearly right now. It's all too close, too immediate. But we'll find out. We have to."

He moved away from me, walked over and checked the locks on the door one more time, stepping around the blanket and its contents with a sigh. "Let's try to get some sleep. I have a feeling we'll need to be fully rested for what happens next."

NINETEEN

I would not have thought that I could sleep after all that had happened. But when I lay down next to Mitch, the scent of his skin and the solidness of his body comforted and relaxed me. I curled up next to him, wrapped an arm around his waist and a leg around his leg, rested my head on his shoulder and fell asleep almost immediately.

I walk in the ruins, naked, the moonlight gleaming on my white skin, giving it an eerie glow. On either side of me are two women. They are naked also, but none of us are ashamed. These are our true bodies, I sense. Beautiful and real.

One of the women is small and blond, her hand is light, cool in mine, her laugh is like the sound of wind chimes.

The other is tall and dark, her hand burns mine, and her laugh is like the low rumbling of a cat's purr. I love them both. I have no choice, I must love them both. And although I do not know them, I recognize that they are indeed my sisters.

The blond woman tugs on my hand. "Come, sister," she says, her voice high-pitched and melodic, "the night and everything in it is ours. It is our legacy."

I hear her words and sense the truth in them. The night is mine. I veer over in her direction.

Now, however, the other woman, the dark one, pulls on my hand, exerting a pressure equal to the blond sister. "You are changing, even now," she says and I feel the lure of her voice. "You can feel your body adapting, evolving. Turn your back on the legacy and come with me to watch the sunrise."

Ah, the sun. I have not seen the sun for so long and I crave its warmth, its light. I head in the dark sister's direction.

But I find I cannot choose between the two of them. So I stand still and lock my feet together. They each retain their holds on my hands and they pull, harder now with each passing second, both of them urging me to join them. Night and day they are and I cannot decide.

My sisters pull on my hands harder still, and I feel a small ache begin in the center of my forehead. From there it spreads, crackling down my body like a fracture in ice.

I tell them to stop, but they continue pulling, until my skin is divided down the center. Blood trickles and then gushes as they rip the skin from my body, half for one and half for the other. Each sister takes the piece of me she wanted and moves off in her own direction.

And I am left, skinless and crying, alone in the ruins and the dust.

I woke with a gasp. My heart pounded in my chest and I breathed deeply, attempting to calm myself. *Only a dream,* I thought, and ran my hands over my still intact skin and body. Only a dream.

Stealing a glance at the clock on the mantelpiece—only another hour to go until sunset—I lay back into the pillows and tested the edges of my memory. My oldest memory now seemed to be my arrival on the East Coast soon after the opening of the Empire State building. The year was 1931. So almost a hundred years of my life had already vanished, surrounded by a seemingly impenetrable wall. And although I knew that something existed on the other side of that obstacle, it was engulfed in a thick fog that obscured reality.

I could live with all of that, if only the wall were not slowly but surely encroaching on my present. Unless a way could be found to stop the progression, soon everything I remembered would be forgotten.

And then, I thought, *who would I be? What portions, if any, of me would be left?*

My thoughts were interrupted by a soft knock on the door. I checked the clock again. At least another fifteen minutes remained until sundown, but this upper part of the building had no windows except for the ones in our apartment. I could open the door safely without exposing myself to any stray rays of sunlight.

But why would I want to open it? It was too early for Vivienne and Sam to arrive; it most certainly would be Maggie or Phoenix and I did not wish to see either of them. Ever again, if the truth be known.

Whoever was there knocked again. Paused and then knocked for a third time. *What the hell,* I thought, got out of bed and opened the door.

The boy stood there, arms at his sides, fists clenching and unclenching. Tears streamed down his face, silent tears he made no attempt to hide or wipe away. His clear blue eyes met mine seeming to plead for admittance to the room. He gave a sad smile and put a hand out to me.

I hesitated and he pushed his hand at me again. This time I grasped it and he entered the room, falling down on his knees next to the wrapped bundle by the door. Shaking his head violently, he pulled the blanket back, picked up the head of the dog and hugged it to him.

"Oh, Phoenix." Despite the knowledge of who this boy was, my heart went out to him. There could be no questioning of the truth of his reaction and I found now I could not believe that he had done this deed. But somehow, he knew it had been done. And he may have known why and by whom.

"I wish you could speak," I said quietly. "But your mother says that you can read and write. Could you tell me like that? Do you know who did this?"

He gave me a sidelong glance, then set the dog's head down reverently on the floor, tenderly tucking the blanket back around it.

No, in spite of the clearness of my earlier vision, I now could not believe that this child, no matter whose son he was, had killed the dog. He wiped his eyes and nose with his sleeve, then touched my hand again and pulled me over to the small desk on which the computer sat. I noticed as we passed the bed that Mitch was awake and silently watching, his eyes glowing with interest.

Phoenix sat down in front of the computer, his fingers poised over the keyboard. He looked up at me, expectantly, his expression saying as plain as day, "Well?"

"Do you know how to use a computer?" I asked him. In answer he rolled his eyes and pressed a few keys, bringing up a blank screen in which he typed: *of course. dont you?*

I laughed. "No, actually I don't. But I am old-fashioned. Where did you learn?"

special school.

"I thought your mother taught you at home?"

He shrugged and typed. *used to go to school, then we moved. i liked school, but she didnt want me there. they made fun of me.*

"Because you don't speak?"

He nodded. *other children are cruel she said. and get used to it.*

I nodded my agreement. "She is right about that. Perhaps not about the getting used to it. But it is a cruel world, Phoenix. Do you know who killed Moe?"

He sniffled a bit. *not me, i didnt do it. i know you probably think i did, but i didn't.*

"I do not think you would kill Moe. It's all right, Phoenix. Just tell me the best way you can what you think might have happened."

He started sobbing and his fingers flew on the keys. *i woke up and got dressed and saw that the door was open and i heard the water running and i knew something was wrong. she was at the market, she left a note telling me so and i know i shouldnt have come upstairs but the door was open. the door should not be open, should never be open, Uncle Pete told her so the first night we came. and i came up to close the door and looked inside and saw the head. i got scared and mad.*

"Because of the dog," I said, brushing back his fair hair, "because you loved him too?"

He nodded and began typing again, crying as his fingers talked. *you killed the dog, i thought, i dont know why i thought that but i did. so i knocked down the tv and threw the phone into the fire.*

He stopped for a moment and sniffed, wiping his nose on his sleeve again. I grimaced slightly and walked across the room, bringing back a box of tissues for him. He ducked his head and grabbed one, wiping his eyes and blowing his nose.

thank you, he typed, *im not a baby but the dog . . . he was my friend.*

"I know." I hoped my voice was soothing and comforting. "Sometimes it's a good thing to cry."

He rolled his eyes. *only babies cry.*

"Fine, if you say so."

He nodded.

"And then, after you threw the phone into the fire and knocked down the television, what happened then, Phoenix?"

and then i saw what was on the computer and i got scared again and typed the note but i heard someone coming out of the shower and i jumped up and knocked the monitor down while i was trying to get away. but its not broken, nothing is broken and if you didnt kill the dog then you wont kill me and maybe you wont be mad and youll let me stay.

I stared at the words he had typed. It all made perfect sense, I supposed. "Of course I didn't kill the dog. Why would you think that?"

she said you might have. dottie just might have done it herself, she said, because she is mad at us.

"Well, Phoenix, I am not angry with you. Even if I were, I am not in the habit of killing children. Or dogs, for that matter."

He seemed to relax a little bit in his chair, then tensed up again and typed: *she said you might kill me. you might kill us both. will he kill me?*

"Who? Will who kill you?"

mitch. he will be mad that i made a mess. will he kill me?

I managed to suppress a laugh, he was so concerned that someone would kill him. When I thought about it more, though, I no longer found it comical; instead I found his worries heartbreaking. What sort of upbringing, what sort of damage did Eduard and Maggie do to this child?

I smiled down at him tenderly and brushed his fine hair away from his forehead. "I hardly think so, Phoenix. And I promise that Mitch will not kill you."

He seemed satisfied by my answer.

"Now, tell me one last thing, if you typed that note, what did you mean? Not his son?"

something he used to say to her. he was not a nice man, he was mean and cruel. not my son, he would say, not really, neither of them are mine. and she would cry. i dont belong, i never have. and he never liked me because of that. he only wanted me because i might be useful. the boy might be useful one day, he would say. he never liked that i can remember things that never happened.

"What sort of things, Phoenix?" I asked softly.

Before he could answer, Maggie's voice called from outside the door. "Phoenix? Phoenix! Answer me right this minute! Are you here, baby?"

He jumped and before I could stop him, hit a key that erased everything he had written.

"He's in here, Maggie," I called.

"Oh, thank heaven," she said, rushing over to him. "I worried that maybe he'd wandered off again. I hope he wasn't bothering you." Her eyes darted to the bundle by the door. "Or that he wasn't getting into something he shouldn't have." She gave him a little push. "Haven't I told you not to come up here? Didn't I tell you that just this morning?"

He nodded sullenly.

I flew to his defense. "He was fine, Maggie. He was showing me how to play a computer game. No harm was done. He was not doing anything wrong. And"—I looked down and met his eyes—

"he's welcome to come back and play some other time. So long as he is polite and knocks first."

I was rewarded with a small smile from the boy. As he raised his head, I saw for the first time the scar across his neck. I reached out and touched it, thick and heavy like all of the Others.

"From the operation," Maggie said quickly, her eyes darting away from mine quickly, "when he was a baby. It never healed properly, those damned doctors. We usually try to keep it covered or people stare." She grabbed his hand roughly and practically dragged him out of the room. "Come on, boy. You have bothered Dot long enough and we have work to do downstairs."

I followed them to the door and watched her hurry him down the stairs. When they reached the bottom landing, she let go of him and he turned around and gave me a small wave. He mouthed the words "I'll come back."

I nodded and gave him a little smile. Then I closed the door and locked it, walked back across the room and sat in front of the computer again, gently running my fingers over the blank screen.

TWENTY

"What the hell was that all about?" Mitch came up behind me, as I peered at the now blank screen, wrapped an arm around my neck and kissed me on the shoulder. "You and Phoenix were playing a game?"

"You know we weren't, Mitch. He told me a lot of interesting things, though. He wasn't particularly thrilled with having Eduard as his father, which easily explains the 'not his son' message. He didn't kill the dog, but he admitted to the rest of the pranks. He was frightened, he said, and angry because of Moe. He wrote it all out, but then deleted it when Maggie showed up."

"Here." He pulled the chair back. "You get up and let me sit down. Maybe I can find the file." He pushed a few keys. "Yes, here it is. Give me a second to read it over."

At one point he chuckled while reading. "Poor kid. Do you think he really thought we were going to kill him?"

"Yes, I think he really did expect that we would, for a little while at least. I gather he has not had the most pleasant of childhoods up until now."

"Do you believe him about all of this?"

"I do, indeed, Mitch. Most especially about how he didn't kill Moe. No child, no matter what his background, could be that good an actor. Nor am I that bad a judge of character. Most of the time."

Mitch smiled briefly. "And now you think he's not a monster?"

I sighed and rubbed my hands over my eyes. "I don't know what he is, Mitch. There's no question about one thing: he does bear the mark of the Others. Maggie can deny it all she likes, but I know what I saw and I know what I felt."

Shivering slightly, I hugged my arms to myself. "That scar is not the mark of an incompetent doctor's scalpel. So he cannot be what he seems. Physically, he may be the son of Maggie and Eduard, and he may seem a child, but he carries another soul, a mature soul, the soul of one transferred at birth. He could be anyone." I shook my head. "I feel sorry for him, Mitch. He seems so lost and frightened. He remembers things that never happened."

"What sorts of things?"

"I asked him, but Maggie came looking for him before he could answer."

"Interesting. And speaking of memories, dare I ask?"

I gave a small humorless laugh. "I still remember you, my love, you need not worry about that." The unspoken "yet" hung in the air. "But other periods of my life are not as vivid." My voice softened. "I seem to be missing about one hundred years so far."

He fell silent, most likely calculating, as I had,

how many more days until my forgotten past would catch up to the present. The answer to that equation was not favorable. When he spoke again, his voice was low and husky. "Other than that, sweetheart, how do you feel?"

I thought for a moment. "Not bad at all," I said, surprised as I said it to find it was true. "But I am famished. I feel as if I haven't eaten for months."

"Then get dressed. We'll bury poor Moe somewhere and go out and find you food. Shouldn't be too difficult, it's Saturday night and all of the other pubs will be crowded. We'll want to get back early, though, because Sam and Viv should be here no later than two or three o'clock. They're catching the nine o'clock flight from Paris, then renting a car and driving up from Manchester. The train left too early in the day for Viv to board it safely."

I nodded. "Travel arrangements were certainly easier in the Cadre days. All we ever had to do was grab a private jet. I wonder how the others are getting here."

"Lily and Victor are taking the trip in stages. They'll fly to New York and stay with Claude overnight. Then the three of them fly to London and stay in a hotel, driving up here the following evening. Lily was quite outspoken about what a pain it was to get here."

I gave a rueful smile. "I'm sure she was. I have always been an inconvenience to her, to say the least."

"Stop it. She's gotten over all of her revenge

issues, years ago. And she was only joking and sends her love along to you until she can be here. It sounded like she was actually looking forward to the trip, pain or no. And Victor sounded like Victor, inscrutable as ever."

Neither one of us had to say what we were thinking: unless Sam was able to perform a miracle, I might not remember who either of them were by the time they arrived.

"I've decided not to open the pub tonight," Mitch said. "Maggie's not capable of handling a Saturday night crowd all by herself."

"I feel fine for the moment, Mitch. We shouldn't lose a night's income because of me. We need the money."

"Money be damned. All I want is to be with you. In fact, I may close down indefinitely, or at least until Pete returns. We've more than enough cash from the last two assassins to keep us and the pub going for a while."

"I suppose you know best, Mitch. To be honest, I don't much want to spend my next couple of evenings pouring out stout and whiskey."

He nodded. "Then it's settled. And after we feed, all I really want to do is settle in with you on the couch and watch the fire until Vivienne and Sam show up. I will not leave you alone again. Not until this matter is settled. And you, young lady, are not allowed to sneak off anywhere by yourself. As I said earlier, I'm sure that Moe was killed to leave you unprotected."

He turned back to the computer again. "Here's

yet another e-mail from George Montgomery. He's a persistent bastard, isn't he?"

I peered over Mitch's shoulder and read the letter; it was exactly the same as the previous one, with a paragraph tacked onto the top that said *I fear my previous communication (quoted below) may not have arrived. If this is not the case, I apologize for the duplication of mail. Please answer at your earliest convenience.*

"Persistent, yes, but he seems sincerely interested in helping." I laughed. "Even after I drank his blood and left him wandering around aimlessly not one time but twice. Fortunately he doesn't seem to have remembered either of those encounters, despite the fact that he keeps coming back for more. I almost wish I had given him his interview; at least that way some of my memories would remain, if only in print. I wonder . . ."

"Hmmm?"

"If we talk to him and he publishes his article, do you suppose somebody else might read it and know a solution to my situation?"

"We don't need Montgomery's article. Once Sam gets here—"

"Mitch," I interrupted before he could begin his hopeful speech, "we need to face the facts. Sam is a fine doctor and a wonderful friend, but this whole thing is probably out of his league. Don't put too much responsibility on him for finding a cure."

He sat silent for a while. "You're right, Deirdre. Do you want to talk to Montgomery?"

"I don't see that it can hurt our situation much. And it may even help."

"Okay." He typed in a few lines and hit the return key with a flourish. "I've asked him to meet us at his hotel, tomorrow night around seven."

After we dressed, we headed down the stairs. The first thing Mitch did was make sure the sign on the pub door read closed. Then he locked and bolted that door and turned off all the outside lights.

"Mitch?" Maggie came around the corner, wearing an apron over her tight jeans. "You locked the door?" Her voice trembled and she cleared her throat. She looked genuinely frightened. "Why?"

"We're not going to be opening tonight, Maggie. And possibly not for another day or two. Neither one of us is going to be here and we both thought you could use a night off. You've been working so hard and we've all been keeping crazy hours. A night of rest won't hurt any of us one bit."

"Well, that's true," she said, visibly relaxing, "but is it a good idea just to close down?"

Mitch shrugged. "We'll manage."

"Besides," I added, "we have friends coming in from Paris later on this evening."

At my mention of Paris, her eyes acquired a hard and angry edge. With good cause, I realized. Talk of Paris would most likely bring back sad memories of Eduard. Quickly following that thought was the certainty that she knew exactly who these friends were and that she might well have reason to hate Vivienne. Or all of us, for that matter.

I wanted to laugh. What an interesting experiment in tightrope walking we had unfolding before us. Mitch and I knew what sort of creature she was and she most certainly knew what we were. And none of us were willing to reveal our knowledge. Yet. Instead we danced a complicated pattern around the issues, ensuring that every word said could be interpreted two different ways.

"We can entertain them in our apartment, if you'd like," I said, "so that we don't disturb your rest."

She smiled, and the expression seemed effortless, guileless. "There's no need for that. Once Phoenix falls asleep he stays asleep. Even if he does get up and walk around every so often. As far as the pub goes, well, I don't mind a little time off, I'll admit that, even though I haven't been here all that long. Maybe after Phoenix gets to sleep, we could all meet here for a drink of something."

"We'll see," Mitch said. "They may be too tired following their trip. But I'm sure," and he gave her a twisted smile, "you'll meet up with them eventually."

Maggie nodded again. "That would be lovely; any friends of yours are likely to be friends of mine."

I glanced at her and she gave me an angelic

smile. "Really, I mean that," she said, and then she hesitated for a moment. "And why that reminds me of this next, I've no idea." Giving a short laugh, she shrugged and continued, "Maybe I'm more like Pete than I'd ever have imagined. In any event, Phoenix tells me that he found Moe," and she frowned, suppressing a shiver, "or at least the rest of him, hidden away up near the abbey. He was most anxious that we reclaim him and give the poor creature a decent burial. And I was hoping that the two of you would take him. I don't think I have the stomach for it, poor creature."

"Not a problem," Mitch said, "but I'd like to get an early start on all of it. Is Phoenix around?"

"Always." Maggie smiled. "At least until you want him for something. But isn't that always the way?" She turned her head and called to the back of the pub, "Phoenix? Honey? Did you want to go with Mitch and Dottie now?"

Phoenix appeared next to us and touched Mitch's hand shyly. In turn, Mitch looked down at him and gave him a warm smile. "Come on, then, boy," he said, his voice much softer than the words. "Why don't you go behind the bar and get me the flashlight? You know," he said when the boy looked at him, confused, "the torch?"

Phoenix nodded and fetched the object, holding it proudly in front of him.

"Good job," Mitch said. "Now let's get moving."

* * *

The dog's body had been hidden away outside the abbey, just as Maggie said, surrounded by a clump of sparse but thorny shrubs.

Mitch walked around the site for a while after Phoenix pointed it out, checking the ground and searching, I assumed, for any evidence that might help determine the identity of the culprit.

"The dog was definitely killed in this spot," he said after a few moments, "but there's not much else in the way of clues. Now if this were a human corpse, it would all be different. The local police would be involved and a crime laboratory would be able to find out a lot more. Unfortunately, we're the only ones likely to care about this murder. And all we've got to go on is a puddle of dried blood and one shoe print with no way to analyze any of it."

He directed the flashlight beam at the ground again and shook his head. "There's absolutely no sign of a struggle, which leads me to believe that our perpetrator must have sedated or drugged the dog before killing him. No way would Moe have just lain down and let someone do this to him. Friend or stranger, it wouldn't have mattered."

He knelt down next to the body, licked his finger, ran it over the severed neck and put it to his mouth to taste. After a second he grimaced, then nodded. "Not the most sophisticated of methods, I'll grant you, but there is a slight medicinal taste to the blood."

He got up, and brushed his hand on his jeans, looking over at Phoenix, who stood about five yards away, refusing to come any nearer. "If it's any consolation, son," Mitch said with a nod in his direction, "I'd be willing to bet that the dog didn't feel anything at all. He most likely went to sleep and just didn't wake up again. Think of it that way, if you can. And thank you for finding him for us; you've been a regular trooper and I appreciate your help."

The boy nodded and gave Mitch a tentative smile, his eyes wide with admiration and gratitude.

"Okay then," Mitch said, "I'm finished here. Think fast, son," he said and tossed the flashlight to Phoenix, who managed to catch it. "You take that for me. And I'll bring the poor old boy home." He knelt down next to the dog again, wrapped up the body in his jacket and without a word carried him back, Phoenix and me trailing along behind like a gruesome and dismal parade.

We buried Moe in the small yard behind the pub. As Mitch was digging the grave, Phoenix crept up next to me, his small fingers working their way into mine. We both stood solemnly, brushing away our tears and watching as Mitch finished the job. He reverently laid the dog in the hole, filled it all back in and patted the dirt down.

"Poor dog," Mitch said by way of a eulogy. "He was a great protector and a good friend." The boy next to me sniffled and nodded, his hand still gripping mine tightly.

He did not let go as we went back into the

pub, determined, apparently, to stay as close to me as possible. It almost seemed as if he was trying to take the place of the dog he'd always seen with me.

TWENTY-ONE

Despite the desperateness of our situation and the sadness of having to say good-bye to a good friend, that night stood out in my mind as being a near perfect evening. *Of course,* I reminded myself wryly, *you have far fewer nights against which to compare it than you did a week ago.* Even so, I enjoyed the time. Every small detail grew to be important, more poignant with the knowledge that this too could and probably would disappear without warning.

We did not go out after all, but rather ended up sitting in the closed pub. Maggie and I worked behind the bar, rearranging bottles, washing glassware and polishing the mirror. With the recognition of what she was, a breeder for the Others and as such an enemy, she had lost most of her appeal for me. She seemed more subdued than usual, moody and morose. It was as if she had an inner switch and could turn her charm and magnetism on or off at will.

Oddly enough, through it all we managed to reach a kind of mutual admiration. We worked well together and talked of commonplace things, avoiding all the important issues. I was grateful for her presence, actually. Had it been just Mitch and I, we'd most likely have spent the evening running through the same old circles of thought that had, thus far, gotten us nowhere.

"Looks like we need more port, Dot." Maggie looked up at me from where she knelt on the floor taking inventory of our stock.

"Which kind?" I asked, making the list.

"Both, I think. And some more of that merlot that you like. Plus a bottle of Irish whisky."

I glanced over to where Mitch and Phoenix were playing a game of darts. "How's our supply of scotch?"

"Quite good, actually."

"I'll write it down anyway; I have a feeling that we'll need to have a lot on hand fairly soon."

"Oh? Is it something your friends from France drink?"

"No," I said, without thinking to whom I was talking, "it would be for Mitch. He drinks it when he gets angry."

She laughed. "Is he planning on being angry any time soon? Is it something he schedules on the calendar? No wonder the two of you get along so well."

I laughed along with her.

She stood up and dusted off the knees of her jeans, then leaned both of her elbows on the bar, staring at Mitch and her son. "They're quite the pair, aren't they? Funny, because he doesn't usually take well to men. His father was a strict man."

They had moved away from the dartboard and Mitch was now patiently explaining the fine art of shooting pool to the boy. Phoenix, it turned out, had a natural ability for the game, in spite of the fact that the pool cue he insisted on using was almost twice his size.

I watched the scene in front of me for some time, marveling how to anyone looking in the pub windows at us, we would have looked like a normal human family.

Finally, Maggie looked up at the clock, slipped off her apron and laid it over the bar. "Bedtime, Phoenix."

He looked up at her and bit at his lower lip.

"Don't give me that look, young man, we're actually hours past bedtime. So say your good nights and off we'll go. I'm rather tired myself, so I'll tuck you in and stay with you."

He nodded reluctantly, touched my hand in farewell, then walked back over to Mitch and hugged him, tightly.

The shocked look on Mitch's face gave way to an expression of happiness and he hugged the boy back, then ruffled the top of his hair. I wondered if Mitch had any idea that he'd just thrown away any credibility he might have had with his hostage idea. Anyone seeing the interaction of the two of them would know he had no intention of ever hurting Phoenix.

And when I saw the love on Mitch's face, as Phoenix walked dejectedly down the hallway to his little cot in the room off the kitchen, I felt a huge responsibility leave my shoulders. When the poison ran its course and the person that I was disappeared into nothingness, Mitch would have someone to carry him through.

"Good night to the both of you," Maggie said. "I'll be seeing you tomorrow evening some time."

We heard the two of them moving around back in their room, and then there was silence.

"Have you noticed," I said quietly, all too aware of the presence in the other room, "that there have been no attacks on us since Maggie arrived?"

Mitch looked over at me. "Now that you mention it, yeah. They came on pretty hot and heavy for a while there, but now, other than Moe's accident, there's been nothing."

"A coincidence?"

Mitch laughed. "I told you when we first met that I didn't believe in coincidences. I may have had to add a lot of beliefs to my original short list, but coincidence is still not one of them. I have also noticed that you only became sick after Maggie arrived."

"Obviously, then, she is connected." I stopped for a second, then shook my head and gave a wry laugh. "Hell, of course she is connected. About as connected as one can get, without being in charge of the whole operation. But," and my voice grew wistful, "it's easy to forget all of that when she's present. I do not want to believe she's an assassin of any sort."

"Protective covering," Mitch said with a nod.

At that point, there was a knock on the front pub door. I got up to answer it and opened it to the hurricane that was Vivienne.

"Oh, *ma chere*." She pulled me into her arms

and held me close. Then, drawing back a little, she deposited a long kiss on my lips. "It is so good to see you, my sister. And good to be out of that car. Four hours of English countryside? *Merde,* I do not know how you stand it."

She studied my face, her easy smile turning into an angry frown. "But I see that the bastards have done their dirty work to you, Deirdre. We will not speak of the hair, since it seems you have done that on purpose. Otherwise, though, you look positively green, *mon chou;* like a walking case of *mal-de-mer.*"

I laughed. "It does feel like that sometimes, Vivienne. And I am glad to see you too. Where is Sam?"

"Here." He appeared in the doorway, his black doctor's bag in hand. "Just getting some stuff out of the car. Viv's right, it was too long a trip from the airport. But unlike Viv, I kind of enjoyed the scenery."

Sam came into the room, gave me one quick worried glance and set his bag on the table. "Mitch." He nodded, extending his hand. "Good to see you as always. You, at least, are looking well."

Mitch clapped him on the shoulder. "I can't even begin to tell you how welcome you are. Can I offer you a drink of something?"

"Coffee would be wonderful at this point. About an hour outside of Whitby I suddenly got very tired and I'm still a little groggy."

Vivienne laughed. "It was most exciting. We

veered all over the road before he woke up just in time to avoid hitting some silly cow."

"There was no cow, Viv."

She stuck her tongue out at him. "And exactly how would you know that, *mon beau morsel*, you were asleep at the time."

I walked around behind the bar and poured Sam a cup of coffee. "Mitch, do you want coffee?"

"Sure," he said, "that will be fine." I fixed Mitch's coffee and stirred it, handing it over to him. Looking at the second mug, though, I frowned. "I fear I don't remember how you drink this, Sam."

He took it from me. "This will be fine, as is." He took a sip, then stopped. "You don't remember? Has it progressed that far already, Deirdre?"

"No," I said quickly, "it's not that." Pouring two glasses of red wine, I walked back out from behind the bar and handed one glass to Vivienne. "I truly do not remember."

"Good." He sat down at one of the tables. "So here is what I propose we do. It's too late in the night to do anything now. But tomorrow, at sunset, you'll need to report to my clinic."

I sat down next to him, sipping my wine. "Your clinic?"

"Well, okay." Sam laughed. "Calling it a clinic is a bit of an overstatement. What I have set up is really just a couple of rooms with a few beds and some rented testing equipment. Nothing particularly fancy, but it was the best I could throw together on the short notice."

"How did you manage that?" Mitch joined us, followed by Vivienne.

Sam shrugged. "A few inquiries here or there, a couple of favors from European colleagues called in. And a whole stack of cash."

"Cash?"

Vivienne gave a giggle. "You do not think that I have lived so long, Mitch, by trusting in banks and society, do you? My little swan's nest is quite properly feathered."

"But you should not be spending your money on me, Vivienne," I said, secretly pleased that she cared. "You will need it to live on."

"Oh, foo," she said with a wave of her hand. "It is only money. And there are ways to get more, there are many ways. I have plenty, as it turns out, and even if I did not?" Vivienne gave a pretty little shrug. "It would still be well spent. I have only one sister in the whole world and we must stick together, *mon ami*. Besides," and she laughed a bit, "this puts you firmly in my debt. And there is nothing wrong with that."

I touched her hand. "Thank you," I said, feeling tears begin to fill my eyes. "It means so much to me to have you here now."

She gave me a sharp glance and placed her other hand on top of mine. "How long has it been since you've fed, my sister?"

"A couple of days, I think, since our last big feed. To be honest, I've lost track of time. Why do you ask?"

"Because your skin feels warm, hot almost, as if you had just fed. Sam?"

"I'm on it," he said, rummaging around in his black bag and pulling out a strange instrument. "May I?"

I nodded.

Sam reached over and inserted the instrument in my ear. "A new kind of thermometer," he said, "much more sensitive than the older kinds." It beeped and he pulled it away. "Quicker, too."

He looked at the thermometer's display screen. "Hmmm, let's try that again, shall we?"

The second reading was no different from the first. "You, young lady," Sam said, "are running a fever. Not particularly high, really. And if you were human, I'd say it was nothing to worry about. A low-grade infection, maybe. Or the start of a cold or flu. But you are not human. Who the hell knows what sort of damage is being done to your system?" He looked over at Mitch, who had stayed remarkably silent, staring down into his coffee cup.

"I wish you had called me in sooner, Mitch."

He shook his head. "I wish I had too, Sam. But all of this came up out of nowhere. One day Deirdre was fine, the next she was sick and losing memories right and left. We'd never had any reason at all to believe that was even possible."

I gave a laugh. "That's true, Sam. Please don't scold us. Immortality makes one rather cavalier about all sorts of things."

"No more," Sam said, standing up. "We start tomorrow night. Sunset."

"How about two hours past sunset, Sam? I have

an interview with a newspaper reporter scheduled for early tomorrow night."

"You have a what? What happened to the keep-a-low-profile rule?"

"The rules have changed," Mitch stated firmly.

Vivienne laughed. "But of course, *mon cher,* what else are rules for?" Then her eyes opened wide, staring beyond the table and down the hallway into the back of the pub. *"Bon soir, mon petit gamin.* Oh, Deirdre, what an adorable urchin. To whom does he belong?"

I turned in my chair and saw that Phoenix was standing there, looking lost and frail in the darkness. Even with his unfocused eyes, though, he managed to find Mitch and crawl into his lap.

"This is Phoenix," Mitch whispered. "He walks in his sleep. Be quiet and don't wake him. But take a look at this." Gently he grasped the boy's chin and raised his head, exposing the ugly scar.

"Mon Dieu." Vivienne jumped up from her chair. "He carries their mark."

I nodded. "Yes, he does."

"Phoenix?" A sleepy voice carried down the hallway and a light turned on.

"He's in here, Maggie," Mitch called softly and she came out into the room, dressed in nothing but a white cotton nightgown, almost completely sheer in the backlit doorway. She looked every bit an angel.

Vivienne gave a small gasp. When I looked at her, I saw that she was biting her lip and staring at Maggie like a drowning man dreaming of dry land. Sam, too, seemed fascinated with the new arrival.

Completely unperturbed with the obvious hunger in Vivienne's eyes and stance, Maggie nodded to everyone and picked the boy up from Mitch's lap. "I'm sorry to interrupt." She gave a low laugh. "One would think that with all the occurrences of this boy walking in his sleep, I'd learn to lock the door. It would be lovely to meet your friends, but I am tired. And I'm sure"—she smiled at Vivienne, exposing her even white teeth—"you all have important things to talk about. So let's save the introductions for later, if that's okay. Good night."

We all stared after her until the light turned off and we heard the door close.

"Interesting," Sam said, sinking slowly into his chair.

Vivienne shook her head and smiled, her dimples deepening. "So," she said, her eyes glowing as she looked to Mitch, to me, then back again to him, as if we had just done something incredibly clever, "you not only have one of their children here, you have a Breeder as well. And tamed, although just barely."

"There's more to it than you see, Viv." Mitch took a sip of his coffee. "And I hesitate to mention it for fear of bringing up bad blood."

She made a clicking sound with her tongue. "There is no such thing, Mitch, *mon gars,* and you know it. Tell me now, or I may burst. I do not care if we stay until after the sun rises—this is a story I simply have to hear."

"Indeed you do, Vivienne," I said, draining my glass of wine and setting it back down on the table. "Maggie Richards is none other than the widow of the late Eduard DeRouchard."

TWENTY-TWO

Vivienne sat for a moment, staring off down the hall after Maggie and her son. "Eduard's widow? And here? Staying with the two of you?"

I had feared her reaction. Eduard was, after all, an ex-lover of hers. Beneath the soft and frivolous surface of my blood sister lurked wildfires and tempers, ordinarily kept banked and under control. But by her own admission, she had adored Eduard, even to his death.

Her face was totally still for a minute. I reached over and touched her hand in a gesture of support. She looked back at me, her expression unfathomable, until she began to laugh that delightful high-pitched giggle of hers.

"Were you afraid that I would crumble to pieces out of grief over Eduard's defection? Over hearing that he married another woman? My dear sister," she said, fanning herself with her hand, "it is sweet that you should be concerned with the state of my heart. But I assure you that I am free from the fascinating spell of Monsieur le Docteur."

I shrugged. "It was possible, I thought."

"No," she said, still laughing, reaching over to

take Sam's arm and hugging it to her. "And no again. One doctor in my life is quite enough, *merci."* Then she sobered just a bit. "But the boy? Surely you do not believe that he is Eduard, reborn? The last time we saw him he was nothing but smoking ash and cinders. There is no resurrection from that."

"We don't know who the boy is," Mitch said. "But we intend to find out."

Sam cleared his throat and glanced at the clock over the bar. "It's not an issue for me, folks, but I suggest we either tell this story quickly or save it for another time. Viv and I still need to find our house and unpack a few things from the car before dawn. And, Deirdre"—he gave me a discerning glance—"you look tired, if such a thing is possible."

I sighed. "You're right, Sam. Let's hold this discussion until tomorrow night sometime. I am weary and hungry."

"Oh, damn." He slapped himself lightly on the head. "That reminds me. I brought you a gift, of sorts." Sam got up and headed for the door. "Hold on just a second and I'll go get it."

On his return, he was carrying an ice chest. "My mother always taught me that every self-respecting guest comes bearing drink and food. And in this case, I've brought both."

I lifted the lid and smiled, seeing the rows of plastic blood bags lined up in the chest. "Thank you, Sam."

"Enjoy." An expression of disgust flitted over his handsome face for a second. Then he set the

chest down on a table and smiled at me. "Keep
it cold," he said, "and keep it safe." He gave me
a small hug. "Keep yourself safe, as well."

Sam broke the embrace, touched my forehead
briefly and frowned. "Get some rest, okay?" He
turned away from me. "Ready to go, Viv?"

"Lead on, my darling, and I will follow," Vivienne replied as Sam and Mitch headed for the
door. She leaned over, wrapping an arm around
my waist. "For one thing," she whispered in my
ear, "the view is so enchanting, don't you think?"

Laughing in response, I gave her a wry smile
and a kiss on the cheek.

Mitch opened the door for both of them, shook
Sam's hand, ruffled the top of Viv's hair. "Thanks
for coming," he said. "If nothing else, the company will be good for her. Maybe with more people she knows around, she won't be as likely to
forget."

He closed the door behind them and the room
felt empty.

"That girl," Mitch said with a smile for the
irony of the word, "is like a breath of fresh air.
She sure hasn't changed in the last three years,
has she?" Mitch picked up the ice chest and
started for the stairs. Realizing I was not following,
he turned back to me. "Deirdre? Are you coming
to bed?"

"I suppose I should."

"But?"

"I don't want to sleep. Every time I wake up,
I'm missing a piece of my past."

His eyes reflected his worry. "Well, we don't

have to sleep. Come on, love, I'll serve you breakfast in bed."

I trudged up the stairs behind him, stepped over the two dogs at the door, looked around the room and sighed. "I'll build up a fire," I said, forcing a smile, "and slip into something more comfortable. You can fix breakfast."

Unfortunately, the something more comfortable turned out to be nothing more than an old plaid flannel nightgown. The wood Mitch had brought in earlier seemed damp, giving me no end of trouble with getting a fire started. It seemed the possibility of a picture-book romantic moment was lost. Not that it mattered. We had never needed the trappings of love.

When Mitch emerged from the kitchen, he bore a tray that held two of our best wineglasses and a small vase that held a single red rose. The glasses were filled with heated blood. In the cold air of the fireless apartment, I could see the steam rising from them.

"That is lovely, Mitch," I said, accepting my glass.

"Careful, it's hot," he warned. "I tried to warm it differently this time. Running hot water over the bags seems to take forever, but I let the fire get too high under the pan. Wasn't paying attention, I guess, because I was searching for the vase." He chuckled. "Which emphasizes what I've always thought: never let ambience get in the way of the food. But I think it's still drinkable, at least it hadn't reached the boiling point."

"And the rose? Where did that come from?"

He laughed. "A gift from Vivienne, I think. It was tucked into the ice chest."

I sipped and then drained the glass. "It's fine, Mitch. Thank you."

He drank his and set the empty glass on the nightstand next to mine. "No fire?" he asked.

"The wood was damp. And I hadn't the patience."

"Allow me," he said and in what seemed like no time at all he had a crackling fire going. "Turn out the lights, sweetheart, and join me."

We settled down in front of the fire. "While I was fixing the blood," he said, "I started thinking about the time I found you in your bathroom drinking from one of those stupid little plastic bags. Do you remember?"

I smiled at him, from where I was snuggled into his arm. "Yes, quite clearly. You thought I was crazy and couldn't get out of there fast enough."

He lean over and kissed me. "I came back, though, because I loved you so much that I didn't care. I fought so hard against believing the truth about you. The obvious answer was staring me straight in the face, and I chose not to see it. Human nature, I guess."

I gave a low laugh. "Vampire nature, too, I think. We all deny what we don't want to accept."

We fell quiet for a second or two, watching the flames leap and fall. My sigh broke the silence. "That all seems so very long ago now. And although it is hard to believe, life was so much simpler then. How did it all get so complicated, Mitch? Was there a point in time when all of this could have been averted? A specific action taken that, if undone, could change everything?"

"Somehow, Deirdre, I can tell where this conversation is headed. And we've been there before."

"I know. And I did not bring it up to assume the blame this time. Rather, I'm just thinking out loud. I have been dreaming of Max, you see. And I wonder if my subconscious is trying to go back and change that one pivotal moment."

"That sounds like a question for Sam. I'm still just a dumb cop, struggling through the best I can."

"Do you miss it, Mitch? The police work?"

"Deirdre—" he started in a warning tone, but I interrupted him.

"Yes, I know what you're going to say because you have said it before—I am more important to you than the work."

"Damned straight."

"Even so," I said with a smile, "try to imagine life without me. Would you return to the force if you could?"

"In a New York minute," he said.

"There," I said, "that didn't hurt a bit, did it? Why have you never spoken of it before?"

"For the same reason I don't talk about Chris. Let it go, sweetheart, please just let it go."

I sighed, thinking that soon I would have no choice but to take his advice. We lay in silence again for a while.

"Mitch?" I shifted my position slightly, and traced my fingers down his chest.

"Hmmm?" He was more than half asleep already.

"We need to talk about this."

"About what?"

"About what we are going to do when Sam fails to find a cure."

"If." He sat up and looked into my eyes. "And notice that I said *if* Sam can't help, we'll use Maggie and Phoenix as hostages against the Others providing an antidote."

"And if that doesn't work? What then?"

"Hell, I don't know, Deirdre. Maybe I'll get them to poison me too and we can live together, both of us with no memory and rediscovering each other every day."

I laughed. "The way you say it makes it sound rather exciting."

"I hope so," he said, leaning over to kiss me. "I'd hate to think that I was getting boring in our old age."

"You? Boring? Never."

I responded to the kiss; he began to run his strong hands over my body. And with an inner smile I thought, *No, we definitely do not need to rely on romantic trappings.*

Afterward, I did not sleep; instead I occupied myself with cleaning up our small flat, washing dishes, changing the bedsheets, dusting. Then I sat on the sofa, with my legs curled under me. Watching Mitch sleep in front of the dying fire, I shed more than a few quiet tears.

* * *

Mitch had arranged to meet George Montgomery in his hotel room shortly after sunset. I wondered as we took the elevator up to his floor if he had any clue at all what he was about to hear.

George met us at the door, wearing jeans and the same suit jacket he'd worn when I first met him in the cemetery by the abbey, the occurrence of which he obviously had no recollection. As far as he was concerned this was our first meeting.

He shook hands with Mitch, then took my hand and gave it a kiss. "I'm so glad to meet you at last. And I can't thank you enough, both of you, for agreeing to talk to me."

I sniffed the air and noticed a tray with a half-eaten plate of food sitting on the desk. "Did we interrupt your dinner?"

"No, I was done. Hotel food is not the most appetizing thing in the world. But it's quick and easy."

"Smells like fettuccine Alfredo," Mitch said appreciatively. "I haven't had that for years. Deirdre, do you remember that little restaurant we went to on our first date?"

"Yes, my love, I still do." But for how long? I wondered.

George put the cover back on his plate. "The chef had a heavy hand with the garlic on this dish. I'll just set it out in the hallway and then we can start."

As he walked past me with the tray, an overwhelming wave of nausea washed over me. "Bathroom?" I managed to blurt the word, and ran for it when he pointed.

When I finished vomiting up the blood I had drunk that morning, I rested my feverish head against the cool porcelain until I felt strong enough to stand. I splashed water on my face and stared at myself in the mirror.

I looked like hell. And Viv was right, it was not just the hair. My eyes were heavy with dark circles and my skin was blotchy, discolored. Sighing, I dried my face and hands and went out to join George and Mitch.

"Deirdre?" Mitch got up from the chair he was sitting in and took my arm, guiding me to that same seat.

I smiled up at him. "I'm fine, Mitch. Must have been the smell of the food."

George nodded knowingly. "My ex-wife was like that when she was pregnant. When's the happy event?"

I looked at him in shock at first. "Pregnant? You think I'm pregnant?" Mitch caught my eye and we both burst out laughing.

George glanced back and forth at us, giving us a sheepish grin. "Well, it was just a hunch. A nice young couple, newly married, and she throws up at the scent of food. Made sense to me, but I guess I was wrong."

I wiped the tears of laughter away from my eyes. Poor man, he really did have no idea what we were. He had built up this image in his mind of a young American couple being persecuted by

some sort of international conspiracy. He believed
we were human, he believed we were innocent.

"You have no idea, Mr. Montgomery, how
wrong you are. Now please sit down and I will tell
you why."

"May I record this?"

I nodded. "That would be the best idea, I think.
If for no other reason than that I would like to
have a record of it."

He pulled out a handheld tape recorder,
checked to see that there was a cassette loaded
and ready to go, then clicked the button and set
it down on the table next to me. "Fine, then,"
he said, "this one's for posterity."

TWENTY-THREE

I told him everything I could recall of my life. A much shorter story than it would have been yesterday. But certainly longer than it would be tomorrow. At first, he kept interrupting with questions and exclamations, but as the telling progressed, he grew quieter and more thoughtful.

"So here we stand, Mr. Montgomery. My memories are being pared away with each passing day. We are a species being hounded to extinction with no understanding of why. Our lair has been discovered and infiltrated by members of the Others' organization. All we have to bargain with is a woman and her mute son, both of them with far more appeal than is conceivable, making it nearly impossible for us to take action."

He sat still, his hands folded in his lap, his eyes searching my face for confirmation that this story was all true.

"You have just handed me the story of the century," he said finally. "Unfortunately," and his mouth twisted into a reluctant grin, "I can't use any of this for my article. If it's not true, I'd be crucified. And if it is true"—he chuckled a bit—"I'd still be crucified. Printing anything you have told me, true or not, reduces me to the level of sensationalism of *Real-Life Vampires.* And, regardless of how you may feel about my profession based on Terri and Bob, I have some integrity."

Sighing, I got up from my chair and stretched. "I understand, Mr. Montgomery. I'm not sure what I had hoped to accomplish by talking to you. I'm not sure of anything at this point. Except that my time is running short."

He reached over for the tape recorder, removed the cassette and handed it to me. "A gesture of my good faith."

I took it, stared at it lying in my palm, then pushed it into the back pocket of my jeans.

"I am sorry," he continued. "If I could do more to help you both, I would. And for what it's worth, I do believe your story. However, as a detached bystander, I have an idea or two."

Mitch ran his fingers through his hair. "Whatever you have to offer is probably more than we already have. Go ahead."

"Should you discover that no others of your kind have been pursued as relentlessly as you, maybe you need to think 'Why us? Why me?' If you, Deirdre, are being specially targeted, and it seems that you are, then there must be a reason. There always is. It may not be a good reason, but still . . . So if all of this were happening to me, I'd go back and check the source. There are no coincidences in life. Just series of connected events."

Mitch chuckled a bit at that statement, but I sighed.

"Easy enough to say that, Mr. Montgomery, but all too soon my ability to think things through to their logical ends will be completely erased by my inability to remember. Thank you, however, for your time."

We walked almost as far as the address Sam had given us before I spoke again. "That was a complete and utter waste of what little time I have left. I sincerely hope that Sam will have more to offer."

"I don't know," Mitch said. "Montgomery was right about one thing. We do need to get to the source of all of this. And that won't be accomplished by hiding out here in Whitby. I'm going to leave you with Sam and Vivienne for the rest of the night and do some investigation of my own. Now that we have Maggie in hand, we might as well use her if we can."

He checked the paper on which Sam had written the address. "This seems to be the place."

I rang the bell and could hear Vivienne's excited call from inside the building. "Yes," I said with a smile, "it is indeed."

Mitch took me into his arms and held me in a long embrace, not moving away when the door opened, but tightening his hold on me. "I love you, Deirdre," he whispered into my hair, "and I don't want you ever to forget that."

"I will try, my love."

"Secrets?" Vivienne's light voice rang in the air. "I love secrets."

"Not a secret," Mitch said, his voice shaking. "I love this woman."

"Oh, foo," she said, with a pout and a little shake of her shoulders. "That is not a secret. We all know that. And of course you do. She is, of course, absolutely wonderful. Being, as she is, my sister. Now come in, both of you. Sam is fussing around in his lab, as happy as a child with a new toy. He'll be glad you are here finally so that he can try it all out."

Mitch shook his head. "I can't stay. I have some investigation to do." He kissed me, hard on the lips. "Do what Sam tells you to do, sweetheart. I'll be back long before dawn to see what's happening."

Watching him walk away, I tried to hold back my tears and almost succeeded until Vivienne put an arm around my shoulders. I broke down then and cried, as she held me there in the open front doorway; she stroked my short hair and whispered nonsense words of comfort. When my sobbing subsided, she held me out at arm's length, wiped away my tears and smiled.

"Feel better now?"

I sniffed and gave a small choked laugh. "Actually, I do."

Vivienne pulled me into the house, closing and locking the door behind us. "See, we are still more female than we are monsters. Sometimes a good cry is all we need. Come now, Sam is waiting for you."

The layout of their house was similar to the one of the pub, with the substitution of a waiting room

for the bar area and a sterile-looking laboratory
in place of the kitchen. Apparently, I would be
secluded in the room beyond the lab.

I looked around. "This is amazing, Vivienne,"
I said. "I cannot believe you set this all up in just
a few days. You must have spent a great deal of
money."

She shrugged. "It is not as impressive a feat as
you are thinking. This building had been used as
a doctor's office before we bought it and so we
changed it not at all. Mostly, we had it cleaned.
Sam has been working all day to set up the equipment that was here waiting for us when we arrived. So," and she gave me a wicked little smile,
"you are not so much in my debt after all. Which
is a shame, *ma chere*. I like having people in my
power."

Sam came out of the back, pulling on a pair of
latex gloves. "How's my patient this evening?"

"Nauseated. Anxious. Frightened."

"Good." He smiled at me. "At least that gives
us something to work with. Come on back. No,
not you, Viv. I'll give you a call if I need you."

She flounced out to the waiting area. "I did
not live for over three centuries, Doctor Samuels,
so that I could wait here at your beck and call.
Perhaps I will take a tour of the town."

"That's a good idea." Sam nodded absentmind-
edly. "Have fun, but be careful."

With a few choice words, in her native language, she flew out of the front door.

I waited until it closed, then gave him a stern
look. "You have done a very bad thing, Sam."

He looked surprised and just a little guilty. "I have? And what have I done?"

I laughed. "You have unleashed Vivienne on this poor little unsuspecting town."

"Oh," he said, smiling, "is that all? I suspect if Whitby survived Dracula, it'll survive Vivienne." Then he laughed. "Maybe."

He had me take off my clothes, put on a hospital gown and then started with a basic physical exam. My weight, height, temperature and blood pressure were taken and recorded. He listened to my heart with a stethoscope and tested my reflexes with a little rubber hammer.

As he worked, he talked, keeping up a running stream of commentary to accompany his actions. "I ran all these same tests on Vivienne earlier, so that I'd have some sort of control results. There are no textbooks written on vampire physiognomy. In fact, there's probably only one doctor in the whole world capable of documenting the phenomenon." He laughed. "And Viv would kill me if I tried such a thing. Still, it's very tempting, especially when you consider that I started out in med school primarily to become a hematologist."

"Really? What moved you into psychiatry?"

"Contingencies. During my first year, a full scholarship became available; I fit all of the qualifications except for my medical concentration. And so, since I needed the money, I changed majors. But I've kept up as much as possible in the new advances of the field, even to the point of doing private research for interested individuals."

I smiled. "Such as I?"

"Exactly. Among others. In fact that's where I get the blood from—my other research assignments. I take two or three bags from each shipment and put them into storage. Vivienne says that I am a larcenous squirrel, hiding away acorns for the winter." He laughed. "Now," he said, getting back to business, "I am going to take some of your blood. I've never been able to draw blood from Viv's veins with a needle, so I've had to devise another method. She says it doesn't hurt much."

With a scalpel, he made a small incision in the crook of my right arm and inserted a tiny glass tube that ran into a larger glass cylinder. He pushed a button on the cylinder and I heard a rush of air. "This creates a vacuum," he explained. "Otherwise we'd be here all night waiting for a drop or two. Ah, there we go."

I felt the suction on my arm and watched as the cylinder filled with my blood. *Odd,* I thought, *it looks no different than any other blood.*

He pulled the tube from my arm when the cylinder was almost full and turned to move the blood out to the lab.

"Sam," I said, staring at my arm and trying not to panic, "am I still supposed to be bleeding?"

"What?" He turned and looked at me, watching for a moment as a small red flow trickled down my arm. "No, you are not supposed to be bleeding. Viv always dried up to the point of it being difficult to even get the tube out of her arm. Interesting."

He set the cylinder down and held a small wad of cotton to the spot. "Here," he said, bending my arm up, "hold that there for a bit while I get ready for the next test."

He wheeled in a small machine and began to attach small round disks to various portions of my head and body. Each disk was attached by a wire to the machine. "Before we start this," he said, "I want to see if I can draw blood from you the normal way. I should have done that first, without relying on the anomalies I'd previously discovered with Viv."

"More blood?" I said. "How much do you need?"

He shook his head. "This is not for the blood, actually. I just want to see if your blood behaves as Viv's does. So I won't take much."

I held out my left arm and he slid an empty hypodermic needle straight into the same general area as he had hit on the other arm and drew off about half a tube. "No problem," he said, sounding rather pleased with the result. "Interesting," he repeated.

"What does it mean?"

"For now, it merely means that your blood is different than Viv's. Not necessarily good or bad, just different. Relax, Deirdre."

I tried to do as he asked through all the prodding and poking. But after several hours, I grew restless.

"Will we be finished soon?" I asked. "What else can you possibly do to me, other than slit me open and take a good long look at what is inside?"

His mouth twisted up into a grin. "Now, there's an idea . . ." Then he laughed. "But no, on second thought, Mitch would skin me alive. And Viv would eat my liver or something equally as horrible. Actually, we're almost done. Only one more test, a polygraph. I'm just going to ask you some basic questions about things you should remember but don't. And then I'm going to hypnotize you and ask again. But before we do that you can take a break and walk around or something."

"In this gown?" I blushed. "I think I would prefer to get it over with, if you don't mind."

He laughed. "Whatever you say."

The questions he asked were simple enough, but for most of them I had no answer. Finally, I sighed. "Don't ask me anymore, Sam. The sheer volume of things that I have forgotten is depressing."

"It's okay," he said, "I've got enough to go on already. Do you remember how I hypnotized you during the Larry Martin situation?"

I nodded. "Yes, that time frame is more recent."

"Good," Sam said, holding up a pen, "now just stare at the pen and listen to me as I talk."

He used the same type of procedure as I did when hypnotizing my victims. And it was just as effective.

I opened my eyes to see Sam turning off the tape recorder he'd used during the session. "Well?"

"I'm not sure what it means, Deirdre, but I think it's probably good news. The memories are there—under hypnosis you can pull them up without hesitation. That tells me it's not a permanent block and not a physical problem."

"So you can fix it?"

"Theoretically? Yeah, I believe so. But you can't rush research, Deirdre, so this may take some time."

I sighed. There it was again, time I did not have. "That's wonderful news, Sam, thank you for all of your effort."

"Viv came in while you were under," he said. "She'll entertain you until Mitch shows up. I've got work to do."

When Mitch arrived, I was exhausted emotionally and physically. I had dressed and was sitting quietly talking to Vivienne in the outer rooms. The clatter of beakers and tubes and the clicking of the computer keyboard signaled Sam as being hard at work in the lab.

"So?" Mitch came over and gave me a kiss.

I shrugged. "He is working on it, right now. 'These things take time, Deirdre, you can't rush research.' " I mimicked his words and Vivienne laughed.

"Sam always says that and then, *voila!* He comes through." She reached over, took my hand and held it up to her cheek. "You will be fine, *ma chere*, I feel sure of it. Now you and Mitch should get home before the sun rises. Have a little something to drink—I swear, Sam takes more blood than any of us ever do. And they call us monsters."

Mitch laughed and I gave a weak smile.

"Ready, Deirdre?"

I kissed Vivienne. "Tell Sam I said good night and thank you. And that I will come back tomorrow night if he needs anything else."

TWENTY-FOUR

I could tell that Mitch had news for me, but did not want to speak about it in the open. The dogs greeted us at the door of the pub and for a second I looked around for Moe, then sighed when I remembered that he was gone.

"Poor fellow," I said. "I don't think I appreciated him enough."

"Who?" Mitch looked up from the attentions of the two mongrels, then seeing the expression on my face, nodded. "Yeah, he was sort of a fixture of the place. Doesn't quite seem the same without him. Kind of like Pete."

I smiled sadly. "Yes, but Pete will be coming back." It made no sense in saying that when he did, I would not know him.

We mounted the stairs and locked ourselves in.

"Hungry?" At my nod, he went into the kitchen, opened the refrigerator door and took out a bag of blood. "I'll warm it up for you. And then I'll tell you what I found out. It was all I could do not to come running over to tell you."

I gave a brief laugh. "Sam wouldn't have liked that; he wouldn't even let Vivienne into the room."

He called out to me, over the sound of running water. "So what did he do to you?"

"Besides draining all my blood, you mean?" I smiled when I said it, though, for hadn't Sam made amends with the gift to replace it? "He connected me to a lot of machines. It was all tests and little graphs on computer screens. None of it meant anything to me, but he seemed pleased and content that he had enough to work with. And he hypnotized me. He believed that the memories were not gone forever. Just blocked."

Mitch came out of the kitchen with a large glass tumbler filled with blood and handed it to me. "That's good. Now drink up."

I sniffed at it and took a long sip. "It's not quite the same thing as getting it fresh. But it will do, I suppose." I drained it and he reached for the empty glass.

"More?"

"No. That was more than enough. Now tell me your news."

He gave me a broad smile.

"Well?"

"I found out who is in charge of the Others. And it appears that we are holding a larger bargaining chip than we initially thought. Maggie Richards is more than the widow of their dead leader. Much more. She is also the mother of the current one. Such a nice direct connection, don't you think? Blood ties run thick in their organization, apparently."

"I thought the eldest son was staying with his father's family, learning the funeral business.

Oh." I shook my head. "Of course. Where better to take care of their transfers of souls? So who is this man? And how do we get in touch with him?"

"Steven DeRouchard currently resides in New York City. I have a phone number."

"Just like that? How could it be so simple? How did you find this out?"

"Phoenix paid me a visit." Mitch smiled in remembrance. "I'm getting to like that child more and more with each passing day. Which I should not, I guess, considering his origins. But we had a nice talk, until Maggie came to interrupt us. We'd already guessed that the boy hated his father, but apparently he's not particularly fond of his brother, either. He was more than willing to answer my questions and was able to find the De-Rouchard Mortuary on-line listing for me."

The whole thing seemed too easy to me, too much of a coincidence, somehow. Then it hit me. "I don't like it, Mitch. It feels like a trap, as if he wanted us to find him."

"Yeah, of course he did. But we'll use the information to our advantage, not his. Besides, what else can they do to us now?"

To me, such a statement was challenging fate, but I said nothing, letting Mitch rattle on with his plans to contact the DeRouchards, how we would catch a flight to New York City with Maggie and Phoenix in tow, how he felt sure that they would cooperate fully, how he felt sure that the solution to my sickness was just a day or two away.

I loved him for many reasons, not the least one being his refusal to surrender. Unfortunately, I did not share the feeling, being frightened and totally weary. I had not slept at all the previous day, for fear of losing more of myself. Ultimately, though, I knew that I could not stay awake forever. Leaning my head on the back of the sofa, I closed my eyes for just a second. Nothing made sense. Nothing. And I was so tired.

I get off the plane in the city alone; I do not mind the solitude. It seems natural to me. The way it should be. And I know that somewhere, he is waiting. I will find him when it is time and then things will be made right.

I love being on these streets again, enjoy staring up at the tall buildings and the crowds of people rushing past me. Putting my head back, I inhale the city air. It smells of gasoline and car exhaust, it smells of flesh and blood and life and death. And home.

As if I were invisible, the people ignore me when I walk by, laughing. And when I hear the voice call, they must not, for they do not react, do not respond.

The voice is filled with pain and betrayal and it tears at my heart. I follow the voice, I have no choice, my feet move of their own volition and I follow.

I know the building. I have been there before, dreamt of it before. But now it is different; there is no one to greet me at the door. There is no music playing, for there is no one there to dance. The room is dark and silent and empty.

Except for the voice that calls.

It calls a name. And I follow, down a hallway. I push on a door that hangs heavy. Even with my full strength I can only open it halfway. Stepping into the room, I think that it is empty also.

But the voice calls me and I turn around.

He is here. There. On the door, held up and pinned by a long piece of splintered wood.

Here, I think, *is the answer I have sought in my waking life. I need only undo this act and all will be right.*

I put my hand to the wood and pull it away.

And the world seems to rise around me again. There is music playing somewhere, sounds of voices filter in to this room and the lights grow bright.

He moves away from the door and walks over to me. I am frightened, but he smiles.

"Have I done well?" I ask.

He nods and smiles and encircles me with his arms. His embrace is soft, comforting me like black-feathered wings. His grasp is as strong as steel and holds me captive.

"Once more, little one," he says as I stare into his eyes, "once more and all will be right."

I woke panicked and completely disoriented. The dream seemed so real, so natural. It hurt to be back here, submerged once again into a body that did not react as it should, into a mind that was failing.

Looking over at Mitch, sleeping, I breathed a

sigh of relief that I still knew him. Testing the edges of my memory, though, I discovered that all of my years prior to my arrival in New York City as Deirdre Griffin were gone. As if I had been born the night I had arrived there.

Fewer than twenty years were left to me. And so much had happened to me during those years, so much of what made my life worth living. Mitch, of course, comprised the bulk of that worth. But there was Lily, the daughter I had never known, had never had a chance to know and now never would. And Vivienne and Sam and even Phoenix. Gwen, Victor, Claude, the memories of Larry Martin, of Chris, of the cabin in Maine, of Elly, who plied me with herbal tea and scented candles.

Also rising to my mind were the memories of all of the countless victims from the past twenty years, those from whom I had stolen a portion of their life, so that I might live to reach this point in time.

One more sleep, one more dream, and all of them would be gone.

I had not the optimism of Sam, nor the perpetual gaiety of Vivienne, nor the hardheaded stubbornness of Mitch, who refused to give up even in the face of truth. All I had was love and the past events that served to make me the creature I was; when that past no longer existed, there would only be love.

I feared that it would not be enough to weather this storm.

Inwardly I raged. These bastards would pay although I did not know how I would exact my revenge. Deep inside, I felt the anger of the Cat; she had not deserted me, I realized, but had only drawn further into my being. I visualized her, retreating as if into a dark cave from the pain and the sickness.

And although she'd retreated, she was not beaten or cowed; rather she stood facing the entrance of her lair, snarling her defiance. Biding her time. Her spirit and her inner fire still burned. As did mine.

Years ago, Sam had theorized that the Cat was merely my subconscious way of dealing with anger. Despite his then denial of the physical manifestation, he was, in a way, quite correct. She held on to feelings with which I could not deal, and it was with her that I kept my rage and my frustration, feeding her basest instincts.

I reached deep inside and walked into her lair. She came to me and I caressed her fur, searching for her mind, attempting to touch the mind of the Cat. When I did find her and touch her, I also filled her with my hatred and my anger, feeling it drain out of me and into her.

Soon, I whispered to her, *soon we will find a way. We have to find a way. Until then, my pet, sleep and heal. And do not forget to hold true to the anger as I will try to hold on to the love.*

The phone rang, startling me out of my meditation, and I jumped from the couch to answer it.

"Hello?"

There was a pause. "Mom? It's me. Lily."

"Yes, I know. Where are you?"

"London."

"Did you have a good flight?"

She laughed. "It's too goddamned long a trip. And we barely made it to the hotel. But we're here. And we'll be leaving shortly after sunset to drive up there."

"Is Claude driving?"

"Shit, no. I am. There's no way I'd trust this journey to anyone else."

"Well, please drive carefully, Lily. You do know that they drive on the other side of the road here, don't you?" I shook my head and rolled my eyes when I said the words. Apparently mothering was not an entirely foreign concept to me after all.

She sighed. "I wasn't born yesterday, Mom. And I'll manage fine. But why do you always have to pick these god-awful out-of-the-way places? Like that place in Maine? It was barely a dot on the map." She paused, remembering, as was I, that she had come to our cabin in Maine with the sole purpose of destroying my life. And remembering that she had almost succeeded. "Oh. I'm sorry. I probably shouldn't have brought that up, huh?"

"Lily," I said, trying to sound motherly and comforting, "don't worry about that time. It's over and done and"—I gave a harsh little laugh—"practically forgotten."

"Oh." She sounded like she understood. "That's okay, then. I need to go now, Mom, so that we can get started on time. See you in about five hours or so."

"Lily?"

"Yeah?"

"Vivienne says there are cows on the roads. So be careful."

She laughed again. "Come on, Mom, Viv wouldn't know a cow if it jumped up and bit her on her cute little French ass. Jesus. Cows."

I smiled to hear the sarcasm in her voice. "It was not your"—I hesitated—"ass that I was worried about, Lily. Rather it was the car and the occupants."

"Okay, okay," she continued, "I get the message. And I'll be careful, promise."

"Good. See you soon, then."

"Yeah. And, Mom?" I heard a trace of mischievous laughter in her voice.

"Yes?"

"I'll be bringing some good news when I come. Bye."

I hung up the phone, laughing at how she had to get the last word, while at the same time brushing away a few tears. No sense in crying over this relationship. I had no time in which to repair it.

Mitch came over and put an arm around my waist. "Was that Lily on the phone?"

"Yes, they will be leaving London soon."

"You knew who she was?"

"Yes, Mitch, I knew." I did not want to tell him that I had lost more memories in my sleep. His worry and sorrow would not delay the inevitable. "Of course I knew her."

"Good. I'm going to take a shower now. Join me?"

I reached up and kissed him. "In a bit."

He went into the bathroom and I heard the water start. "In a bit," I repeated softly, "but I have something now that I need to do before it is too late."

TWENTY-FIVE

While Mitch was in the shower, I hurriedly dressed and went downstairs to the pub. The time for subtlety had come and gone. It was time, long past time, to confront the enemy. Before everything I'd ever known faded from my sight, it was important that there be honesty between the two of us, Maggie and me.

Phoenix was standing at the pool table, pushing the balls around with his hand and watching the caroms they made. The dogs we'd shut out of our room that morning flopped around his feet.

"Hello," I said to him with a smile when he looked up at me, "perfecting your game?"

He nodded.

"Well, how would you like to go upstairs and keep Mitch company for a while instead? I want to have a private talk with your mother."

He gave me a doubtful look and I smiled again. "It will be all right with her, I promise. I'll tell her where you are. Mitch is in the shower right now, but I know he won't care if you go in. You can even use the computer if you want. How does that sound?"

His eyes lit up and he nodded, starting for the stairs.

"Wait," I said, "take the dogs with you. And tell me where your mother is before you go."

He gestured with his head to the back of the pub. "Room." He mouthed the word and grinned at me, then whistled to the dogs and bounded up the stairs, opening the door I'd left unlocked.

Now, I thought as I headed to the small room that was Maggie's, *now I can say what needs to be said. And do what needs to be done.*

I knocked on the door but did not wait for her to answer; instead I tried the doorknob and found it unlocked.

"Maggie," I said, the tone of my voice low and controlled, "you really should be more careful. Almost anyone could have just walked in here."

She sat on the end of the narrow bed, slightly hunched over, but her profile showed clear in the light. "I don't care," she murmured, "I don't bloody care anymore." Her shoulders quivered.

"I have come to ask you an important question, Maggie."

"Go ahead." Her muffled voice sounded small and sad, but I did not allow the emotions it aroused to deter me.

"Tell me, Maggie, is there any particular reason why I should not kill you right now? Right here where you sit?"

"No." She turned to me and I saw that she had been crying. Her beautiful face looked old and ugly. For the first time since we'd met, she had no magnetism, no pull on me.

"Just get it over with." She wiped away her tears impatiently with the heel of her hand, a small photograph of a child clutched between her fingers.

I took a step closer to her and looked at the picture. It was not of Phoenix, that much I knew. And there was something odd about the eyes of this child.

"What are you waiting for? There is no reason for you not to kill me. I won't fight you, Dot. In fact, it would be a blessing."

"What?" This was not the answer I had expected to receive. That she would call me on a threat I had no intention of carrying out shocked me beyond belief.

She rose up and dropped the photograph. I watched it as it fell, fluttering slightly and landing on the floor between us. She stepped over it and stood in front of me, her hands clasped in front of her and her eyes downcast.

I did nothing, said nothing. The silence grew between us and the moment seemed to stretch to years.

Eventually her eyes rose from the floor and met mine. She was not afraid, that much was plain. Not afraid, no, but I also saw she fully expected to die. I could almost taste the hopelessness and despair in the air.

"How do you propose to do it, Dot?" she asked. "Will you just drain me of every drop of my blood? I'd imagine that would be a painless way to die. In fact it might be downright pleasant, I'd probably just slowly drift away. Or you could take the quicker approach, I suppose, and simply rip my throat out. Leaves more of a mess behind, though, and"—she gave a small laugh—"I won't be around to help you clean it up."

"Or—" She unbuttoned her shirt, slowly slid it off her arms and dropped it to the floor where it lay crumpled next to the photo. She removed her bra next, exposing her white breasts, nipples slightly crinkled from the cold. "You can tear out my heart. Go ahead, take it. It's never done me much good anyway."

"Maggie," I said softly, "put your shirt back on. I am not going to tear out your heart."

"And you're not going to kill me either, are you?"

"No, I cannot kill you. I wanted to; I came down here to do exactly that, I think. But I was lying to myself. Even if your death at my hands would solve all my problems, I could not do it."

"Why not? I came here to spy on you and Mitch. I brought with me the ingredient needed to catalyze the poison in your veins."

"Catalyze?"

"Oh. You didn't know that part, did you? I thought maybe Sam would have figured it out. If I had never come here, if you had not taken my blood, you would have been fine. And so would your memory."

"You know about that?"

Maggie sighed and picked up her bra and shirt from the floor, sitting down on the bed to put them on again. "I know everything. About you and Mitch, at least. And I know who is calling the shots. I wish I didn't."

I nodded. "It's your oldest son, is it not? Steven DeRouchard?"

"No! My son would never do these things. He'd never call for the death of so many. He was loving and warm and entirely mine. Until . . ." Her voice trailed off and the expression in her eyes grew distant.

"Until?" I prompted her, picking up the picture from the floor and placing it once more into her hand.

Maggie looked at the picture and held back a sob. "Can you even understand what my life has been like? I was raised to be a Breeder; it takes a certain sort of woman, you see, a certain upbringing to enable you to birth children and give them up."

"Give them up?"

She gave me a sharp look. "Okay, you're right. And we should be honest, you and I. It is not giving them up, that would be pardonable. No, instead I've given birth to children only to put them willingly into the hands of murderers."

Maggie started to cry again, ugly tears streaming down her face. I did not know what to say; I moved toward her, my intentions unclear even to me.

"No," she said, "don't touch me. If you touch me, the lure will begin to work on you again. You won't want to kill me. And I very much want to die. I deserve to die."

"Why, Maggie? Why do you want to die?"

She pressed her fingers against her eyes. "When Steven was born, I was so happy. I loved Eduard, I loved my baby, I was doing what I had been raised to do. They took him away from me all in a hurry one day and when he was brought back he had the scar. But they didn't tell me the truth. Eduard explained that as a result of that night's work, the baby would have an incredibly long life span, he would never get sick, he would grow and thrive and be a powerful, influential man one day. Every mother's fondest dream.

"I believed him. Of course I did. To think otherwise . . ."

Once again her voice trailed off. But I made no move toward her, knowing that she would continue.

"Steven grew quickly. In the case of Other children, that growth is not just a trick of time, not just the perception of a mother who does not want to lose her children. They do grow at an accelerated pace. It's not a standard rate; it varies from child to child. Phoenix is growing much slower than his brother did. I asked Eduard about it once, noticing the phenomenon in our own two. 'A difference in the life force of the soul,' he told me, 'and their strivings. Some of them just want to be alive again more than the rest.' And still after that statement, I didn't understand what was really happening, what the awful truth was.

"Then, one day without warning, the soul that dwelled inside the boy I knew as Steven came to life. I watched it happen. We were sitting at the dinner table and I asked him to pass me something. Peas, I think it was."

She looked up at me with a twisted smile. "Isn't it funny how the commonplace things can acquire such importance? That bowl of peas changed my life. Changed the way I looked at the world and not for the better . . ."

I waited patiently.

"I asked him to pass me the peas, Dot, and between the second he turned his head to get the bowl and the second he handed it to me," Maggie continued, "he changed, completely transformed into someone I didn't know right there before my eyes. Suddenly, in the body of my son, the body that I bore and fed and bathed and comforted, there dwelled a stranger. He spoke then, I heard his voice for the first time since they'd taken him away from me as a baby. 'Mother,' he said, just that one word, and he smiled at me. The smile of a demon, it seemed to me, with an uncanny and unholy knowledge shining out of his eyes. No child can smile like that. I dropped the bowl of peas and Phoenix began to cry, silently."

She stopped suddenly and looked around. "Phoenix? Where is he?"

"He is safe, Maggie. I sent him upstairs to stay with Mitch."

She gave me her angelic smile then, turning on some of her near-fatal charm. "He likes Mitch. And you. More than one would think, considering the circumstances. It's almost as if he'd known you before." She shrugged and tossed back her hair. "Who knows? Maybe he did in some other lifetime."

"Whose lifetime, Maggie?"

She looked away from me and dropped her head again; this time, however, it seemed less a response than a deliberate gesture. "I don't know. Eduard never told me. And I never asked." She glanced up at me from under her black lashes. "Oh, I know what you're thinking. I should have asked. Once I knew the truth, how could I not have asked? It's possible that Eduard might even have told me. Maybe I just didn't want to know. I guess we'll find out soon enough, anyway, when the soul they put into him comes to life. But then he won't be Phoenix anymore, will he? He'll be as dead as Steven is."

She gave me a hard look. "I don't want to lose another child that way. Not him. They'll take him away, just like they took Steven. And I will be left with nothing."

"Why are you here, Maggie?"

"He sent me. That man who used to be Steven. God forgive me, he still holds enough of my heart and soul to move me. And I obey him as I always obeyed Eduard. It's the only life I've ever known."

"But why did he send you here? He had to have known he was putting you in danger, you and Phoenix both."

She gave a bitter laugh. "He's not human, you know. None of them are. You and Mitch are more human than they will ever be, regardless. So I doubt he cared, for either my safety or his brother's. My coming here served his purpose at the time."

"And other than the complete and total extermination of my kind, what is his purpose?"

Her face closed up completely and she would not answer.

I should have pushed her, I suppose, pressured her to answer my question, but she turned her eyes to me and I saw the pain that she bore. She was already broken. Nothing could be accomplished by hurting her more.

I sighed. "Thank you, Maggie. I'll bring Phoenix back down to you. And I would suggest that the two of you stay in your room tonight. Lock the door. There are some visitors arriving I do not think you should meet."

TWENTY-SIX

Mitch and Phoenix looked up from the computer in tandem when I opened the door to our flat.

"Have you two been having fun?" I asked, absently, thinking not of how they'd been spending their time. Instead I noticed for the first time how similar the two of them looked. There was something about the shape of their mouths and the way they both looked out of their eyes.

They smiled and Phoenix nodded, typing something out on the keyboard. Mitch read it and laughed. I walked up behind them and read the words on the screen.

hello, deirdre, how are you tonight? want to play some pool with me later on? i know youll beat me again but i dont mind. much.

"What is it with you and pool, Phoenix? Since Mitch first taught you to play, you have done nothing but, every chance you get. And I don't believe that you and I have ever played together, although I would probably beat you."

we played, yeah, we played. it is one of those things i remember. you and me and

He stopped typing for a second and glanced over at Mitch.

mitch, he continued, *in the bar. we were drinking beer.*

I laughed. "If you were drinking beer, young man, that explains all of these false memories. Now you had better get downstairs and go to your mother."

He got up from his chair, but kept his fingers on the keyboard.

i want to stay here with the dogs. shes mad at me again. its not like i can help the memories coming, can i?

Mitch stood up and took the boy by the hand. "For now, son, I think it's best if you stay with your mother. She needs you."

Phoenix pulled his hand away and angrily typed something. Then, without a backward glance, he ran to the door and down the stairs.

Mitch stared off after him but I read what he had written.

you always say that. and its just not fair.

"Typical child," I said, as if I were an authority on the subject.

"Yeah," Mitch agreed, "he's quite a kid. I was surprised to find him here, but he'd typed out a note and slipped it under the bathroom door while I was showering. He told me you and Maggie were having a little talk. And he said you didn't seem too happy and that was okay because neither was she."

"That," I said with a sad smile, "is the understatement of the year. Poor Maggie. I cannot help but feel sorry for her."

"What did the two of you find to talk about?"

"I asked her to give me a good reason why I shouldn't kill her. We have all been dancing around this issue for too long, all three of us pretending that there wasn't some kind of crazy game going on. A game in which none of us, apparently, know the rules." I sighed, trying not to think about tomorrow night, when I might know nothing at all. "I don't have time for subtlety anymore, Mitch."

"Did you lose more memories, Deirdre?"

I walked over to the fireplace and built up the fire. "No," I lied, not wanting him to know that tonight might very well be our last together, "but it's bound to happen again. And so, in that light, I thought that honesty would be best."

"And what did Maggie say in response?"

"That she wanted to die, she deserved to die. For allowing the Others to murder her babies."

"Her children are still alive."

I shook my head. "No, Mitch. You forget, I think, what her children have become. Even Phoenix, as good a child as he seems, is an unknown. So while the bodies of her children are still alive, their souls, their personalities, their very life comes from somewhere, or rather, someone else.

"In a way, I suppose, it is the exact opposite of the situation with Lily. I gave birth, thought my child was dead and discovered years later she lived. Maggie gave birth, thought the child was alive and found out years later that *her* child really was dead. How can you not feel pity for her?"

His mouth tightened. "I'm trying not to. What else did she tell you?"

"Steven DeRouchard is in charge of the Others, as we already knew. He sent her here to act as a catalyst for the poison."

"Interesting," Mitch said, "considering that Sam called earlier with some initial reports and said that there seem to be two separate foreign elements in your blood, the poison and something else."

I gave a soft laugh. "He did? Then what Maggie said confirms his findings. He should be pleased."

Mitch nodded. "Very pleased, I'd say. He and Viv are on their way over here now and although he wouldn't say anything about it all on the phone, he sounded happy."

I gave a small snort. "Of course he's happy. He has a vampire guinea pig at his disposal again. There is nothing else on the face of the earth that he loves more."

"Except for Viv."

I shrugged. "Who knows? The possibility of research may be what attracts him to her."

"Yeah, right. I'd believe that only if he were over the age of seventy and maybe not even then."

"Any more news from Lily?" I was pleased to hear that the note of desperation I felt did not show in my voice. "I hope she will still be driving up tonight?"

"No news. So I assume she's on her way."

"Good."

I walked over to the dresser and pulled open one of the drawers. "Damn."

"What's wrong?" Mitch hurried over and put an arm around my shoulder. "Do you feel okay? What are you looking at? There's nothing in there."

"Exactly. I wanted something nice to wear when Lily and the rest of them showed up. Victor always makes me feel so shoddy; if I had a pair of fresh jeans to put on, at least I would feel clean."

"Why the hell should you care how Victor makes you feel?"

I shook my head. "You're right, of course. We have way more important things to think about. But it would have been nice to feel beautiful again, to feel like Deirdre Griffin for one"—I paused—"night."

Mitch laughed, not understanding. "But you *are* Deirdre Griffin, sweetheart. And you are always beautiful."

I kissed him. "Don't lie to me, Mitch. You never have before and this is a bad time to start. It doesn't matter, really."

There was a light knocking at the door. "Let me in, let me in," Vivienne's slightly muffled voice pleaded. "it's an emergency."

"Bloody hell," Mitch said, flinging the door open and expecting the worst. "I wonder what's wrong now."

There stood Viv, carrying a small cosmetic case and a large garment bag.

I could not help the smile that crossed my face

and quickly turned into a laugh. "Come in, Vivienne," I said. "You must have read my mind."

She looked beautiful, as always, and was dressed in a pink sheath dress that showed off her white arms and magnificent neck. Taking one look at Mitch, she shoved him out the door. "Go," she said, swinging the case at him. "Go downstairs and talk to Sam. He's been forced into playing a game with that boy. Deirdre has a party to attend this evening and I know she wants to look her best."

She closed the door behind him and leaned up against it. "Men." She giggled. "They just cannot understand that a girl needs to feel pretty. And that what we see in the mirror is not always what they see in their beds."

"You are a lifesaver, Vivienne."

"Foo," she said, "I am nothing like that. I just did not want my little sister looking, well," and she hesitated, rolling her eyes slightly, "looking like you. Now get out of those awful clothes and see what I have brought for you."

When Viv had finished, the woman in the mirror had little resemblance to the woman who had greeted her on her arrival. Makeup covered the dark circles under my eyes and the fever-blotched skin. She even managed to style my short dyed hair into something less marinelike.

"What did you do?" she'd said, clicking her tongue, "chop it all off with a razor? And then pour bleach on your head?"

I nodded. "Damn close to that, actually. We were in a hurry."

"When one's looks are involved, one must never be in such a hurry, *ma chere.* However, do not fear. I have fixed you, have I not?"

And she had, bringing a red velvet dress, matching heels and a short jacket made out of black fur.

I had looked at the dress, stroking the fabric between my fingers, and said, "I'm glad it's not green."

She cocked her head to one side. "But green would be lovely on you. Had I anything that color, I would have brought it."

"Green," I said with conviction, "is an unlucky color for me." Then I broke into tears.

"Bad memories, *mon chou*?" At her questioning look, I shook my head.

"No, no memories." I wiped the tears away. "I have no idea at all why I would even say such a thing."

"So," she said then, "are we done with crying? I will do your makeup."

Viv gave me one more appraising glance now, applied a little more mascara to my lashes and stood back. *"Voila!"* she said, giving a little wave of her hand. "And you are transformed!"

"Thank you," I said. "No one else will understand, but this has meant so very much to me."

She came up to me and held my hands. "I could not bear to think of you spending what might be your last night dressed in denim and flannel."

"My last night?"

Her gray eyes met mine and all trace of laughter and gaiety had disappeared. "Do not lie to me, sister. I may spend most of my time convincing the world around me that I am trivial and stupid, but I am not. And I know that you have one, maybe two nights, before your memory is gone. Sam is hopeful that he has found something to reverse the damage—"

My eyes flew open. "He has?"

She put a finger on my lips. "He will want to tell you all about that himself. And hopeful is not the same as sure. But he is sure that with time—"

"Time that I do not have."

Viv nodded sharply. "*Oui*. And Mitch, he would protect you with his very life if what threatened you came from outside. But he is powerless in this. I thought, the last time I looked in your eyes, that you knew exactly what was happening, better than either of them. And that you were going to fight this with all your might and heart. But how can you fight that which is flowing through your veins?"

I started to answer, but she continued. "You cannot, of course, not even you, my indomitable sister. So, I see my Sam trying to solve the problem with his brains, and you and Mitch, with your strength and your love. And I think, what have I to offer? Nothing." Viv giggled now, burying her emotion again under a frivolous gesture. "Nothing, except a new dress and some makeup to lighten your spirits."

"Hardly nothing," I said. "Now I can face Victor and the rest of them without feeling shopworn."

"I will make a confession, *ma chere*. He makes me feel just the same. Victor is very good at making one feel his inferior. He always reminds me without a word that I was nothing but a cheap whore when we met."

"Vivienne." I looked back into her eyes. "I will venture a guess that you have never been, nor will you ever be, cheap."

She gave a little flip of her shoulders and took my arm. "But of course, you are right. I was, and am, very, very expensive."

We laughed together as we walked down the stairs, arm in arm.

Mitch hovered around the entrance to the bar, alternating between watching Sam and Phoenix playing pool and waiting for me to come downstairs. He turned to see us and smiled at me, his eyes glowing with love.

Vivienne let go of my arm as we reached the landing and gave a small curtsy. "See, Monsieur Greer, I have delivered your wife, much improved."

"There was nothing wrong with her before, Viv." He laughed as she shrugged and sauntered past him. "You have just gilded her a bit. Her true beauty is not kept on the outside."

I gave him a sharp glance, wondering if he knew how painful those words were, but quickly realized that he'd meant no hurt to me. He still had hope, I knew.

I could not afford hope. But I smiled at him and we went into the room, joining Vivienne at the bar.

TWENTY-SEVEN

I accepted a glass of wine from her and sipped it as we watched Sam with the boy.

Vivienne applauded when Sam sank a particularly difficult shot to win the game. He solemnly shook hands with Phoenix and walked over to us, holding out his cue to Mitch. "Your turn," he said, "and Vivienne will cheer you on, won't you? I want to have a private talk with Deirdre."

"Doctors," she said, with a pretty pout. "They are so fickle, no? But if you insist, Sam, *mon amour*, I will leave the two of you alone."

Sam gently cupped his hand on my elbow and led me over to a table in a far corner of the room, handling me so delicately that I laughed and pulled away from him. "Whatever else I may have forgotten, Sam, I have not forgotten how to walk."

"I'm sorry," he said sheepishly, sitting down across from me, "it's that bedside manner. It never goes away."

I nodded. "Vivienne says that you have news for me. And good news at that."

His eyes flicked over to her and then back to me. "She shouldn't have said anything. I may have found something in your blood, some element that can be isolated, that is responsible for blocking your memories. And if I've found it, then perhaps I can neutralize it. But it's going to take a lot more research and a lot more time."

I sighed. "Time? I have plenty of time. And I suppose if the memories are only blocked and not erased, that they can be brought back?"

"In theory, yes." He reached over and took my hand. "But there is nothing I can do for you now. Not even in a week or a month. And at the rate at which you are losing recall . . ."

"There will be nothing left of me by tomorrow night. I understand. I have seen this coming for a while, Sam, and I will survive it. I will beat it. I am holding on to what matters most. My love and my anger."

We fell silent for a while, watching Mitch and the boy. "They look like fast friends, don't they?" Sam said, and I nodded, giving the two of them a loving glance.

"Yes. Regardless of what and who he is, Phoenix has been good for Mitch. An ill wind, as they say."

"What will you do, Deirdre?"

I raised an eyebrow. "Do? About Mitch and the boy?"

"No, what will you do when it's all gone?"

"Stay here, I suppose." I gave a grim laugh and held out my arms, lurching from side to side in my chair and making a low growling sound. "Terrorize the townspeople with my zombie impression, perhaps."

"Well, that sounds like fun." He shook his head and gave me a full smile.

"Oh, yes. I can hardly wait."

"Excuse me." Maggie stood over us, an unopened bottle of wine in her hand, an extra glass and a small corkscrew, with which she proceeded first to peel the foil from the bottle's neck and then to remove the cork. She set the wine, the glass and the implement on the table.

"May I join you before the party starts? I won't interfere, I promise. But I can hear you talking and laughing from my room. I'm not good company for myself tonight. And now that we are no longer enemies, or," and she gave a sad smile, "at least now that I am a known evil, I can't hurt you anymore. Besides"—she smiled and a fraction of her previous charm came through—"you could always say that you let me join you so that you could keep an eye on me."

Her eyes, still red and moist from crying, were vacant and kept darting erratically over to her son and then back to us. Her smile seemed hesitant, not the full alluring expression that normally painted her face.

"Please, Maggie," I said, somewhat remorseful of my earlier treatment of her, "sit and join us."

She moved like an old woman and sat with a sigh, tearing her eyes away from Phoenix. "You must be Doctor Samuels," she said, holding her hand out to him, a little of her old charm surfacing. "I'm Maggie Richards. But you know that already. You know everything, I suppose."

He shook her hand and gave a small laugh. "Not everything, I'm afraid."

She gave him a searching look and stared at the hand clasping hers before breaking the grip. "But you are still human, aren't you? How strange that he would be wrong about that."

"Excuse me? I don't quite follow you."

"Steven. He felt sure that Vivienne would have transformed you by now. 'If they call in reinforcements,' he said, 'most likely you will need to deal with Samuels as well. I cannot believe that Vivienne would let him slip through her soft little fingers.' " She gave a short barking laugh. "Isn't it funny that he could be wrong? I thought he was invincible and omniscient. And he's not."

"Maggie, why are you telling us this?"

"It doesn't matter, don't you see? I've already done what he asked me to do. And you know all of it. Soon he will have everything he wants and this will all be over. And when Phoenix changes, there will be nothing left for me anyway."

I glanced over at Sam and he gave an almost imperceptible nod.

"Why do you say that, Maggie?" he prompted. "You're a young, beautiful and vibrant woman. You can have more children if you want—"

At that point there was a call of triumph from the pool table and she jumped visibly, for the voice was not Mitch's.

"I got it," Phoenix shouted. "Did you see it? I shot it right in and won the game."

Silence fell on the room, deathly and grim, as

the import of his being able to speak registered with all of us.

The change had begun.

Maggie stared at him, grief-stricken, holding a hand to her throat. "Too soon," she whispered, "this is too soon." She gazed around the room, looking at each of us in turn, drawing us into her sorrow, her grief. "He's too young and I'm not ready, I'm not prepared for this, not now. I cannot stand the thoughts of losing another child."

Her hands shook on the table and she knocked over her glass, splashing herself with red wine. Taking no notice, she rose slowly from her seat, pulling herself to her full height and straightening her shoulders.

"Phoenix," she called, her voice clear and commanding despite the tears that streamed down her face, "look at me."

The boy turned and began to walk toward us. Even in that short span of time, he had changed. The host body conformed to the awakened soul within and brought about subtle changes in facial structure. I could plainly see the skin move, making room for the rearrangement of bones and muscles, transforming his face to match the original. But the eyes, the eyes stayed the same.

I gave a small gasp of recognition. I knew him, I should have known him all along. What had seemed a great puzzle was now so very simple. It was as I had told Mitch, we had actively fought to deny the obvious.

And although I could not fathom how or why

it had happened, it appeared that Eduard DeRouchard had given Mitch a priceless gift.

From the body of a boy named Phoenix, Christopher Greer had been reborn.

"Oh, my God."

Next to me, Sam also registered the transformation. "But how?"

Maggie sobbed quietly, still standing, staring at the creature who, not even five minutes ago, had masqueraded as her son. But her son was dead, he had died a little over four years ago on the same night that Christopher Greer had died.

"He was buried out of their funeral home." Her voice was emotionless now and deathly quiet, but we heard every word. "DeRouchard Brothers Mortuary, in New York. When Eduard saw the name on the death certificate he was very happy.

" 'Here's my chance,' he said, 'here's my leverage over the Cadre. I can hold Greer's son as hostage for their compliance.' "

Mitch gave a small intake of breath and stepped forward. He had not seen the change, I realized, for Chris had been standing with his back to him. Mitch was just now understanding who the boy was; I saw a great joy and relief leap into his eyes. He moved in his direction.

I caught his eye and I shook my head slightly. Now, in the face of Maggie's great distress, was not the time for their reunion.

Mitch nodded his agreement and held back.

Maggie continued her story. "Eduard reached for my baby then and I protested.

" 'You told me that this one was to be mine,

that if I gave Steven to you, I could keep any other children that followed. And you have Steven; he's not my child anymore. He is one of your Others now. But this one, Eduard, this one is mine. You promised.'

"Eduard looked into my eyes. His expression seemed cold and lifeless to me. There was no love in those eyes, no mercy, no regret for what he was about to do. 'I know, Maggie,' he said, 'and I am sorry, but this is too big an opportunity to ignore. And there are no other babies right now. I can't afford to pass this chance by. There will be others. Now, give the baby to me.' "

She looked around at us, her expression panicked and wild. "You knew him," she said, catching Vivienne's eye, "you know what he was like. I loved him. And I hated him. And I couldn't say no. God forgive me, I just couldn't say no."

She collapsed into her chair and Chris walked up to her, hesitantly. "Mum," he said, his voice cracking. "It's okay, Mum, it really is. I'm still here, the little boy you raised, your baby. Mum? It's Phoenix. I'm still here. And I won't be like Steven, I promise."

Maggie's shoulders shook convulsively and her sobs grew louder, more uncontrolled. "He promised, too. And then he broke them; all of his promises, one by one, proved worthless. And you, you're just the same as he was, just the same as your brother is. You're not human, not normal. I'm sorry I brought you into this world."

"Mum? Please don't say that, you don't mean it. I know you love me. And I love you."

I saw the glitter of her eyes through the dark curtain of her hair. "Love? Not that, Phoenix, don't talk to me about love. You are a De-Rouchard, you know nothing of love."

Before I knew she had even moved, her hand shot up to the table, she grabbed the corkscrew and stabbed at the boy, aiming for his heart. He ducked to his right and the implement pierced his arm instead.

He gave a loud cry and Mitch flew across the room and knocked the object from Maggie's hand before she could strike again.

The smell of blood permeated the air. Sam rushed to Chris's side as he stood there, swaying slightly, blood spurting from between the fingers of the hand he had clasped to the wound, the corkscrew still protruding from his arm.

"Mum?" His voice was quiet and confused. "Mum?" Louder now, his voice reached her.

Maggie looked at him. Her face turned deathly white when she realized what she had attempted to do.

"Oh, Phoenix," she moaned, "I didn't mean it. Honest, baby, I didn't know what I was doing." She reached over and grabbed my hand. "You don't think I meant to kill him, do you, Dot? He's my baby, my little boy. I couldn't hurt him, not ever."

Sam looked up from tending to Chris's arm and over at Vivienne. "Get my bag," he said to her calmly, "and give Maggie a sedative. Valium should work just fine. You remember how to give a shot, right?"

"But, of course, *mon cher.*" She fetched the bag, prepared a hypodermic needle and injected Maggie. Then Viv tugged on her arm and coaxed Maggie to her feet. "Come now, little lamb, and take a walk with Nurse Vivienne. She will tuck you into your bed, all safe and secure. Do not worry, your Phoenix will be fine and so will you."

Maggie teetered a bit and Viv looked over her shoulder. "Mitch, could you help, please?"

The look of love on Chris's face as he watched the three of them walk back to the room was heartbreakingly familiar. When they reached the room, he turned his attention back to Sam. "She'll be okay, won't she, Doctor Samuels? She really didn't mean to hurt me."

Sam shrugged. "If she'd actually hit your heart, Chris, she'd have done some real damage. But maybe she didn't mean to. We'll continue to think that, hmmm? Now keep still and let me get this bandaged."

TWENTY-EIGHT

Mitch and Vivienne came out of the back bedroom. In answer to my questioning look, she smiled briefly. "Poor little lamb," she said, "she reminds me so of Monique. Not a huge surprise, I suppose. Eduard leaves his mark, does he not? Bastard that he was." Her eyes grew hard. "And I fear his malice will live on for years and years. But Maggie, she will sleep for a while yet. What she will be like when she awakens is, I believe, a question for our doctor."

Sam finished bandaging Chris's arm. "Hard to say," he admitted. "I've no idea what sort of trauma this situation could cause." He gave a shaky laugh. "I may need to tranquilize everyone."

Mitch stood for a minute, just looking at the boy who had been Phoenix. Then he crossed the room and clasped his newly reborn son in his arms. "Damn," he said, his voice thick with emotion, "you're alive. I can't believe it, you're actually alive."

Chris winced from the pain in his arm. "I don't know, Dad, not five minutes after I get back, the woman I thought of as my mother for so many years tried to kill me again. Maybe it's not such a good idea, after all." But he smiled as he said it to soften the words.

"What's it like?" Mitch asked him. "To be dead and then to return?"

"Confusing." Chris shook his head. "It's going to take me a lot of time to adjust. And to be a child again? I'm not sure if I'm ready to talk about it; I can barely remember being Phoenix now. As if it were a dream I had just woken up from. And at the same time I have all the old remembrances and emotions from my previous life, jumbled up inside me. I can't seem to sort any of it out in my mind. . . ."

Something about the mature words coming from the mouth of the child was disconcerting and I could well understand that Chris would be overwhelmed.

"Take your time," I said, "we are none of us going anywhere. But know that you are welcome. And"—I looked at Mitch—"much loved."

There was a knock at the pub door then and I went to answer it. Through the window I could see one of the largest men I'd ever seen with a slim redheaded girl at his side, a backpack slung across one shoulder. Lily and Claude had arrived.

I opened the door.

"Hi," Lily said, giving me a brief hug. "Sorry we're late. We had some trouble getting started in London." Then she pulled back and took a long look at me, her eyes searching my face.

"Hello, Lily," I said, totally at a loss for words.

I never knew what to say to this girl, my daughter. Except for the truth. "I'm glad you're here."

"Are you okay? You look different." She reached over and touched my hair. "Might be the new style, I guess. Although, I don't think it suits you."

I shrugged. "Vivienne doesn't like it much either. But we thought at the time that a disguise was a good idea. Even Mitch dyed his hair. It didn't help much, they still found us. How they do it, I don't know, but they always find us."

"But no more." Lily reached into her backpack and pulled out a videotape. "I come bearing wonderful news. Amazing news. Terri and Bob have recanted. And the Others have called off their vendetta, because of a recent change in leadership. The silent assassins with sharp sticks won't be stopping at our doors anymore."

She peered into the pub. "No television? Shit, Mom, this is like living in the Dark Ages. Anyway, do you think we could come inside? Or are you going to leave us standing here all night?"

I laughed. "I'm sorry, please, come in." She walked past me, grabbing my hand as she did and giving it a quick squeeze.

"Hey, kiddo," I heard Mitch say as Lily entered into the lighted pub, "how've you been? You're looking good. And where's Victor?"

"Back in London," she said, her voice flat.

"Well, never mind about that. You've managed to come late for all of the good stuff. Come meet Chris."

Claude cleared his throat, pulling my attention

away from Mitch and Lily. He smiled at me, took my hand and kissed it. "You're looking well, Deirdre."

"And you are a liar, Claude. I have never looked worse. However, you are welcome. And yes," I said to the question in his eyes, "I still remember you. For now."

I took his arm and led him into the pub. "Mitch?" I asked, "can we bring the television down here? I would very much like to see this tape that Lily brought us."

"Good idea," he said, "I was wondering where we would find room for everyone upstairs. I'll be right back. Chris? Do you want to help?"

The two of them headed up the steps and Sam began rearranging chairs for the viewing. Vivienne poured wine for everyone and Claude came back to my side after taking one.

"So who's the kid?" he asked. "He has the scent of an Other about him."

"With good cause. Four years ago, Eduard apparently thought he could use a hostage, and so he borrowed the soul of Mitch's son and planted it into the body of his newborn child. We are all still adjusting to the idea. Chris only came back to life tonight, forced out earlier than he should have been, I think, because of the presence of Mitch. Such a strange situation. And where's Victor? I had hoped he could shed some light on all of this."

Claude reached into his pocket and took out a handkerchief, dabbing at his face. "Victor decided he did not want to accompany us. He had other business, he said."

Lily walked up to us. "Yeah, he's a stubborn old man. That's why we're late. After we saw the tape last night, he refused to come. 'No need now,' he said. And 'He's making his move.' That's all he would say. He seemed inordinately pleased about the whole thing, though. Ecstatic, I'd say. And not so much because we were all safe now, but more because of the change in leadership. When it was time to go this evening, he told us to come ahead without him. No reason, no explanation. Just do this because he said so."

"Typical," Mitch said, walking down the stairs with the television in his arms. Chris trailed after him, followed by the two dogs. Lily coaxed them over to sniff at her fingers.

"Somehow," she said, laughing up at me, "I'd not have taken you for a dog person."

"I'm not. Curly and Larry belong to Mitch."

She laughed at the names. "So where's Moe?"

"Dead," I said. "Which reminds me. Chris?"

"Yeah?" He looked up from where he was attaching the video player to the television.

"Who killed Moe?"

"Moe?" Chris straightened up, a confused look on his face. He struggled for a minute; then recognition and sadness came over him. "Oh, yeah. Moe. Poor dog." For a moment he looked like the boy he had been, his eyes haunted and frightened. "I really don't know for sure, Deirdre, he was that way when I found him. I think Phoenix knew who did it, but I just can't remember."

"I suppose," I said, "given her recent penchant for violence, that it could have been Maggie."

"No." He shook his head vehemently. "It wasn't Mum. I know that for sure."

"Well, I'll have to take your word for that. Perhaps it was one last parting shot from the Others."

"Maybe." Chris reached down and turned on the television. "Okay, Lily," he said, "let's see this tape."

The opening was the same. The same overly dramatic organ music, the same beginning credits, the photos of famous and infamous vampires. But from there everything changed. The *Real-Life Vampires* logo appeared briefly, then was covered over in a wash of black. The theme music stopped midnote and all was silent.

The camera cut to Terri Hamilton, wearing a dark suit and an extremely somber expression, as if she had just come from a funeral. And perhaps, in her mind, she had.

"This," she said without one trace of her former smile, the smile we had all wanted to wipe off of her face, "will be our last show. And one that we taped with great trepidation and sadness. But it must be said that we have always been dedicated to the truth. We have dedicated ourselves, putting our careers and our lives on the line to expose things that had been kept hidden and secret. Things we felt you had a right to know."

Mitch gave a half laugh. "She still manages to say all the keywords, doesn't she?"

"And now, dear friends, we have received news of great import. News that affects both Bob and me personally. News that affects a great many of our listening audience.

"We have . . ." She paused, her eyes briefly darting to the script in front of her. ". . . been duped. All of us. There are no such things as vampires." At this point, her voice cracked and she looked over to Bob, who picked up the speech.

Vivienne giggled. "This is very good, Lily. Perhaps they can both be more humiliated?"

Lily snickered. "It gets better, Vivienne. Just wait."

"That's right, Terri." Bob looked authoritative as usual and about as comfortable as a man forced to eat his words on national television could be. "New evidence has been brought to our attention that completely discounts the vampire scare. Medical reports have been falsified, documentation and film footage that had been certified as genuine are now proven nothing more than the basest fabrications. Most especially," and on the screen behind him came the film we had viewed no more than a week ago, "this most recent report, depicting the murder of four men by supposed vampires, turned out to be nothing more than a prescripted staging, a fake."

"Oh," Viv sneered, "was that a sham? But it looked so real. *Merde.* I cannot believe that people would be so stupid as to believe their propaganda."

"Let us hope, Vivienne, that they are," I said with a half smile. "If they believed what they were told earlier, then those same people might just believe this as well."

"We are horrified," Terri continued, "that we played a part, no matter how innocent, in the persecution of certain people. In our defense, I can only say that we were expertly and deliberately misled by the leadership of the Others, the group responsible for this widespread hysteria."

"The Others," Bob continued, the screen behind him now changing to a large photo of an extremely handsome, blond-haired, green-eyed man, standing and waving at the door of an airplane, "an international group of supposed philanthropists, had previously been under the direction of this man. Eduard DeRouchard."

Chris gave a short gasp. "I do remember him," he said, his voice tight and angry. "I remember him quite clearly."

Terri spoke again. "The campaign against the Cadre, another international group, had been Mr. DeRouchard's brainchild. And although no one fully knows what he had hoped to achieve, since he died shortly after the initial attacks on his rival organization, his plans were continued for years by his seconds- in-command. Recently, though, his eldest son, Steven DeRouchard, took control of the group and the truth came out. Eduard De-Rouchard, a wealthy and influential man, was in reality a delusional madman, who fully believed in the righteousness of his actions, wrong though they were."

"Here, here!" Vivienne raised her glass to the television set. "That is the most truth Miss Terri Hamilton has ever spoken in her life."

Bob cleared his throat and took a sip from the

water glass sitting next to him. "Steven De-Rouchard has declined to appear on camera or to have his words taped. But he has given us a statement to read."

" 'People of the world, esteemed colleagues and most especially my wronged and persecuted brothers and sisters of the Cadre, I know that the pain, sorrow and fear caused by our organization can never be fully repaired. But with Mr. Smith and Miss Hamilton's gracious assistance, I can at least set the record straight. I honor the memory of my father as a son should, but cannot allow the atrocities committed through his orders and in his name to go unrecompensed.

" 'Therefore, I have authorized the return of all monies and properties seized to their original owners. In addition, damages will be paid to those who lost loved ones in this unnecessary strife. The fallacy that vampires can exist, side by side with humans in our world, should be dismissed as nothing more than the ravings of a madman.

" 'Mostly I offer my sincerest apologies for the wrongs that have been done in my father's name. And I urge the alliance now of both of these organizations, the Others and the Cadre. Together we can rid the world of many woes and evils; together we can make this world a better place for us all.' "

The camera panned over to Terri. She was smiling now while dabbing at her eyes with a lace hankie. "Such beautiful and brave words, Bob. Thank you for sharing them with us. And thank

God for Steven DeRouchard. Somehow I think he will make the world a more wonderful place."

Mitch laughed, a rich hearty sound. "I think we're all supposed to join hands now and sing a song about the brotherhood of mankind."

Lily reached over and turned off the tape. "And that's it, except for a rather boring recap of it all. Now, I think a party is in order, don't you?"

"If you can trust him, that is," Chris said. "I have vague memories of him having a very cruel streak when he was younger. He seemed to enjoy making lesser creatures squirm. He was good at hiding it, though, and Phoenix's bruises and scars healed quickly, so Mum never suspected. But Eduard knew. And he encouraged the behavior."

"That does not surprise me," Vivienne said, "but still, if Terri and Bob have fallen, can the empire of DeRouchard be far behind?"

TWENTY-NINE

Lily went behind the bar and motioned for Vivienne to join her. Within a few minutes, I heard the pop of a champagne cork and the splash of liquid hitting the bar.

"Listen, you two," Mitch called to them, "I don't mind you helping yourself to our inventory, but don't make a mess unless you plan on cleaning it up."

Vivienne giggled and stuck her tongue out at him. "We will clean it up, Monsieur Greer. But only after we celebrate. This is a very special evening for us all, is it not?"

Lily found the champagne glasses and began to pour one out for each of us. Then she hesitated, looking at Chris. "I'm not sure what the drinking age is here, Chris. But out of all of us, I'd say that you most deserve a glass of this."

"Just a small one, Lily, no more than half a glass. I sure don't need to face Mum tomorrow morning with a hangover. You've all forgotten that when everyone else retires for the day, I'll be left here alone with her."

"We could keep her sedated, if you're worried

about your safety, Chris," Sam said. "Or I could come over and keep watch."

Chris's face reflected more sadness than fear. "I don't think you understand, Doctor Samuels. She's not going to attempt to kill me again. That was just the shock of the transition."

I looked at him. "I agree, Chris. Her violence was a mistake, similar to her dropping the bowl of peas with Steven's change."

Vivienne held back a giggle. "How could it be like a bowl of peas?"

"It's a long story, Vivienne," I said, half smiling, "and I suggest we hold off on it until another time. It's not really appropriate material for the party mood you're trying to establish."

Chris rubbed his right hand across his eyes. "Yeah, I think it was like that, Deirdre. Did she tell you that story?"

I nodded. "Yes."

"Maybe tomorrow night you could tell it back to me. I can barely picture it, and I think I'm going to need every trick in the book to pull her out of this. I'm hoping that once she discovers I am not going to turn into another like Steven, she will adapt."

Sam nodded. "That would be the ideal solution."

Chris gave a short laugh. "It's not as if she's lost anything, not recently, at least. It was always me, inside, in spite of the illusion that Phoenix and I were different people. She'll learn that with time."

I knew, of course, that what he said was not

really true. Maggie *had* lost her baby and she would carry the guilt for that the rest of her life.

"We all hope that she adapts, Chris," I said. "I don't believe that any of us could wish her ill."

Lily came around then and distributed champagne to everyone. Finally we all stood with glasses in hand.

"In Victor's absence," Vivienne said, "I am the eldest, although"—she gave Sam a wink—"I will kill the first of you who suggest that I look it. Even so, I shall propose the toast." She paused for a moment, to catch our attention and to collect her thoughts.

"To life." She held up her glass. "May it always be good. To love, may it always be true. And to truth." Her eyes acquired a wicked glint. "May it never be delivered again into the hands of the likes of Terri and Bob."

"Cheers!" We all laughed and clinked our glasses together, moving back into the conversational groups we'd been in prior to the toast.

I did not participate fully in the party, although I sat at the same table with Sam, Vivienne, Claude and Lily, drinking with them, and producing a smile or a laugh at the appropriate times.

"So, Viv," Lily said, "Mom told me you ran into cows on the road on the way here."

Vivienne laughed and started telling her the story of Sam and the cow, embellishing the tale until it was so far removed from the truth that it was unrecognizable. Then she stood up and sang a song in her native language. "And that, *mon amis,* was the song of the earl and the milkmaid,"

she said when finished. "I used to sing it centuries
ago. It is the cow's fault, of course."

"Viv," Sam said dryly, "there was never any cow
on the road."

I watched them all as they laughed, and I put
on the appearance of joining in the fun. In reality,
though, I was doing nothing more than counting
the minutes ticking by. I wondered how long I
could manage to avoid sleep. Looking around at
this small group of people that I loved, I knew
that, no matter how long, it would not be enough.

Mitch and Chris sat away from us and talked
quietly together for most of the night. The undis-
guised joy on my husband's face brought joy to
me as well, and I found that I could not begrudge
him the time spent with his son. Instead, I was
content to watch, more than content to pore over
my remaining memories as if they were jewels or
golden coins.

The Others may have promised recompense,
but I doubted that there was any cure for me that
they would share. It was all too easy, the recanting
of Terri and Bob, the brave words of Steven De-
Rouchard that sounded so noble, so uplifting. *No*,
I thought, as I watched the celebration around
me, *there is something else happening here. Something
else to which all the hardship we have experienced is
just a preamble. Something more terrible, perhaps, something more permanent.*

About an hour before dawn, Sam went back to
check on Maggie and reported that she was still

sleeping soundly. Chris got up from where he and Mitch had sat talking, stretched and yawned. "I need to get some sleep, too. I'm totally exhausted. Night, all."

He walked back to the bedroom he had been sharing with Maggie and once again I marveled at his reappearance and the intellect and experience of a man in the body of a boy. It's an ill wind that blows no good, I had told Sam earlier. And although that was certainly true, I could not help worrying about what the payment for this particular miracle would be. For payment would be required. Of that I was quite sure.

Lily left Vivienne and came over to sit next to me. "You're being awfully quiet, Mom, are you sure you're okay? Can I get you something else to drink maybe?"

"I am fine, Lily. Just a little tired and hungry. And that can easily be cured with sleep and blood. Tomorrow night I will be right as rain."

She gave me a sharp look. "If you say so. Anyway, Claude and I should be getting back to the hotel before dawn. Maybe some of the rest of the Cadre will be joining us tomorrow night, although I tend to doubt that now that the dogs have been called off. We are, as a group, very self-serving."

I gave her a weak smile. "True. If you should hear from Victor, please give him my regards. You are happy with him, are you not?"

"Yeah."

"That's good." My eyes went to Mitch and he sensed my gaze and smiled at me from across the room. "A strong relationship can make all the difference in the world."

"Well, about that, Mom. It's not really what you think. Our relationship is strictly platonic, we've never progressed to anything even remotely sexual."

I blushed and turned my head away. "Oh," I said, "I had rather thought it had."

"Well, to be honest, Mom, I wanted you to think that. Because I knew it bothered you." She laughed. "Hey, I'm a pain in the ass most of the time, Victor always says that. Why should I treat you any differently?"

"Why should you, indeed? I certainly have never done anything to deserve your love or your respect. Perhaps, in the future, we can change that." *If I have a future.*

"Sure." She kissed my cheek and patted my hand. "I'd like that."

"We could do some sight-seeing tomorrow night, if you would like," I lied to her, smiling. "You'd probably enjoy roaming around in the ruins. And the cemetery."

"It's a date. And now I'd better go, before sunup. Good night, Mom." She kissed me again and waved to the others. "Mitch, Sam, Viv, see you all tomorrow night."

She and Claude left, followed fairly quickly by Vivienne and Sam.

"I should know more on the test results, Deirdre. I'll call if there are any new developments. Failing that, we'll both see you tomorrow night as well." He shook Mitch's hand and moved to open the door for Vivienne.

"Bonsoir," she whispered in my ear, "and do not worry, sister. It will all be made right."

I shivered at her words. *That, my sister,* I thought, *is exactly what I fear.*

I stood for a while staring at the door after they left, wishing that I could make this particular moment in time stop and stay.

Mitch came over and draped an arm around my shoulders. "Quite an evening, wasn't it?"

"Yes," I said, "it was that. I think, though, that I might miss having Terri and Bob on the air. If it hadn't been so pointed an attack at us, they might have been amusing."

Mitch chuckled. "At the very least, their scripting was original. Now come, wife, it's almost dawn."

I reached up and kissed him. "I love you. You must know this, Mitch. That no matter what the future holds," *or does not,* I thought, "I will always hold that love for you deep inside me. It will never die as long as I live. Every time you see me or every time you look in the mirror I want you to think, 'Deirdre loves me.' "

He said nothing, he did not need to. Instead, he picked me up, carried me up the stairs and through the door as if we were newlyweds. He set me down on the bed gently, and checked the locks on the door and on the window shutters.

Then he turned on every light in the place and we made love. There was no darkness in which to hide and the love we felt surely must have shone from our eyes.

When it was over, I laughed and stretched. "That was wonderful, my love. Just like the first time and the last time and every other time rolled into one."

He smiled. "Glad you liked it, Mrs. Greer."

"I did not merely like it, Mitch. I loved it. As I love you."

He kissed me. "I love you, too."

We talked for a time about the events of the evening; Chris's return, the Others' abrupt and unexpected turnabout, even Vivienne and her nonexistent cow. Eventually, though, his responses came further apart and his voice grew sleepy.

"Get some rest, Mitch. We can always talk more when we wake up." I forced a cheerful tone to my voice, wanting to get through this last meeting without tears. I did not want his last memory of me to include red eyes and a sniffly nose.

"Yeah," he murmured, already dropping off. "Good night."

"Good night, Mitch." I kissed him and he rolled over and slept.

I lay awake for as long as I could, watching him sleep, capturing this feeling of love and hiding it away in my heart. I had promised him I would.

Then sleep overcame me, as I knew it would, and I fell into what seemed an endless dream.

Come home, it said, *and leave all of this behind.*

THIRTY

And when I woke, it had been done. I opened my eyes to a strange place, to a stranger sleeping beside me, to a world that held no place for me. I quietly slid out of bed and looked at the man I had left behind. I knew what we must have meant to each other, but the memories were gone, along with the years—*had it been years?*—we had shared.

Instinctively, I knew that there must have been good times and bad times, tears and laughter. And love. I felt sure I would not have stayed with him if there were not love.

I sighed and looked at the clothes draped across the furniture and dropped on the floor. We had, I supposed, shared a time of passion, before we had slept. But if he had ever held me, had ever kissed me, the touch of him had been completely washed away.

Come home, the dream had said. And so, quietly, I put clothes on my body, not the ones that had been on the floor, but some others that I found: jeans and a sweater and a pair of heavy boots. As I sat down to put the latter on, I felt something in the back pocket of the pants, reached in and pulled it out. It was, I saw, a small cassette tape.

Why it was there, I hadn't a clue. What it contained, music or voices or silence, was a mystery to me. Yet, it had obviously been important enough for me to save, so save it I would. I tucked it back into my pocket and finished lacing the boots.

I unlocked and opened the door, peering out into the hallway. Two dogs slept at the door. They opened their eyes as I stepped out and rose to their feet, stretching and yawning. They followed me down the stairs and then surged ahead of me, showing me the way to a back door. As I passed through a kitchen, I saw a woman with dark hair and sad eyes, sitting at the table. Just sitting and staring off into nothingness.

I should have known what sorrow she was nursing, should have known why she sat here, like this, all alone and crying softly. And my heart broke that I could not remember.

She jumped as I stepped into the room, then relaxed. "Hello, Dot," she said, not smiling, "did you have a good sleep?"

Dot? I thought, *is that really my name? No, that does not seem quite right.* "Fine, thank you," I said, with what I hoped was an appropriate smile. "And you?"

She gave a small humorless laugh. "You should know well enough that I did. Vivienne gave me enough Valium to drop a cow, I think. But even at that, I feel better now."

"Good," I said, "I'm glad."

I stepped over to the door and put a hand on the knob.

"Going out?" she asked. "Shall I tell Mitch where you've gone?"

Mitch. That was his name, then. A good name, strong and confident. Perhaps it matched him, but I did not know, I could not remember.

However, the state of my mind and memory were none of this woman's concern, so I smiled and played along. "Yes, if you would please. Tell him that I am just going for a short walk and I should be back soon. He shouldn't worry; I'll be fine."

She nodded, seeming to understand much more of this conversation than I did. "That's right, your kind is safe again. The vendetta has been called off by Steven. Phoenix told me. Or Chris told me. We had a very long talk today, while the rest of you were sleeping. And I think, we think, everything will be fine."

"Good," I repeated, "I am so very glad for you and Chris." Reaching over, I opened the door, letting the dogs out into the night. "And I will see you later, then. Good night."

"Good night, Dot." Her eyes glinted up at me. "Enjoy your walk."

I closed the door and looked at the dogs. "Where to?" I asked them and then laughed at my own folly. They could not tell me.

I began walking, just walking. Admiring the rows of tidy little houses, sniffing the sea air appreciatively, I decided to move uphill, to get a better vantage point of this town. Perhaps a glimpse of it as a whole would trigger some glimmer of remembrance.

As I reached the top of the steep cobblestoned street, I was greeted with a glimpse of ruins, of moonlight shining through empty windows, of rows of graves. Somehow, it felt appropriate, it felt right that I should find my way here.

"Is this home then?" I asked the question.

"No," came an answer from behind me, "you are not home yet, Deirdre, but I promise you it will be soon."

And a hand clapped down on my mouth and I felt a needle slide into my skin. My mind dissolved and my eyes fluttered shut.

I did not know that I had slept, so little time seemed to have passed. I had closed my eyes in the old church ruins and opened them here. Where was here? Was it real or a dream? And now that there was nothing left of me, did it matter? Would it ever matter again?

The surface upon which I lay was smooth and soothingly cool. I rubbed a hand against it. It was leather. My hand dropped farther and my eyes began to focus. Black leather, I saw, and supported by chrome.

And I was dressed in different clothes. Instead of the jeans I had been wearing, I had on a black silk nightgown with a plunging neckline and a billowing skirt. Oddly enough, this garment seemed as familiar as the jeans, shirt and hiking boots. *Perhaps that was the dream,* I thought.

The room was dark but even as that thought crossed my mind, the shadows retreated somewhat giving me limited vision. A large room, it smelled of new leather and fresh paint.

I sat up on the couch and looked around me at this new place. *It must be a dream,* I thought, *since it seems familiar. And now only dreams are real.*

Feeling more comfortable in that assessment, I relaxed. No matter how terrible the dreams were, I knew, they never hurt me upon awakening. I studied the room again. A bar stood in one corner of the room, black and chrome and sparkling. On the bar top, stood a bottle of opened red wine and two clean glasses of delicate crystal.

"Why not?" I said with a quiet laugh. "I'm very thirsty."

I rose from the couch on unsteady legs; once standing I discovered that I felt dizzy and slightly nauseated. *Odd,* I thought, *I normally feel well in the dreams.* However, I managed to cross to the bar and pour myself a glass of wine.

The first sip brought tears to my eyes. It was not that the wine tasted bad; on the contrary it was wonderful, sharp and rich. No, the tears had nothing to do with the wine's quality. I cried because I knew I'd drunk this vintage before, in happier times, perhaps, although I could not remember.

Glancing at the empty glass, I wondered for whom it was meant. My head ached and I sighed, turning around with the wine in my hand and leaning my back against the bar. I faced a different view of the room now and saw across from me that there was one door, a heavy wooden one. And deeper in the shadows, back in a dark corner, there was a massive desk, so black it might have been carved of onyx. On the wall next to the desk, seeming horribly out of place in this sea of modern furniture, stood a huge ornate and antique armoire. And behind the desk sat a man, so completely engulfed in shadows that had it not been for the glitter of the eyes that watched me, I might never have seen him.

"So," I said unsteadily, trying to peer through the shadows to see the face of the man sitting at the desk, "you are Steven DeRouchard."

Attaching the name did me little good. I knew the name, recognized it the same way I knew the difference between my foot and my hand, but the recognition was academic. Cold and emotionless. The name represented a man, no more and no less. He meant nothing to me. Like all the rest of them, he meant nothing.

The voice laughed. "Truly, little one, you have named me. Or have you? The name DeRouchard is, perhaps, unimportant. I like to think of it and the body it represents as a vessel, or," and he paused, searching, I thought, for a word or perhaps only for dramatic effect, "a bottle, if you will. Its importance, its value does not lie in external trappings. Its true worth can only be determined by that which it holds. The essence of the vessel is all."

"Then I am nothing," I said, following his logic, "since I have no essence."

"Not necessarily, my dear. You have potential. A bottle that is empty can easily be filled."

Suddenly the peaceful feeling I had been enjoying exploded into anger.

"If I am empty, you bastard, it is your doing." I picked up the wine bottle and with all my strength threw it at his head. It came up short and struck the edge of the desk, splashing him with bits of broken glass and wine.

I opened my mouth to speak again but stopped, dead in the water and drifting. For one second, one very short second, I had a flash of memory. Something about the violence, the tinkling sound of shattered glass and my anger all blended into the vision of this man and he was . . .

No. The memory vanished, washed away in his laughter. The moment disappeared and was gone.

"There," I said, moving forward a step, "why don't you see if you can fill *that* bottle? Bastard."

He brushed the slivers of glass from his coat. "See? You are not empty, little one, you still have your anger."

"I have held on to my anger. And I have saved it for you. I'm glad you are pleased."

"More than pleased, actually." He got up from behind the desk and began to move toward me.

Although I did not want to show my weakness to him, I could not help my reaction. I shrank back into the bar, fearing his approach.

"Why have you done this to me?" I whispered the words as he came closer to me. "What have I done to make you hate me, hate us, so much?"

"Hate?" He stopped about five feet away from me. "This has nothing to do with hate and everything to do with love. I saved your life, Deirdre."

At the mention of that name, I shivered. I had heard his voice say that name, my name I now knew, in dreams and in life.

"How did you save me?"

"If you could remember, you would know. I stopped the attacks on you. I brought you here. And you are alive."

I shook my head. "I do not think I am alive, not here, not in this time and place. I am dreaming, all of this. You have been in my dreams, since . . ."

"Always. I have always been in your dreams. That is where I belong." He moved toward me again and I saw him, clearly, and as if for the first time. His face with its finely sculpted lines, his mouth, his hair, the way he walked—all of it was real. This was no dream. Something deep inside me knew this man. Only one thing was different, only one detail seemed strange.

He stood in front of me now. Close enough so that I could reach out with a trembling hand and touch the scar that spread from one side of his neck to the other. "DeRouchard," I whispered. "It is the mark."

"Yet still, you've missed my true name. Try again, little one. The memory is there and you must find it if you are to survive. And once you do, I can save you. I alone hold the key; only I can fill you again and make you whole."

He gently grasped my chin in his hand and lifted my head to meet his gaze. I knew his touch. I knew his eyes. Straining for the memory, I stood on the tips of my toes and stared deeply at him.

And then I began to cry.

His arms pulled me into him. "It's been a long road, Deirdre, but now you are back home where you belong. The rest of it is much better forgotten. Now, say my name."

"Steven DeRouchard?"

"No, that is wrong." His mouth came down on mine and he kissed me, causing a thousand memories of him and him alone to stir and rush to the surface.

Oh, dear God. Somewhere deep inside I heard the roar of a caged animal. Somewhere deep inside me a woman was weeping over a lost love, a perfect love. And from somewhere far away I heard a voice, a well-loved voice, say "remember me . . ."

Gone. All gone. *I must get them back,* I thought, *the anger and the woman and the memories.*

But all I had left was here and now.

And I said his name.

"Max."

ACKNOWLEDGMENTS

Thanks go out as always to my family, Pete, Brian and Geoff, for their help and support during the writing process. Special thanks to Barbara for keeping a space at her kitchen table open for me when I most needed it, to Jim for his photographs and stories of Whitby and for the use of his scanner, to John and his evil alter-ego David for always being able to make me laugh, to Joyce and Tim for caring, to William and Phyllis for being there, to Kelly for her bathtub-battered copy of Blood Secrets, to Jack and the other sff.net regulars for their late-night virtual hand-holding, and to Cherry, my agent, and John, my editor, for their patience and understanding. Last, but not least, I wish to give heartfelt thanks to all the fans and readers of The Vampire Legacy—you make it all worthwhile.

BOOK YOUR PLACE ON OUR WEBSITE AND MAKE THE READING CONNECTION!

We've created a customized website just for our very special readers, where you can get the inside scoop on everything that's going on with Zebra, Pinnacle and Kensington books.

When you come online, you'll have the exciting opportunity to:

- View covers of upcoming books
- Read sample chapters
- Learn about our future publishing schedule (listed by publication month *and author*)
- Find out when your favorite authors will be visiting a city near you
- Search for and order backlist books from our online catalog
- Check out author bios and background information
- Send e-mail to your favorite authors
- Meet the Kensington staff online
- Join us in weekly chats with authors, readers and other guests
- Get writing guidelines
- AND MUCH MORE!

**Visit our website at
http://www.kensingtonbooks.com**